the ballad of west tenth street

the ballad of west tenth street

marjorie kernan

HARPER PERENNIAL

NEW YORK • LONDON • TORONTO • SYDNEY • NEW DELHI • AUCKLAND

HARPER PERENNIAL

This book is a work of fiction. The characters, incidents, and dialogue are drawn from the author's imagination and are not to be construed as real. Any resemblance to actual events or persons, living or dead, is entirely coincidental.

HarperCollins books may be purchased for educational, business, or sales promotional use. For information please write: Special Markets Department, HarperCollins Publishers, 10 East 53rd Street, New York, NY 10022.

FIRST EDITION

Designed by Aline Pace

Library of Congress Cataloging-in-Publication Data has been applied for.

ISBN 978-0-06-166917-0

09 10 11 12 13 OV/RRD 10 9 8 7 6 5 4 3 2 1

to Andre

the ballad of west tenth street

1

On Fifth Avenue, in lower Manhattan, at the corner of Eleventh Street, stands the First Presbyterian Church, a gloomy edifice made of blackened sandstone. Should you turn there and walk along West Eleventh, you will pass the row house the Weather Underground blew up while dabbling in explosives, then the New School's glass and steel building, and finally Gene's Restaurant and the back dining room of Charlie Mom's, where couples glumly eat sautéed broccoli and mu shu pork.

Cross Sixth Avenue to West Tenth Street, past where the old Jefferson Market courthouse stands on an island, its clock tower a finger raised to the sky and its booming note a reminder to passersby that they are either late, on time, or free of such cares.

West of Seventh Avenue the cross streets run off at a southerly angle. With this shift comes a sense of entering another New York, an older and less orderly one. The names of the streets change as well, from utilitarian numbers to names evoking distant landowners, orchards, and inns. The noise of traffic recedes. Sparrows chitter in the trees.

The remaining Federal townhouses of the West Village keep company with every conceivable architectural fad: high Victorian apartment blocks with Gothic porticos, brick cottages with a galleon in stained glass on each window, stolid Civil War–era merchant's houses with stables behind, engine companies with arched red doors, twenties white brick garages and brownstones. Most of the buildings have an expensive, well-groomed air but a few tenements survive, brazenly declaring their poverty, their stone facades coated in dingy beige paint and a row of dented trash cans chained to their front.

Go a little farther and you'll cross Bleecker Street, with its boutiques and French pastry shops. Near the end of the next block stand a pair of fine old brick townhouses. One has a blue door with a tarnished brass knocker in the shape of a dolphin. The other is empty. A handsome sign declares it FOR SALE. THE CAVENDISH GROUP, it reads, IS PLEASED TO ANNOUNCE THIS VERY FINE PROPERTY. A telephone number is obligingly given below.

From the house with the blue door, a bang and a clatter comes from the narrow kitchen area below the street. The door opens and a boy with long reddish hair hauls out a carton. "Seven, eight," he counts as he drops bottles from the carton into a bin, the bottles clanking. He shakes his head and goes back inside.

Clumping, making as much noise as possible, as is the nature of boys, he climbs three flights of stairs to the attic floor. There he flops down on one end of the blue leather sofa in front of the TV, which is blank.

"Eight," he announced to his sister, who sat at the other end of the sofa. "Eight in one week. She's drinking like mad again."

"Uh-huh," Deen said, not really listening.

"I'm gonna draw a picture of her liver, all green and purple, and paste it up in her bathroom. Or maybe I'll do one of her puking it right out." He took a pad of paper and a box of colored pencils from the table and began some preliminary lines.

"Hey, Deen?"

"Yeah, Hamish?"

"You have noticed she's acting pretty weird again lately? When's the full moon, do you know?"

"No. Oh, I get it. Okay, I'll check—the paper's right here, hang on a sec. Oh geeze, it's Saturday."

"Aw, shit! And she always drinks more on weekends. What if she goes bonkers again with the pills and all, and this time they don't pump her stomach out in time? What if she dies and we're poor pitiful orphans and have to be adopted by some Mormon family or something, some people who do good works and all that shit, and you'll have to wear gingham dresses down to your ankles and marry some old lech named Jezekial?"

"Geeze, Hames, what'd you eat for breakfast, a bowl of raw paranoia? Munster'll be fine. She only lost track of how many pills she'd taken that one time. Besides, Uncle Brian would adopt us."

"Yeah, then why'd she bake a tennis shoe for dinner last night? With tomatoes, for Christ's sake."

"Okay," Deen said wearily. "I tell you what—we'll get up in the middle of the night to check on her. We can take turns. I'll find a little mirror to hold over her mouth to make sure she's still breathing."

Hamish responded with a dissatisfied sigh. He began a new drawing. Deen went back to her book.

"Hey Deen?" he said. "You think we'll grow up to be like them?"

"Lushes and pill poppers, you mean? Or junkies?"

"I've got a theory about it all, you want to hear it?"

"Be my guest. I'm sure it's highly scientific."

"Well, it is. It's this: You and I got Pops's hair, right? And sort of his looks. And Gretchen's got Munster's hair and totally her looks. So Munster's crazy and drinks and Gretchen's crazy, so that means you and I are more likely to turn out like Pops."

"Dead of an overdose at thirty-nine? Thanks, Hames. But I'm happy to inform you that it's not all that simple. For one thing I'm going to be a classical pianist, not some crazed rocker. And Munster and Gretchen are crazy *because* Pops died. You and I aren't, because we were too little to miss him."

"I guess. So what do you think I'll be when I grow up?"

"I dunno. You're too young to tell yet. An artist of some kind probably. What're you drawing?"

"Pops dead in the hotel room. I made his skin just ever so slightly green, see?"

"It's pretty good. You think he really made that big a mess in the room when he died, though?"

"Naw, he ran around messing everything up before."

***

Hamish Hollander, sometimes called Hames, was twelve. His sister Ondine, whom everyone called Deen, was nearly fourteen. They both had wavy reddish blond hair, pale skin, and long faces with green eyes. They liked each other well enough, finding it convenient to have in each other an ally. Childhood is often a battle waged by two alien nations—one with experience, power, and money; the other with nothing much in the way of weaponry but guile. Deen, of course, sat on her high horse about being so vastly much older, but Hamish was an even-tempered boy and took her loftiness in stride. They pooled their worries and their jokes about the frequently inexplicable behavior of adults.

***

Below them, in the basement kitchen, a slender blonde stood swaying barefoot, her feet dusty from the brick floor. Her name was Sadie Hollander. She had a loose-jointed, rackety look, and her tangled hair fell constantly over her eyes and just as constantly she pushed it back, making it even more disheveled, but somehow not diminishing her charm. She had a loopy smile and vague, dark blue eyes. Her white, somewhat grubby jeans rode low on her hips and the man's shirt she wore had a tear in one sleeve. She exuded wafts of the bygone sixties the way a woman's scarves are haunted by traces of perfume.

She looked around the kitchen, unsure what she'd come there to do. She shrugged and went to the counter to make herself a vodka rocks. She sliced a lime and squeezed a wedge over her drink, letting it fall in. "Plop," she said.

She took a sip and let out a sigh of pleasure. Ah, the first of the day. Just then a sleek brown mouse raced across the floor, leaped over her feet, then disappeared beneath the dishwasher. It peered out, its eyes like drops of India ink and its nose twitching.

"Hello," Sadie said to it, leaning down. "I'm going to have to think of a name for you. Something rather distinguished, I think. Aren't you lucky I don't live with some fussbudget husband who would lecture me about leaving food around, or put out traps? Gawd, what a dull life that would be."

She stood and said to herself, "I think Mommie'll have just one more drink before the hellish bore of making dinner." She often talked to herself, felt it quite a natural thing to do.

The mouse rose on its hind legs and climbed into the burrow it had made in the yellow insulation. It turned several times then curled up, its tail over its paws. It scratched its belly then slept, dreaming of waving grasses above, of moving below the verdant canopy, silent and hidden, fresh earth letting loose its scent. The mouse let out a squeak and dreamed of a ball of dried grasses tucked among some roots, inside which lay a knot of pink, hairless offspring, his drive solely to care for, their eyes still dark spots beneath their wrinkled skin.

Sadie, the impatient variety of dreamer, could never bear hanging around waiting for dinner to cook, so after she'd put together the meal she took her drink out to the back garden, to the table under the mulberry tree. September had nearly gone but she could still hear the creaks and whirs of the few remaining insects. The twilights were falling more swiftly, the light fleeing the sky with a whisper.

Her husband, Ree, had been the first, really the only person to notice her habit of watching the end of each day. How she'd drift away to be alone in the garden, or rooftop or balcony. How she never left the beach till all the light was gone, or in winter positioned herself by a window. And he'd understood that it wasn't because she was an addict of the pyrotechnics of sunset, but simply needed to observe each day's slide away from the sun. "Leave her be," he'd say to friends who tried to follow her. "She likes to watch it by herself."

Lights came on in the apartment to the west and she got up. "Deen, Hamish!" she called up the stairs. "Dinner's ready."

"Coming!" they yelled back.

She'd taken a bit of trouble with dinner, a pork tenderloin with rosemary, apples, and bacon, with potatoes and veg. She was vaguely aware that she hadn't done great things with dinner lately. She did not, in fact, recall the incident of the baked tennis shoe à la Provençal because she often didn't remember much about the night before, and her children had tactfully not mentioned it. But she did think that perhaps she'd done something silly again. That's how she always thought of it, as having done something silly. It never particularly bothered her—either the other party would get over it or they wouldn't.

Deen and Hamish came down the stairs, Hamish clumping. They looked rather worriedly at her.

"Oh, don't give me that look, all that bug-eyed nonsense," she said to them. "It's a perfectly good dinner. You should see what I had to eat growing up. The fifties were the most grisly era ever for cooking."

Deen got out napkins and silverware while Hamish put out glasses of water and lit the candles. As Sadie served the food, he uncorked a bottle of wine she'd left out and poured her a glass, sniffing it with an air of expertise.

When they sat down Hamish asked, "Munster, can I play Pops's Telecaster?"

"I wish you wouldn't call me that. No. Adolescent boys and rare, finicky guitars don't go together. No, now shush."

"How was your visit with Gretchen yesterday?" Deen asked her.

"Didn't I tell you last night?" Sadie said, surprised.

"Not really."

"Hmm. Well, she's drawing a lot, which is good, but you know how she's stuck on that dog drawing. I've been racking my brains to think what it means. The doctors have all kinds of idiotic ideas about it, but I think it has to do with a toy your father gave her when she was quite small that was tragically lost. She wept for days, it was heartbreaking. The younger doctor there though, he seems to have taken a real interest in Gretchen and says its meaning doesn't really matter, she simply needs to be given bigger paper.

"She was the easiest child," Sadie sighed. "Never a problem. We used to carry her around when she was a baby, in a sling I'd made out of an old paisley shawl. All the band members used to beg for a turn carrying her. She went everywhere with us and never ever cried during rehearsals and the noisiest parties you can imagine. She was our good luck talisman."

"Maybe she inhaled too much secondhand pot smoke," Hamish suggested.

"Certainly not. I know everyone's trying like mad to teach your generation that drugs are evil, but have some sense. A couple of joints do not make a person crazy. And as the children of someone who died of a heroin overdose I hardly feel the need to stuff your heads with a lot of nonsense from the D.A.R.E. handbook. Stuff's tommyrot anyway."

Above them the front door opened with a bang. Heavy steps were heard overhead.

"Oi!" a voice called down the stairs. "Where's the missus?"

"Uncle Brian!" Hamish cried, and charged up to meet him. He returned to the kitchen with an aging but still jaunty Englishman in a black leather jacket, gray jeans, and boots.

"Lo, Saids, how're you, love?" he said, kissing her. "Hames, fetch us a beer, there's a good lad. My little Deen, Deen-deenie, give us a kiss too."

Deen gave him a peck and he grabbed her, trying to draw her onto his lap as he sat at the table. She squirmed away from him.

"Oh ta very much," he said. "Forgot I was contagious."

"Oh, for Christ's sake, Brian, stop trying to molest Deen. She's getting a bit old for you anyway," Sadie said.

"Thanks ever so much, Saids. I'll have you know I draw the line at sixteen. Nice way to welcome me back, and here I was thinking you'd all be glad to see me. Well, I know where I'm not wanted, so I'll just nip back upstairs, grab my kit, and be gone." As he spoke in highly injured tones he pulled the platter of food toward him and began picking at it, then stole Deen's fork to eat some potatoes. "Anyone going to give a poor old man a bloody plate?" he asked.

Sadie laughed and set a place for him.

"You have some too, love," he said to her, noting that her plate had hardly been touched. "Come on, there's a good girl, have a tiny piece, you look like you could blow away in the first wind."

Brian Brain, né Brian Burker, was honorary uncle and protector of the Hollander clan, having been Ree Hollander's best friend, rhythm guitarist, and collaborator in writing most of their songs. He had dark, sad, exophthalmic eyes and runnels down his cheeks that seemed stained with coal dust. His still dark hair stood up from his scalp and his yellowing, crooked teeth still echoed his famous boyish grin. He now managed bands and had a key to Sadie's house, where he stayed whenever he was in New York. He sometimes invented reasons to be in the city, so that he could keep an eye on them.

He looked around the table, his sad, gummy eyes taking in everything. Deen, it was true, was not such a little girl anymore; he'd better stop thinking he could maul her about. And young Hames was frighteningly like his father must've been at that age, a skinny, pale lad, all hair and the will for passion. It broke his heart to look at Hames. Sadie, well, there was someone who never changed in his eyes. She'd been a wisp of a thing with tangled hair all over her eyes when he'd met her, her fine wrist with a chunky man's watch on it shooting out of a sleeve, a mad princess from a far-off land.

Sadie had eaten a few bites but had gone back to her vodka seconds later, sitting quietly, listening to the children chatter with Brian. She looked fondly at her children, at their bright hair and eager faces. So like Ree's it made her heart ache. They didn't like her giving them what they called "moony" looks, so she could only indulge in them when they weren't aware, but my, how she loved them.

She poured more vodka into her glass, now well into her seventh drink of the day. Then she put the glass down with a thud. She'd tried to set it down carefully but had misjudged the distance.

She'd always done it like that, Brian thought, seemed relatively sober until *bang,* she slipped over the edge.

She stood, putting a hand out to the fridge to balance herself. "Think I'll go to bed now," she said.

Brian got up and put an arm around her. "I'll walk you up, love. Can't have you breaking your neck just yet. Come on girl, up we go."

He came back down a few minutes later. The children were eating ice cream from pint cartons.

"She's been talking to a mouse that lives under the dishwasher," Deen told him.

"She's got a mouse for a friend?" Brian said. He poured himself some more red wine and lit a cigarette. Brian was a dedicated chain-smoker, so he was always about the business of smoking—of lighting one, cupping his hands, flapping out a match, tapping a pack against the back of his hand, taking a drag, squinting, flicking an ash, stamping out a butt, sending one sailing into the gutter, rummaging in his pockets, taking that first puff, his eyes dreamy, throwing his head back to exhale a jet of smoke, crumpling a finished packet into a ball.

"Well, I dunno if it's a *friend,* but she talks to it a lot."

"And she cooked a tennis shoe for dinner last night. With tomatoes and herbs. We had to put her to bed and get subs from Mr. Z's. Again," Hamish said.

"Right. We'll get all this straightened out. I'll have a little chat with her about tennis shoes and mice. Fair enough? Though mind you, talking to mice seems fairly normal to me."

"She's been drinking a shitload lately," Hamish told him.

"Munster's been acting kind of odd, even for her," Deen added. "We're worried she might be losing it."

"Your mother? Our Saids? Never," said Brian. "That woman doesn't lose it, she goes full bore off a cliff, a flaming trail of broken hearts in her wake. No, she holds onto it fast and takes it all with her. Your mum's saner than anyone I know. She's just drinking a bit hard is all. Worried about Gretchen, no doubt. And probably a bit lonely having no one but you two louts about the place. I shouldn't worry, she needs a bit of cheering up is all."

2

Sadie, like many dedicated drinkers, woke early, with a raging thirst. Too hazy to get up to satisfy it, she lay in bed letting her consciousness rise to the surface. She had a vague feeling that Brian had put her to bed—why she couldn't say. She flexed her toes and stretched her arms, chasing the image. She hoped he had, hoped that he was in the house. She felt sure she'd seen him last night, seen his thin, runnelly face at the dinner table. That's right, he'd lit a cigarette and said *last bloody place a man can smoke in this town*.

If he had put her to bed maybe he'd . . . yes he had, he'd left a bottle of apple juice on the floor within reach. Oh, kind genie. She drank a long swallow.

She looked around her room with the drifting interest of the newly wakened, her eye falling on various objects among the jumble. A rosewood cello key, a book bound in yellow cloth, a pile of necklaces, a glass with a smear of some ancient liquid in it, must remember to take that downstairs. A montage of other mornings, other places and times came back to her, powder spilled on a red lacquered tray, burned joints in their roach clips, big flashy earrings, letters from home, leaves caught up as mementos, reel-to-reel tapes, empty bottles. A thousand still lifes in a thousand mirrors of the day.

Heigh-ho, up and to the bathroom, that palace of flowing water. Sp-lash around in the cold first, *then* look in the mirror. She drew her fingers on either side of her cheeks, pulling the skin up and back. The effect was slightly weird but definitely younger. Is that where they would lay the scalpel? No, they never would, she'd never let them cut her for that, for mere vanity. Allow madmen with scalpels to cut her face so that she could pretend, yes, pretend! she shouted at the mirror, to be younger? Younger? She'd been young once and that was enough, thank you very much.

A drawing caught her eye, taped up next to the mirror. Of a crone leaning down to scream into a cauldron. Hamish's latest effort, evidently. Oh, the crone was her. But why did he show her screaming into a white cauldron? Who'd ever heard of a white cauldron for Christ's sake? Cauldrons were black, everyone knew that. Well, she'd ask him later.

It is a known phenomenon among drunks, their minds and their systems hardened to their habits and therefore suffering in no way the depredations of a hangover that a novice drinker suffers, that if they wake early they still have a bit of the juice running through their veins, therefore the sometimes astonishing jauntiness of their behavior in the mornings. Sadie was among this hardy type, and she sang a song as she tied her peacock silk dressing gown around her. "Who knows what evil lurks in the shadow of a society woman's bustle?" she sang. "Perhaps the imps of Satan." Nevertheless, she held firmly to the banister as she went down the stairs.

She read the *Times* and drank coffee, tucking one foot under her, enjoying knowing she would be alone for an hour or more. Hames woke first, clumping down the stairs, making a racket. He kicked the fridge and tangled with chair legs, getting himself breakfast, wanting to talk but knowing she wouldn't, so he clamped his headphones over his ears and munched away, lost in a world of miraculous guitars. Deen came down later, to eat an apple and read a book. Then they grabbed their knapsacks and rushed off.

Sadie looked around her and sighed. She loved this house but it really needed some work. Maybe if she could just get it to a certain point she could feel the courage to do some painting and spiffing up. But like her life, it was too unraveled.

Many people—or perhaps one should say, many people like Sadie, aren't much good at handling staff. A delicate balance exists between employer and employee in the household and a certain toughness and dispassion is needed on the part of the employer, which Sadie, child of the egalitarian sixties, was incapable of. As a result, after having lost a trusted and efficient cleaner who'd been with her for ten years, she'd tried repeatedly to find someone—let us be correct and not call it a woman, to clean her house once a week with any degree of skill, care, or honesty. Or anything like the spit and polish that in the recesses of her untidy soul she cried for, an ancient holdover from her New England childhood and its memories of salt-washed shingles.

Corralled into hiring nearly any applicant by her willingness to give everyone the benefit of the doubt, she'd soon realize she'd made a mistake. She was adept at not seeming to fire them, simply wafting away. "Darling, I am so sorry," she'd say. "But it turns out we all have to go back to London for I don't know how long, ages perhaps. So it simply wouldn't be fair not to let you be a free agent, look around for other work."

There would be a slightly mulish tone to her last sentence, so perhaps she wasn't so bad at firing people after all. But she had to screw herself up for weeks to do it. Meanwhile, the house got rattier.

Into every run of bad luck and poor judgment there eventually comes a whiff of hope. Some weeks earlier Sadie had hired a new woman named Brenda MacFarland. Brenda MacFarland had a churchy, solid air and smelled of starch. Her skin was the color of polished chestnuts and she was very good-looking, but seemed to be trying to hide it. She'd told Sadie, as if getting it off her chest, that she'd come north from South Carolina with a husband thirteen years ago, and that he had left her with their boy to raise. Then she'd looked around disapprovingly and said, "This here's going to take some real thumping and scrubbing to even make a start. Just so you know."

Sadie waved her hand around vaguely. "Yes, it does rather, doesn't it? It's gotten so none of us can find anything."

"Well, I'll have to chip and chip till I get there. Don't go expecting any miracles right away."

Sadie felt a shiver of hope at Brenda's obvious disgust with the state of the house. She thought it a happy omen the way she clenched her jaw as she gave it the gimlet eye.

And things had indeed begun to improve. Each week, after finishing the general cleaning, Brenda attacked a particular part of the house, staring at it first and seeming to breathe smoke as she planned her campaign.

Brenda appeared to prefer to be left alone while she worked, so Sadie kept out of the way. She also liked to give a full report when she'd finished, one that culminated in a triumphant description of her day's special project. These pleasant sessions were conducted in the kitchen.

"I got it into my mind to take the bull by the horns and do something about that front hall," she told Sadie that afternoon. "My, there was a mountain of dust behind that table, and a few things some people have been looking for for some time, I don't doubt. And that light above? Must've been a whole army of dead bugs in there. Been a while since you had anybody knows what they're doing here, hasn't it? Floor's waxed too."

"How wonderful, Brenda. It's getting so I look forward with real relish to hearing about your special projects. I think I'll take my drink up there later to just sit and admire it."

"Miz, uh . . ." Brenda trailed off, uncomfortable at using Sadie's first name, though she'd been asked to more than once. For years she'd worked during the week for an old dragon to whom the rigors of social hierarchy were law, and she was used to addressing her employer formally.

She began again, dispensing with the tricky problem of names. "I was thinking, if all the copper pots and such down here got polished it'd sure be brighter. Now, it'd be years before I could get to that, so I was wondering, what if I bring my boy Liall along next Saturday? He's twelve and can do as he's told. Oh no, I didn't mean for you to have to pay him," she added, seeing the look on Sadie's face. "But it's like this—he's a good boy but big for his age, and he's starting to run after some older boys I don't like the cut of, not one bit. If he were here I could keep an eye on him and sure worry less. I was minding about giving this kitchen here for instance a real going over, and I know I could do it a lot better if there were gladness in my heart and I wasn't worried about my boy."

Sadie thought this as neat a piece of blackmail as she'd ever heard. It also made perfect sense, so she said, "Bring him along, by all means. Perhaps he'll shame my two into stirring themselves to a bit of work. But I'm a little troubled by the idea of a young boy scouring pots down here all day, it seems a bit Dickensian."

"Oh no, I thought he could do some then go off to play in the park, or do some errands. I'll make sure he's no bother."

"Maybe he and Hamish might do some things together. They're the same age. But children are funny about being put together. . . ."

Sadie trailed off. She hoped fervently that the two boys would like each other, but hopes like that were so often dashed.

"Yes, that's the truth," Brenda said. For the first time a look of true warmth was exchanged between the two women.

After Brenda had gone, Sadie sat at the kitchen table marking the calendar she made each week for the children's schedules. Red for Hames and blue for Deen, it was taped to the fridge each Saturday.

Sadie had thought long and hard about education in the city for her children. She'd decided that private schools were too insular, but then the public schools not challenging enough. Homeschooling was out, she was far too flighty and unlettered, besides it had always struck her as slightly creepy to be both mother and teacher. Surely homeschooled children grew up to be socially maladjusted. So she'd hit on a fourth option—she paid certain inhabitants of the Village to give them lessons. The Village was stuffed with intellectuals and artists with time on their hands and a liking for cash money. In fact, the children were getting excellent educations for far less than the cost of private school. The only drawback was that their schedules were complicated and often subject to change. Twice a year they took a test to prove that they'd passed the required state levels, tests they galloped through.

Having taped up the schedule she then turned her mind to planning dinner. Once she'd done that she could have a fucking drink and relax. Brian had said he'd be back, so she'd better go to the market. A limo had called for him at noon to take him to the recording studio. Good old Brian, he still kept rocker's hours, still rushed down at noon to drain two cups of coffee and smoke two fags, acting as if he'd been wrenched out of bed at dawn. He still wore leather and strutted around like a lad, got into brawls, and worked now with other, younger bands. He'd never married and to Sadie's mind it had kept him from ever feeling either the dull weight of responsibility or alimony.

***

Upstairs, Deen let herself in the front door and headed straight for the piano. Elizabeth, her piano teacher, had begun her that afternoon on Beethoven's *Pathétique.* She was itching to keep working on it. She pulled the music out of her case and set it on the stand, looking at the notes, absorbing their pattern. She took a breath, straightened her back, held her chin up and her arms out, relaxed, and began. The solemnity, sadness, and vigor of the piece thrilled her.

She threw herself into playing, letting herself go now that she was alone with it, but knew she must slow down, do what Elizabeth had shown her. To breathe in the sense of the piece then exhale, to create the modality of the dying notes. Slow the chords, use the pauses, timing was everything, breathe with it. She came to the climax of pity in the piece, the fading gasps of some beautiful, broken creature. Two tears welled at the corners of her eyes. She nearly wanted to stop, to lean over and bawl her eyes out over the keys it spoke to her so strongly of the well of human loneliness, but her desire to play was greater.

One level of her mind thought of the music, the other of Gretchen. All alone in that terrible place. Oh, so alone. Cut off from everyone, abandoned, and with all those terrible people wandering the hallways like ghouls.

Did being crazy mean not actually knowing where you were, being all confused, not knowing why you were there? Why all of a sudden your own family sent you away, just that you're lost and it hurts? Like an animal feels, lying in the road after being hit by a car, but not knowing what a car is? Torn asunder and bleeding—oh, stop thinking about that.

Deen could see more clearly now what had happened to Gretchen than in the confused days six months ago. Well, it had started earlier than that, she could see that now, when Gretchen stopped playing the drums. It had seemed like an ordinary teenage whim at the time. But Gretchen loved her drums, spent hours tuning and adjusting them. Then she'd gradually stopped talking. Right up to the time she'd really stopped talking, it hadn't seemed so odd, she'd hardly ever talked anyway.

Now Deen saw how Sadie had tried to keep what was happening from her. The veiled conferences behind sealed doors, Sadie slamming the lid down on the washer before Deen saw what was in it. The people Munster had coming over to the house at all hours to sit with Gretchen, and Dr. Ed skidding in and out. The day it had all boiled over and Deen, thinking she'd heard her mother call out for her, went running into Gretchen's room, though she'd been told not to. She couldn't figure it out; Gretchen was all cut up. All the parts of her that would normally be covered were all cut up. Munster was holding a bloody towel and she threw her head back like she was going to howl, then covered Gretchen with it. Made no sound, which was worse than if she'd screamed. Then Dr. Ed came and the three of them left in an ambulance.

Deen played the final chords slowly, they made her ache with sadness. But Elizabeth had told her that in music mood had two levels, that tears and someone leaving had to have another sound hidden inside them, a faint but inevitable ringing that spoke of joy, return. She'd said that the dominant note could only truly effect pathos if the opposite notes hovered inside it. That there was no certain way of saying how to play this, except that you knew. But scales have it inside them too, Deen thought, obviously. Scales are logic and highly refined systems of numbers, and have two ends that must meet.

And every time her mind, not that she allowed it to often, replayed that image of her sister on her bed, she felt sure that even though the whole world had troubled families and were crying and wailing on

Oprah, that Gretchen had been waylaid and attacked by evil, jealous demons. That they had found a way into her room and out of their rage for her beauty and her pure, trusting ways, had attacked her viciously with knives.

***

Gretchen at that moment was sitting in a wheelchair in the corner of a large room with a linoleum floor, sofas in a nasty shade of blue, and potted plants with broad, dark leaves. Night had fallen and the bank of windows along one wall no longer afforded their calming views of acres of mown grass and trees in islands of pachysandra. She was alone. This pleased her. They'd forgotten to collect her for dinner. She'd sat very still and tried to blend in with the potted plant next to her. Soon they'd figure it out and come looking for her, to put her to bed. She worked harder on her drawing to get it done before they did.

The pad was a large block of Manila paper. It had hairs on its surface that clutched at the pastels she kept in a paper coffee cup by her side. She preferred colored pencils but was not allowed to have anything sharp. She was very careful not to get any pastel marks on her bathrobe, bad things happened if you did. When she moved her mouth up and down fast, like she was talking bat talk, she was thinking bad things. Like how she wanted to color everything over like mad, scream the colors over her face, her clothes, the walls. But bad things happened if you did.

Her drawing, the only drawing she'd made since bad things had started happening, had to be very carefully done. One thing out of kilter and, well, she didn't like to think about that. In the exact center of the page, at the bottom, feet planted along the edge of the paper, stood a dog. A shaggy, brownish, blondish dog. It had long fringed ears and its arms were raised, its paws held out flat.

On each paw stood a smaller version of the same dog. On each of their four paws eight more, smaller dogs sprang forth, and so on until she reached the edges of the page. When she did she would cry helplessly. But because Gretchen didn't talk she didn't cry like a speaking person does, she only made a faint, keening buzz.

3

Sadie had bought the house on West Tenth Street with money her father had left her. The sudden appearance of a large sum of cash in her life had caused her to sit down and think. She thought for a long while and with care, deciding a surprising number of things. The first was that she was tired of living in England. She'd been living in London since she was eighteen, when she'd met Ree. Her father had given her a trip to Paris and London for the summer before she was to go to Sarah Lawrence. Suitably chaperoned by a school friend and her mother, of course. The mother, it turned out, was given to migraines, and as a result was a good deal of the time no threat to Sadie's freedom. And the friend turned out to be a bit of a pill, afraid of cities, foreigners, and the many things she constantly deemed "icky." So Sadie left them at the hotel, blithely exploring the two cities and growing up quite a bit in the process. It was 1968 and if you were young, or had any go in you at all, there were many new experiences to be had. She met Ree just before she was due to fly home, and as a result was the cause of many and more severe migraines, as she refused point-blank to quit London, leaving her friend's mother with the task of relating this news to her parents.

The woman's tears and moans and her friend's shrieks caused her not even the slightest twinge as she picked out some clothes and crammed them into a single suitcase. A thoroughly bad, willful, snot-nosed, evil, uncaring girl by then, proclaimed such in high-pitched American accents, she got on the elevator. The uniformed operator gave her a worried, fatherly glance. He had a postcard of JFK peeking out of his pocket. "A great man, and a poor, terrible martyr," he said, touching it reverently. "Now who's to lead us all to peace and brotherhood? You'll be after a taxi then, Miss?"

"To hell with taxis," Sadie said, picking up her bag and marching through the lobby. "And to hell with Sarah Lawrence!" she cried as she reached the street, where Ree was waiting for her.

They lived in seedy flats in sordid London neighborhoods, dodging angry landladies and never knowing who was crashed on the sofa, or sometimes whose sofa they were crashed on. Or quite where they were on the continent, on bleary mornings in hotel rooms littered with empty bottles. Her mother wrote tearful letters, pleading with her to come home, her father sighed and sent her a check each month. He had to send them care of the American Express office in London, because she and Ree moved so often. Or, rather, were asked to leave.

So when Sadie sat down to think her long think, she decided that after all those rackety years she wanted a house. She strung her thoughts carefully, knotting each to the next. Because Ree had to be in New York often and she now wanted to live in the States, she would buy a house there. The idea grew in her mind until it could not be stopped.

Ree hadn't wanted Sadie to buy the house. He argued that it was too expensive, too much responsibility. Sadie had nodded and not said much, but her mind was made up. She'd decided to have another child, possibly two more, and knew that Ree didn't have the instinct to make a permanent home, so she would have to. She'd let him go off on the tour alone, resigning herself to the probability that he'd sleep with other women but also knowing that Brian would be there to make sure things didn't get out of hand.

So she'd parked Gretchen with a friend and began determinedly walking the streets of the Village, looking for her house. On the second day, exploring farther west, she found it. The gods favored her choice—it had just that day come on the market. She didn't have to see the inside to be quite certain that it was her house—the house had a face, one that seemed to say *Oh Sadie, I've been waiting for you*. She stood and smiled at it from across the street. Its sandstone steps were worn and its windows dull with grime. A crack in the wooden gate to the garden showed a tangle of greenery beyond. She was thirty-one, bounding with energy, and she was going to put everything she'd learned into making this house beautiful. She noted the agent's address and walked there as quickly as she could without breaking into a run, which she felt would be undignified, and besides, she didn't want to go into the office red and gasping—that was hardly the best way to negotiate a price. Two hours later, she wrote a check for the deposit.

When Ree's tour ended he looked around, shrugged, and set his guitars down. The house was draped in canvas drop cloths and filled with building materials. Sadie and Gretchen were camping out upstairs while the work was being done, sleeping on bare mattresses on the floor.

"Got its uses," he said. "Right nice room this is. You going make it a bit posh, I suppose? Well, first thing to do is christen it."

As she bought sofas and rugs for it, he insisted they christen each in turn. In his way of thinking, a sofa, a rug, and sometimes even an armchair weren't properly owned by a couple until they'd made love on it. As a result she only bought pieces a full-grown man could recline comfortably on, with fabrics of a soft but durable texture. And she didn't fuss about cleaning off the marks of their congress, believing that any self-respecting velvet sofa should bear the signs of its history. Ree further marked his new territory by doing drugs off every surface in it.

The house had needed quite a lot of work, so she hired a builder with a small crew. They began with the basement. A warren of pokey rooms took up the back half and a dingy kitchen the front. Not fully below street level, it had windows looking onto a sunken area in front and to the garden in back. She had every interior wall taken down and made a large kitchen modeled after the English country kitchens she admired. It had a herringbone brick floor, two wide step-back cupboards, and a pine table that sat twelve at the end nearest the street. She'd laid and grouted the red Mexican tiles for the countertops herself. At the garden end was a laundry area with basket chairs by the window and a washroom, a small defeat in the battle for open space, but one she'd had to concede. The kitchen had been wonderful in its day and still exuded a certain hippie luxe, though now rather worn and stained by accidents with bottles of red wine.

Upstairs the sitting room also ran the length of the house. It had ten-foot ceilings and rather grand moldings. A pair of tall French doors led out to a narrow balcony over the garden and a pair of fine windows overlooked the street. Double doors led into it from either end of the hall. A fireplace with a handsome Adam chimneypiece sat in the center of the opposite wall. Sadie had put everything she'd learned in the seventies about English decoration into it. Its walls were painted a deep, toasted persimmon glazed with paraffin, its woodwork picked out in gloss white. A large seventeenth-century Flemish curio cabinet of ebony and ivory on barley-turned legs stood on one wall by the fireplace and a tall Dutch secretary on the other, painted black, with scarlet and green parrots among fringed tulips. A pair of boxy modern sofas with deep down cushions sat facing each other in the center, a Parsons table lacquered in white between them. A straw-colored wool rug, rather worn now, covered the floor. Italian painted consoles and black lacquered chests of drawers with rococo mirrors above them stood along the walls, and scattered around them were groups of French fauteuils painted gloss white and upholstered in tobacco brown velvet. A grand piano sat in an island between the French doors to the balcony and the sofas. Large prints by Stella, Motherwell, and Johns in white frames hung on the walls, with skillfully arranged clusters of sketches and photographs of Ree, Sadie, their children and friends, in antique frames between. Richly colored Chinese jars, mercilessly drilled and turned into lamps, were dotted about, with white silk drum shades.

Sadie still felt a swell of contentment whenever she went into the room. She'd thought it a wheeze to create a room like this, one like that of some old doyenne's, but for one still young. And it was so very unlike her mother's, with its chintzes, pastel walls, and timid displays of Minton china.

It was also wildly comfortable and well suited to parties, where people could gather in large groups or small. As a result there was a cigarette burn, a scuff, or a chip on everything in it.

Upstairs the bedrooms, by contrast, were quite plain. Sadie, reverting to her New England roots, thought that children's rooms should be left alone, for surely any child with an imagination would want to fill it with his or her own peculiar collection. She had, though, made a more attractive room for herself and Ree, knocking down a wall and making a long, French-gray bedroom overlooking the garden. After Ree died, she'd had the wall put back up to make a needed guest room and hadn't cared anymore if her room was beautiful. In fact, it was now a mess, not at all like a proper grown-up's, with clothes hanging everywhere and books piled in heaps on the floor.

Gretchen's room was at the front, dominated by a large drum kit now covered with dust.

At the top of the house, on the attic floor, Deen and Hamish ruled. Deen, being older, got the room overlooking the garden, Hames the one on the street. Ree's old music room was between them. He'd wanted it a shade of midnight blue, a night color, and as it was windowless it was a room of perpetual twilight. It had a blue leather sofa and chairs he'd chosen himself. Sadie hated to admit it, but he'd had dreadful taste. Still, she hadn't changed it—it was a bit of a shrine and the children loved it. She'd moved his guitars down to her room, not trusting Hamish to leave them alone, and replaced his reel-to-reel with a TV set. Ree had never hung his gold records, but after he died she'd put them all up in there, covering the walls. She thought they would be a comfort to his children—a dead father was a decided handicap but a famous dead father somewhat less so.

* * *

Ree. Ree Hollander, Ree for Hen-ry. A working-class boy. Not many toffs became rockers. Was it because boys like Ree were brasher, or because they grew up in an age of revolt, and the downtrodden so often lead the charge? Whatever the reason, the deprivations of post-war England created a new warrior class of bluesmen who translated their love for that American vernacular into fierce new music.

Into the vortex of the sixties they leaped, uncluttered by bourgeois values or awe of tradition. Raised in the class-bound, regimented England of the fifties they knew exactly what they were—rough louts who were expected to live lives in service to others, as repairmen, clerks, railway agents, farm laborers, deliverymen, or pipefitters.

Henry Hollander finished school at seventeen. He hadn't done well enough for any teacher to encourage him to try for O levels, but neither had he been at the bottom of the class. His father presented him with fifteen pounds and a gray suit jacket he'd outgrown. He went over and over the plan with his son. Henry would take the train to Sheffield, then a bus to his Uncle Tim's, where his Aunt Cecily would be expecting him. Henry was to be polite and keep his gob shut, then go off with Tim in the morning to see the plant manager. And by God he'd say thanks to any job offered and no lagging about. At the end of this oft-repeated talk, his father offered a simple philosophy of life: *See, it's good work, a large printer like that, plenty of opportunities for a bright lad. Provided he keeps his eyes open and wants to learn, stays on the right side of his betters and does whatever he's asked to cheerfully. Why, a lad like that would get on well, learn a skill like typesetting or become a pressman. Skilled men can always get work, even when times are hard.*

Henry took the fifteen pounds, the jacket, his cheap acoustic guitar, and a small cardboard suitcase and got on the train. He got off at the next stop, took a train back, then bought a second-class ticket for London.

The next few months of young Henry's life were difficult and very lonely. He had quite a rough time of it, in fact. He slept in cars, suffered insults, and was sometimes even hungry.

Then things started to look up. He made some friends, acquired a nickname, and found work at an all-night café. Girls who had their own flats figured in his dreams but he was shy, pale, and thin, and girls ignored him.

When the band he formed with his best mate, Brian Brain, né Burker, also from the north, played their first gig at a pub in Pimlico, he thought he was finally on the way. But the crowd talked through their music and seemed to hardly notice they were playing at all. The band was called the Jesters. They played acoustic guitars and sang of fair maidens on gray palfreys. They were paid with a plate of hot food and two pints each. It was all very dispiriting, and as one gig after another in small clubs on the outskirts of London passed, no one noticing them much or minding them much, he and Brian worked on new songs. They spent every night holed up in the tiny kitchen of a flat owned by a girl Brian knew, working on the songs and a way to make their music and their voices more commanding. They took on extra shifts at the moving company where they both worked now, hoarding their money to buy electric guitars and amps, visiting shops that sold secondhand equipment, and talking all day about various guitars. Then a chap who knew a fellow named Luther said Luther needed to sell his '58 Les Paul for quick cash. With a Bandmaster amp and a reverb unit. When Ree played it he felt like he'd been waiting for it his whole life. In his hands, it felt like a beautiful woman who suddenly, amazingly, turned to him and said, please take me. Brian insisted he buy it, even though it took all the money they'd saved.

Often Ree felt guilty as he played it, seeing the hungry look Brian gave it when he thought Ree didn't notice. And sometimes Ree woke in the smoky gray dawn of a London morning, willing himself to get up and go to work after only a few hours sleep, to see Brian already up, silently fingering their new songs on it. "Just getting practice for when I got my own," Brian would say, looking embarrassed.

A drunken housewife gave them a tenner one day for a tip, after they'd finished moving her goods. They ran all the way to a shop on the Brompton Road that had a secondhand two-tone Rickenbacker in the window that Brian had been lusting after for weeks. Luck often seems to come in waves: at the same time, the owner of the moving company gave them permission to hold band practice in the warehouse at night. Their bass player got his hands on a Fender bass, white with a black back and neck, and they met a drummer who said yeah, he'd give it a go, why not? He actually owned a drum set and suddenly they had a real band.

They practiced every night in the shadowy warehouse, working out the new songs Ree and Brian had written in their kitchen sessions. They gave up beer and cigarettes to pool their money to buy a set of cymbals and a mike. Though they were often asked in later years, nobody could ever quite remember how it had come about, but one night they renamed the band the Royhatten Transference. Every evening they arrived at the warehouse around eight and played until after midnight, to hone their new sound. Gigs were discontinued until they had it right. Nobody had a pot to piss in, and they were all demented with the notion of making real music. Three months later they auditioned for a club in Soho and were given a one-time trial gig.

Ree got his first taste of playing Jesus that night. There were lights at the club and he took to them, and they to him. He was transformed. His transformation looked back at him in the eyes of the people on the floor; they looked at him as if he had something that only he could confer. It scared him slightly, then made him doubly ambitious, made him want to do extravagant moves with his guitar as he played, raise his arms, throw his hair back as he sang. The lights rained down on him, bathing him in their electric glory.

The success of that night and others that followed lit a fire under Ree. He spent every conscious moment thinking the music he was writing. He and Brian grew bitter calluses on their hands, then broke them off playing with newer frenzy; the calluses grew back harder each time until they became permanent. They didn't know how to write music, so they invented their own method of notation. They didn't speak about it, but Randy, the drummer, had to go.

Evan Moore, the bass player, was no worry at all. He was good and kept getting better. Bass players have the reputation of being the stupidest member of the band, and Evan lived up to this. He said he couldn't understand their notation system but in any case didn't need it, he had to just feel it, and they agreed. They could go into a jam and he'd plug right along, had a real feel for their moves. His hands were so big that Ree joked that he could wrap them around the neck twice.

Randy was a perfectly sound drummer of standard beats but too fond of little riffles of snare and cymbals, a style of drumming more appropriate to older pop tunes. Randy eventually went, but only after Ree and Brian had found a new drummer, who they kept under wraps. Randy didn't like being told he didn't make the grade, and before they parted he made his views on their characters, their manhood, and their sexuality plain. But finally, with a last squawk, he was gone.

Giff Loudon, the new drummer, was a kid. A long-haired, skinny, smelly kid. He had a foot that could bang down on the backbeat just in the upswing of expectation, a beat that went right up your ass and into your brain. He was sixteen and no more acclimated to human society than a feral cat. His normal state was so wired that Ree and Brian never let him get his hands on any drugs if they could help it.

Ree first saw Sadie as she walked across the floor of a club. He wasn't playing there, just having a drink as he waited for a band he wanted to hear come on. About to raise a pint to his mouth he stopped, looking at her face, her tousled hair, her small frame. Something about her made him want to know her. She seemed perfectly assured of her place among the crowd yet somehow not at all a part of it. She disappeared behind a mirrored wall. He seemed to wake, cried out, "Wait!" then fought his way through the mass of people. He looked everywhere, jumping up to get a better view, even went around the block at a run. But she was gone. He felt at the same time that he wished to die and that now, having seen her, now at last he knew who she was.

After that night he went out constantly, accepted any and all invitations, took the bus rather than the tube, and sat in the top so he could scour the faces on the street below. He played and replayed the fragment of film in his head, he could see her perfectly, her eyes more inward than outward, her straight spine, the fine hair caught behind her ear, her nose, her jaw, the loose, fluent walk, her moodiness.

Several weeks passed and he alternated between hopelessness and the feeling that the gods could not be so cruel, so insane as to show a mortal a peek, then drop the curtain forever.

In the years to come he always described their eventual meeting as so mundane you'd think there was nothing of the roll and thunder of fate to it. Someone said, *Oh, have you met Sadie?* He was never able to dredge up any memory of who. They stepped aside and there she was. She offered her hand and smiled. She said hello. He learned a thousand things he'd ached to know about her.

The band moved from playing at small clubs to bigger ones, to opening for other bands at concerts, to record deals and radio performances. Ree played for her. He couldn't play if she weren't there. She'd stand in the center of the flailing dancers near the stage, intent on the music. He invented all his famous moves in those months, the leaps, the flourishes of his guitar, a spin that made his hair fly out, for her eyes. He'd look out and see the crowd as a meaningless mass, with her as their still center. The lights rained down, gilding his long, gingery hair and the glints of it that peeked from his armpits, the narrow line of it that ran down to his groin, and his milky white body as it flexed like rawhide to the music.

4

Sadie had a dinner party at the end of the week. She often did when Brian was there. He liked to see his New York friends and though he wasn't much help in the kitchen, preparing the dinner with him in the room was far less of a bore. And dinners with him present were more successful, Sadie had to admit. It didn't occur to her that the truth was, she hadn't had a dinner party without him since Ree died.

The children had entertained the guests before dinner with a poem they'd written called "Fabulosovich." Hamish recited it while Deen played an accompaniment she'd written. The poem was about a lion who is cursed by an evil sorceress and must travel to a land where cows rule, to persuade their king to give him a cloak that will free him from the curse. The cloak is made of grass and the lion must control his terrible urge to leap on the cows and devour them.

The guests had been charmed, the dinner edible, and the conversation wide and amusing around the long table. As was their habit, Brian and Sadie settled in for a nightcap in the living room after the guests had left.

"Right then," Brian said, sprawling on one of the sofas. "That all went off well. You should have company in the evening more often, love, look at you—it's gone midnight and you're not a bit sozzled."

"Don't worry, I'll catch up," Sadie said, pouring herself a large vodka rocks. "Want a brandy?"

"Ta. Those kids of yours are bloody naturals for the stage, you know."

"Gawd, don't I. All three of them." Sadie sat on the other sofa, kicking off her shoes and putting her feet up on the coffee table.

"Remember that first apartment we all rented, with that ballroom with the cracked mirrors? Not a stick of furniture and the place looked as if it'd been looted by soldiers. Bloody great crack in the wall where a bomb had hit the house next door. My word, the partying we did there. Threw us out because of it, didn't they?"

"And that silly girl Mona you were screwing. Always standing on her head with no panties on, waggling it in Ree's face."

"She was a real tart all right. Weren't we all just mad with the excitement of it, sex for the asking, drugs for every psychic journey, biting all the hands that fed us? I feel a bit sorry for kids these days, honestly, what's left to overturn?"

"Oh, don't start getting wistful on me, Brian. Have you got a girl these days, I mean, one you can legally be seen about with?"

"No, there's no one much I fancy these days. There's a couple of birds I take out now and then, silly cows really, don't know why I bother. Got to keep up appearances I suppose. Randy old Brian Brain, still pulling the girls."

"You always did like them singularly stupid."

***

Later, between the sheets in Sadie's guest room, Brian smoked a joint and wished he'd blurted out the truth, that he dated girls he found physically attractive but otherwise completely uninteresting. . . . Oh, why couldn't she see it, that he'd never wanted girls for anything but their bodies, so that he wouldn't have to love them, so that his heart could stay true to her? And why the hell didn't he ever tell her what seemed to him an obvious truth? Maybe if she knew he loved her she'd start to get used to the idea, turn it over in her mind. He knew she hardly ever had dinner parties except when he was there, which meant—here the pot started to kick in, sending his thoughts aloft—which meant she thought of him as a sort of consort, a fill-in husband to preside over the table at her side, didn't it? Why the hell didn't he walk down the hall and into her bedroom right now, draw her arms up and caress them, kiss her, and show her he loved her, in the only way he knew?

He groaned and took the last toke, dropping the roach in the ashtray. Of course he'd never even allowed himself to think like that while Ree was alive, he and Ree were mates. But Ree'd been dead twelve years and here was Sadie, pining right away, boozing and dreaming her life away like some princess locked in a tower. But he was too scared he'd see that look on her face if he tried, of shock and sad resignation, oh no, I trusted you never to do that. . . . And then, worse, her inability to conceal her distaste. No, he didn't have a chance with her, see, because she was Ree's girl, had been Ree's one and only queen. No other woman had ever meant anything to Ree, though many had tried. And she, having been Ree's queen, wasn't likely to take up with his ugly, less famous mate, was she? Step down? Not her. Other women, beautiful women, gave him a whirl gladly, wasn't he Brian Brain, Ree Hollander's legendary collaborator and, some said, the real driving sound behind the band? But not our Sadie. Our Saids had sat on the throne while Brian and the rest of the world had cavorted below, desiring only her approval.

Christ, this line of thinking was just driving him mad. He got up and put his clothes back on. He crept up the stairs and listened at Hamish's door. Sure enough, the lad was still up. He and Hamish had a secret—he'd been teaching him to play guitar. He tapped on the door.

"Who is it?"

"Oi, kid, I thought of some new stuff to show you. Bring your guitar into your dad's room, we'll work on some bar chords."

* * *

In the morning Sadie was washing pots and pans and stacking the dishwasher with the remains of the party's wreckage, mentally looking over her shoulder as she did, wanting to get it done before Brenda arrived. Their agreement had stipulated that Brenda cleaned the house and did not wash sinks full of dirty dishes, do laundry, or iron. Brenda scared Sadie just a little bit, which all in all she decided was a good thing.

The area door opened just as Sadie scoured the last pot. Brenda put her bag down and hung up her jacket. "This is my boy Liall," she said. "Liall, say how do you do to Mrs. Hollander."

Sadie wiped her hands on a tea towel and offered one to Liall, who smiled up at her shyly. He had a very square face, a very nice face, Sadie thought, wondering if he might not grow up to be a handsome man. His skin was darker than his mother's and his checked shirt was starched to a boardlike sheen.

"I'll start him on some polishing right now, then get to doing something about this kitchen," Brenda said. "You sit down at that table Liall and keep yourself quiet."

Sadie said, "Well, I'll leave you to it. Hamish and Deen are upstairs, I'll see if I can get them to do something about that bathroom of theirs. Liall, why don't you come up later, when your mother says you can, and meet them?"

The boy nodded, looking pleased, then looked down.

Oh dear, Sadie thought as she climbed the stairs, children are so tenuous. So exposed, everything flying at them and not yet knowing when to duck, only beginning the process of learning to hide things in order to preserve the inner core of self. These thoughts were rather rudely challenged when she saw her two youngest lolling on the twin sofas upstairs, reading magazines and looking as indolent as pashas.

"You two are going to march upstairs and do something about that foul pit you call your bathroom, this instant!" she yelled. "And I don't mean make any little dainty dabs at it either. You're going to scrub some of that scurf and pestilence off it. Now!"

Deen and Hamish jumped up, startled. They looked at each other and shrugged, oh boy, Munster was on a tear. They mooched off toward the stairs in silence, their shoulders telling a tale of childhood woe.

"I'll send Brenda up with some carbolic soap and a blowtorch!" she yelled after them. "Maybe some napalm!"

Deen and Hamish rolled their eyes and made a gesture known only to them. They drew their mouths back in a leer, showing their teeth, and raised their hands up, shaping them into raptor's claws. It was their secret signal for "Munster's on the warpath."

Slowly, ever so slowly, they cleared some of the clutter out of their bathroom and looked around dispiritedly at the grimy tiles, the scum in the tub, the layers of gunk coating the shelves.

"Look at you two," Brenda said from the door. "Wanderers in a strange land. This is my boy Liall."

"What's the matter with your leg?" Hamish asked him.

"I fell down onto the tracks and it got cut off. See, it's a fake leg," Liall said, lifting his pants to reveal a plastic ankle with metal hinges.

"That is totally fucked up," Hamish said rather admiringly.

"Yeah, and it's white."

"I thought they had all kinds of fancy robotic legs now, and like, well, why'd they give you a white leg?"

"Not if you're on Medicaid."

"Now you quit that, Liall," his mother said. "They gave you a leg, didn't they, and fixed you up the best they could. You didn't die, did you?"

"I could get some paint and make it look more like your other leg," Hamish offered.

"You leave that leg of his alone," Brenda said. "It's got all sorts of parts to it and I don't want it gummed up with any paint. Now, your mother's gone off somewhere, and she's thinking to have this bathroom cleaned, so the three of you get on out of here, it gives me a pain to see you two wiping at those walls with your little hands. There isn't a child on earth that knows anything about scrubbing. Go on, get moving."

"Say, your mother's pretty tough, isn't she?" Hamish asked Liall as the three children walked down Tenth Street. "She like that all the time?"

"I heard your mother yelling at you. Is she like that all the time?"

"She just drank too much lion water last night," Deen told him.

"What's that mean?"

"Means she wakes up all mad and roaring," Hamish said.

"It means," Deen said, "she drinks a shitload of booze each night and wakes up with superhuman powers."

"Why does she do that? Drink so much, I mean."

"She just does. Some mothers do, some don't. What's your mother do?"

"Just always after me to be good, stay on the right, keep clean, no swearing."

"That's what they all do. Like we're gonna listen. The hell of it is, we have to listen."

"Hey, let's go over to Gray's Papaya," Hamish said. "See all the hookers looking tired. They eat six dogs and drink fruit shakes and say really weird things," he explained to Liall.

"Let's go by the park first, see if Cap'n Meat's there," Deen suggested.

"Who's Cap'n Meat? Sounds like one scary motherfucker with a name like that," Liall said.

"He's a bum," Deen told him. "We like him. He keeps a cat in his coat; it has a specially designed pocket."

"Still sounds like one scary mother, name like that," Liall said.

"Look, there he is," Hamish said.

Cap'n Meat sat on a bench, or rather, was spread majestically over a bench. His gray-white hair and beard fanned out over his bulky coat and his knapsack was beside him. He'd placed a copy of the *Post* on his other side and was giving his boots a good polish.

"Ah, my little friends," he said as they approached. "Always a pleasure to see your fresh faces."

"This is Liall, Cap'n Meat," Hamish said to him.

"A pleasure, my boy, a pleasure. Here Deen, sit over here. The boys can stand but a lady must always be offered a seat. I think you'll find someone you know in my knapsack." He opened the flap.

Titus, his ginger cat, lay curled on a sweater inside. Deen reached in to stroke him and felt his rumbling purr.

"That, young Liall, is the best cat in all of New York. It is also the smartest cat that ever was. I have lived from shelter to shelter, from one doss house to another, where no pets are welcome, and that cat has escaped detection each time. Would you like to pat him?"

Liall put his hand in hesitantly, then smiled at Deen. "He has the softest fur, doesn't he?" she said. "You see, he's not a long hair and not a short hair, but has a special layer of soft fur underneath."

"And is the devil for the cleaning of it," the Cap'n said. "He has been an example to me. I'm much neater in my ways than I once was, through the shining example of that cat."

"Tell him the story about how you found him," Hamish said.

"Oh, that's too sad a story for this bright day and your young ears."

"Please?"

"Another time, dears, another time. You see, it makes me sad and today I'm not strong enough. I've had some setbacks lately. No, no, nothing to fear, I'm all right," he added to Deen, who looked worried. He smiled at her to reassure her, his red, porous nose growing fatter as he did.

"My mother said to give you this," Deen said, taking a ten-dollar bill from her pocket.

"Now, that's a generous, good-hearted woman. You sure she gave it to you for me?"

"Yes, I told her we might see you. She said to ask if you needed anything else."

"Oh my, no, this is certainly kind. Please tell her that Titus and I will feast with this."

"What're you gonna tell Munster about that ten?" Hamish asked Deen as they left the park.

"What, that wasn't for that old bum?" Liall asked.

"I'll say it must've fallen out of my pocket."

"Man, my mother'd kill me I did that," Liall said.

***

The story of Titus's early days on this planet. That's how Cap'n Meat always thought of it, on this planet, seeing that cool blue ball floating in nothing, everlasting nothing. A planet that through a series of strange occurrences had come to host animal life. And here we are, the various animals, born to serve out our days on that cool blue ball, struggling as we might, being born on it and dying on it.

Cap'n Meat sighed and tried to get comfortable on his blanket. The underpass in Central Park was damp and smelled of urine but seemed safe enough, so far. Titus was curled up by his side, tucked into his coat. One hand rested on the cat's stomach and the other was outside, cradling it.

Sleep is a strange thing, he thought, not for the first time. That all animals needed to lie quietly for some part of each day and go into another state of being. It seemed, if one thought about it logically, to be something a properly functioning animal ought not to need. In fact, a huge design flaw. Because a creature's first and greatest mission here on this planet is to preserve. Preserve the self. And how exactly was one to do that well if one spent a good part of each day blissed out in a state of near unawareness? Why, he'd known men who'd slept right through a mortar attack.

There wasn't much chance he'd do that, he thought. A bum sleeping rough has to learn to sleep with all preservation systems on high alert. Mainstream man, as he thought of most others, mainstream man knows this and accordingly builds himself a shelter in which to sleep safely. Christ, most animals did too. Bums just have some twist in them that makes them spurn the safety. But he could tell you another thing about bums—they may spurn it but they long and moan for it inside their minds and dreams like babies, set it highest on the pinnacle of longings, spin elaborate pictures in their heads of cozy rooms with polished furnishings gleaming in firelight, of silken eiderdowns folded at the foot of a maple bed, of sunny linoleum shining with wax.

The story of Titus. The Cap'n had been going down hard, a bum on the fall to the lowest rungs of the streets when he'd found him. He was dossed down in an old subway tunnel, in with the screamers and the worst of the underworld, where they lived and fought like the rats that teemed around them. He'd gotten his hands on some horse, not a lot but some, and a mickey of Four Roses and was dreaming the good dream. He'd woken hours later, cold and filled with a hellish despair. Some rat was dying nearby, letting out little cries.

Much as he loved all animals he didn't love rats, and it gradually came to him that a rat couldn't make a sound like that, that a rat was shrill, enraged, and this was weak, soft. He stumbled up, dragging his gear with him—you don't leave a scrap you want to keep in the tunnels—and scented his way to the sound. To a cardboard box lying in a corner, one side bashed in. In it a dead cat lay on its side. Four kittens also lay dead next to it, having tried to suck from its teats to the last. A fifth kitten lay curled next to them, mewing and waving its paws. He picked it up held it in his large hands, warming it. Then he got a flannel shirt from his pack, tore it, and made a square to wrap the kitten in, tying it with twine and hanging it around his neck, to keep it warm against his chest.

He didn't dare go into the veterinary clinic and ask for help, so he panhandled in front. He approached only certain people, the ones who looked kind, and as a result had just a few quarters in his cup. But what he really did was keep an eye peeled for the right one. He was getting desperate when finally he saw her. She had a cat carrier and looked worried. She came out half an hour later, crying. The cat carrier was empty.

"Lady," he said softly. "Lady, please?"

She stopped, looking confused, and he could see it, her instinct kicking in, she stiffened and began to walk away.

"I gotta poor sick kitten," he said. "Please, could you help?" She'd stopped again and he went on, trying to keep his voice nice and pleasant. "They won't let a bum like me in there, and the truth is, I don't have the money, but I do have a twenty. I'm not asking for you to know me or see me or ever have anything to do with me again, but I found this kitten, its mother was dead, would you help it? Please?"

She was a young woman with soft brown hair. She put her hand over her eyes, pushing away the tears. He drew the ginger kitten from his shirt and held it out, letting the flannel fall away from it. The woman touched it, then said, "I'll try. Poor thing. You'll wait here? You won't run and leave me feeling responsible for it?"

"No ma'am, I won't."

It was more than an hour before she came back out. He'd begun to see the worst in his mind, the vet shaking his head and saying there's no point, better to put it down, or the kitten, too hungry and too late, dying as it was looked at.

"They said it should be kept over for four days, treated and fed special formulas. I don't have that kind of money. I told them about you. They fed him and gave him some medicine." She carefully handed him back the kitten, now wrapped in a clean towel. "Can you read? I told them you couldn't pay for it, and I couldn't either, so they gave me these." She waited till he tucked the bundle back in his shirt and then gave him a paper and a parcel. "It's instructions for care and a set of feeding bottles and some formula. You have to keep him warm at all times. Oh, and they gave me this and asked me to tell you, be very clear about it, for you to come back in six months and they'll do the neutering. No charge, it says so on that card. The vet, he's nice. He said you come in and bring that cat and he'll neuter it, that the world would be a lot better place if there were fewer unwanted cats. I have to go now. Nah, thanks, there was no charge. Here's your twenty back, they wouldn't take it. And here's a few dollars, for food." She stuffed some crumpled ones in his cup and walked quickly away.

"Oh my yes, that was a nice lady," he reminisced to Titus as they slept in the underpass, all those years later, his hand tucking in deeper around the cat's side. "And that vet was sure nice. But he's wrong about the world being a better place with no unwanted cats in it. Your mother wanted with every instinct in her to feed you and show you how to mouse. And you and me never would've gone traveling together if things were all peachy and perfect, why that way only rich people with houses would have cats."

The man and the ginger tabby fell soundly asleep in the dark of the underpass, the honkings and swishings and bells of the great city growing quieter as the night deepened toward dawn.

And in the shadows of the tall trees a phantom hunted, drifting between the shadows cast down from the trees, seeking, licking his senses to sniff out another human, one lost in sleep, one whom he could harm.

5

New Yorkers are so wary of personal contact with potentially troublesome or even deadly neighbors that they carry this fear into every corner of their lives. They don't speak to strangers, abruptly cut off chats with shopkeepers, avoid making eye contact with that man in the next building, whom they see each morning. Bums are handed a coin or a bill from a blind hand, receiving no response to their thanks. Immigrants handing out leaflets on sidewalks are as invisible as lampposts. A man passes a shop window, glancing in. His eye, unknowing, catches that of the melancholy shopkeeper within, ruing his poor sales. The man starts, pretending to brush something from his nose, anything to falsify the fact that two strange pairs of eyes met.

The children of the city are warned repeatedly, tirelessly, of the dangers of contact with strangers. They are required to recite a catechism of rules on the subject, to list all the people they mustn't talk to. Even teachers and the parents of schoolmates are not exempt.

Certain preternatural brats, already old in their parents' ways, have the mannerisms down cold—the blind eye and the veil of indifference. But honest and true children have to be scared into it. Deen and Hamish were ordinary children in this way, and they liked to talk to everyone. Sadie for her part had given them a few pointers about scary people and left it at that.

On this morning they were running their own branch of the Secret Service. To determine, by covert observation and the gathering of intel, all pertinent facts regarding activity at the house next door. It had been empty more than a year, the pair of bickering decorators who'd bought it having restored it and decamped.

Earlier that week a van and a truck had pulled up in front and an army of men in white coveralls marched in. The FOR SALE sign was taken down, and from early morning to well into each evening they hung wallpaper, painted, cleaned, and worked on the garden.

That morning a moving van had parked in front. Next, a blond woman with a sharp, lacquered look arrived in a taxi. She stood in the front hall with a clipboard, directing the moving men.

"Do you think she's the new owner?" Hamish asked Deen. He'd taken the front wheel off his bike and they were pretending to fix it.

"God, I hope not. She doesn't look like much fun at all."

"Maybe we should just go over and say we're from the house next door, ask her?"

"You think we should?"

"Sure. What's she going to do, put us in jail?"

"No, let's not. She's got that eagle-eyed look, I'm sure she's seen us, so she'd know we were spying on her. Besides, it's more fun trying to figure it out for ourselves."

The next day she was back, with another crew of men, some with slablike shoulders, others of a more delicate build. They could see furniture being moved according to the blond lady's direction and curtains going up. Agonizingly for Hamish and Deen, each pair was drawn as soon as they went up. A woman in her thirties, Spanish-looking with cheeks as pink as carnations, arrived and began working in the kitchen, which the children could see down into by lurking on the sidewalk.

They talked of nothing else, devising elaborate stories about who was to be their new neighbor. Since the brick row house was the twin to their own, they had a special interest in the matter and they prayed it might be someone more interesting than those cranky decorators. The building on their other flank was apartments and not at all the same thing. And even they understood that having a house done up so quickly was no small feat in New York, and must be costing a great deal of money.

The next night they had a brainstorm. They set up a ladder against the fence in the back garden, then ran into the house to get the binoculars. By looking over the wooden fence they could see directly into the back of the house. All the lights were on and the curtains open. Deen, claiming seniority, went up first. For a long while she was silent. Hamish waited impatiently.

"It's like a museum," she said. "It's all full of neat old stuff."

Hamish yanked hard at the hem of her jeans. "Come on!" he said.

When it was his turn he stared in wonder at the rich rooms blazing beyond the windows. The blond lady was going from room to room, fussing with little things, pillows and objects on tables, patting leather-bound books into place and straightening pictures. Taking turns on the ladder, they could see that all the rooms were now papered in deep colors and filled with heavy, old-fashioned furniture. The curtains were of thick velvet, matching the colors of the wallpaper, and every surface was covered in interesting looking things. Bronze dogs sleeping on red marble plinths, candlesticks with long lusters, ivory chess sets, and Chinese vases. Oriental rugs the colors of old wines covered the floors and the walls were hung thickly with paintings in gilt frames. The lamps all had shades made of red silk. There was an air of deep, sighing luxury to it, they agreed in whispers.

Sadie wandered out to the garden, soundless on bare feet, the only herald to her arrival the ice clinking in her glass.

"What in Christ's name are you two up to?" she said.

"Spying on the house next door," Hamish whispered. "Please keep it down, Munster. All the lights are on and they haven't closed the curtains in back. You can see nearly everything. We've got binoculars too."

"Really? How fascinating. Can I have a look?"

Deen slid down the ladder and handed her the binoculars. Sadie climbed up, propping her arms on the top of the fence. Deen and Hamish waited below, curious to hear her opinion.

"It's somebody with a lot of dough," she said, climbing down. "And extremely old school. You haven't found out who's bought it yet? Hmm. It's not the brittle blonde, I can tell you that. She's a working girl. A decorator I'd guess. On a rush job, for some oil sheik or something. No, that's not right—it looks like old money. Not at all up to the minute or decoratorish. Weird, because I'd swear the blonde's a decorator. And you know what, darlings, that house now looks like it's been owned by the same family for generations. Curiouser and curiouser."

The following day Deen was coming home from her English lesson when she saw something that made her stand still and gape. A long blue-blanketed shape was being maneuvered in the front door of the house. There was no question that it was the body of a concert grand. A concert grand, she shouted inside her head, a concert grand! Only made by special order by the best piano makers. *Oh please let the new owner be someone nice, please let them be nice,* she thought as she ran all the way to the basketball court to tell Hames, hissing the news through the chain-link fence.

***

The dark brownstone church on Fifth at the corner of Eleventh had always stuck a cold finger into Deen's ribcage whenever she walked by it. She'd learned, imitating her mother, to call it "the worst pseudo-Gothic of the worst Victorian taste," which distanced it somewhat, but always it affected her with a dire gloom, even on the brightest of days. In the late autumn the pavement in front of it smelled like sour milk and something worse, a miasma created by the crushed ginkgo fruits on the stones. Bums huddled in the niche made by the entrance on Eleventh, sleeping on rancid mattresses, lying there like rag dolls, thin trickles of urine seeping from them over the pavement and dying into sticky traceries.

She didn't like walking next to the black-painted Gothic fence in front of it, its spikes imprisoning a sward of weedless green grass. As she neared it she planned to cross Fifth, lose a few precious minutes and cross to Eleventh on its southern side. As much as she hated that church, she loved that block of Eleventh, with the house the Weather Underground had blown up and the Portuguese Jewish graveyard hidden behind a wall, its few ancient headstones and shaggy cedar huddled nearly forgotten against the side of an apartment building.

Walking along Fifth, looking at the cans of flowers outside the Korean deli and hearing Chopin's G Minor Ballade in her head, pondering how to get those transitions in it right, she looked up at the Forbes Building. Munster had told her that the Forbeses were devils. How their spawn, a devil among devils named Steve, had made what turned out to be a fortuitously lunatic bid for the presidency some years ago, and that he was a dangerous horse's ass. It was a building that trumpeted wealth, with a great portal, polished granite, and bronze fixtures. Like something the Mighty Oz would hide inside.

A bum was gesticulating next to a steel trash can in front of it. As she drew closer she could make out his words.

“Goddamn, motherfucking *infidels*!” he was screaming. “Shit for brains, shit and you make *more* money, shit, shit, *shit*! I’m gonna fuck with you all, motherfuckers! Fuck with you and see you *sucked* up inside the devil, then shit out of his *asshole*.” He picked a broken umbrella out of the trash can and stabbed it up at the building, then dashed it onto the sidewalk. “No, you listen to *me*! Now, fuckheads, before you die and I *eat* you!”

As she passed him Deen tried to become invisible, the incipient New Yorker in her kicking in. But she was afraid of him. The way you could hear the spit in his words, the way his *f*s cracked like gunshots, scared her. His rage shot out around him, making everyone hurry their steps while trying not to look as though they were.

Now he was picking something else out of the trash can, holding it up. She hoped it wasn’t something sharp. It would be terrible if she looked up and caught his eye—he’d be incensed by her fear. There were too few people around her. With a surge she dashed toward a couple ahead and ducked between them, breaking all the rules about physical contact. Startled, they parted and Deen ran across the intersection. A taxi slammed its brakes behind her.

“Yeah and I saw you, little girly-girl,” the angry bum muttered. “Little girly-girl, all nice and clean and *loved*. Well, shit on *all* of you!” he screamed.

6

For every stack of citizens piled and packed into the buildings of New York there are delis to meet their needs. Palatial ones with marble floors and sushi counters, walls of gleaming steel coolers filled with cold drinks and exotic juices, steam tables and salad bars and a grill counter with short order cooks yelling out orders for eggs and sandwiches. Then there are the small ones, owned by families who work there day and night, with wavy wooden floors and florescent lights, their shelves crammed with tins and packets, bootlaces and pain relievers.

Lily and Ron's deli was of the latter type. They opened it each morning at five on the dot. The deliverymen swarmed in first, ticking supplies off their lists, the engines of their trucks idling outside on Seventh Avenue. Say, Lily, you take care now, they'd call out, jumping back in their cabs. Ron swept the sidewalk first thing but if he had to put the broom down Lily would seize it and carry on. Then, between early customers, they cleaned the inside of the shop, tidied the shelves, straightened the stacks of newspapers and dusted the candy rack.

Everyone loved Lily. She treated every customer as if they were a great and treasured friend. She remembered a remarkable number of their names and gave everyone, regular or newcomer, a smile that blazed with sincerity. Strangers were often seen emerging from her shop, bemused expressions on their faces, wondering what they'd done to deserve such a smile.

Lily and Ron's bagels, it must be admitted, were of rather indifferent quality. But the local workmen and a good many residents of the surrounding blocks would have no other, not even the really good ones at the place on Sixth. There the staff stood on raised decks behind the registers, calling out, "Next!" in bored voices.

Lily was a queen of the cash register. No one ever sighed or rolled their eyes in her line. She made the sales incredibly quickly, all the while chatting animatedly to the person paying, juggling bills and coins, stuffing straws and napkins into the bag, and thanking them. She never made incorrect change, showed deep respect for the elderly, and would chase after a deliveryman running late to stuff a brownie and an orange juice in his pocket, yelling, "You got to take care of yourself, get some energy!" Many of her regulars took the trouble to have small change and ones ready so that they could hand her the exact amount, for which they received what one of them had dubbed "Miss Lily's Special Number One," a smile that followed them as they left and seemed to warm their backs.

Cap'n Meat understood the delicacy of Miss Lily's sensibilities. She naturally did not like bums coming into her shop. Bums would distract her and besmirch the shining cleanliness of it. And more than that, Cap'n Meat understood that she felt troubled by bums. They ruined her smile because they ruined her cheer, her hope that by working hard and keeping things tidy everything would be well.

Cap'n Meat had a deep and true respect for Miss Lily, but sometimes his large belly was so aching with hunger, a hunger that grew worse as it gnawed at him. At these times his sensitivity had to be set aside.

So he'd stand at one end of her orange awning, waiting, trying to look unobtrusive and not bother her customers. Who, me? his body seemed to claim, I just happen to be here, I'm not begging, no, not at Lily's.

"Not so good day, huh?" she'd say, rushing out as soon as she could, her black ponytail swinging as she handed him a bag. "You no tell others! In there egg salad, fruit, coffee, and cupcakes. And you drink water. Water cleans body. Some food for cat too, no one call me a bad woman."

You didn't thank a woman like Miss Lily, you respected her world and said thank you with your eyes, then tucked the bag away quick and moved along, just like some bum that'd been told off. No sirree, you let Miss Lily look like she was chewing you out.

She'd stand with her fists on her hips, staring furiously at his back, beneath her orange awning, surrounded by tiers of tight indigo iris buds, roses, spider mums, and cow-eye daisies dyed cyanic yellow, St. Paddy green, and candy pink, wondering why humans, such miraculous creatures, couldn't get down to it and tidy up the world.

* * *

Sadie danced over to the CD player and turned the volume up on the Velvet Underground's "Sweet Jane." She'd just gotten home, from what she called her "dead man's souk" and was aching for a vodka. Her boots lay on the floor, where she'd tugged them off. Still dancing, she went to the vodka bottle and said, "Hello darlin'."

"Hello, love," it answered. Sadie looked confused. Oh dear, was she starting to hear them talk *back*? Thank gawd, not just yet, it seemed—Brian had snuck down the stairs behind her.

"Pour a man one of those too, will you? Christ, what a muddle of a day. Ta." He raised his glass to hers. "Those oiks at the studio are giving me a pain in the balls. Here, I'll cook tonight, love. But first let's have a few of these. Deen and Hamish are upstairs, doing whatever ungodly things they're up to lately. Let's leave them to it, knock back a few together, have a bit of a natter. How's steak and mashed sound?"

"Like bloody awful English cooking."

"Right, that's settled." He sat, pulling out Sadie's chair for her, and lit a cig. "That's better. Know what drives me mad about rock these days? It's so *old*! These kids now, poor bastards, all they can do is tweak it, add a layer of irony here and there. I dunno, Saids, sometimes I wish rock and roll *would* die. Listen to these guys—the VU pulled all the stuffing out of rock and flung it all about. When was that, back in bloody sixty-seven? Now what's left? There's nothing left to invent, all kids can do these days is pick over the scraps, like bloody hens."

"You're gloomy tonight, Brian. I seem to remember you and Ree having this exact same conversation in the early seventies. What's the big deal? Rock's just the latest incarnation of folk music. Like 'Oh Suzannah' or the pipe songs of the Watusi, it's just popular music. It doesn't have to shift seismically every thirty years. What about rap? What about the bands you're working with?"

"Yeah, rap's all right," he admitted. "But I dunno, the rock bands I'm managing, the damn kids know everything about the history of rock, it's like they're as old as I am somehow. And as used up."

"The problem is, sixties rock got sanctified, made monumental. So that the succeeding generations couldn't keep the idea that it's simply music in focus. Couldn't allow themselves the impure pleasure of kick-ass bass lines and get-down-to-it guitar work. You're right, they're more like curators these days. But rock's not fucking art."

“Fair enough. No, you sit, I’ll fix us another. You know, young Hames is a natural on the guitar,” he said, his back to her as he stood to make fresh drinks.

“I *knew* you’ve been sneaking him lessons, but really, Brian, do you think that’s fair? What kind of life would that be for him, always being compared to his father?”

“That’s not our Saids talking,” Brian said, shaking his head. “When did you ever believe in stomping on creative urges? He’ll become what he’ll become. You don’t need to worry about him. Now Deen, that’s another matter.”

“What do you mean?”

“Now don’t get all shirty on me, Saids, but you haven’t noticed something that’s been happening under your own nose. Deen’s talent needs to be taken more seriously. I know you think I’m a moron when it comes to high class music and all, but that kid’s on her way to becoming a real musician. She needs a different teacher. Now, don’t look at me like that, calm down. Fact is, that skinny, mopey bird she’s studying piano with is all right, all very correct and proper, but face it, no effing genius. Deen sticks with her much longer and she’ll get frozen into her way of thinking. She needs someone with some fire in them. Someone brilliant. Maybe even a bit crazy.”

“Oh, Christ, you’ve got someone in mind, haven’t you?” Sadie said. “Come on, spill it, what’ve you been up to? Exactly how crazy are they?”

“Paul Dresden.”

“Good God, I thought he was locked away.”

“Doesn’t live but four blocks from here, in actual fact.”

“Didn’t he go berserk during a performance? And then try to kill someone?”

“Only his wife.”

“Oh, well, that’s all right then.”

“He’s got a new wife, she’s much younger and I hear she keeps him in line. He only did six months, a token sentence, and that was a long time ago. Poor sod's been skint, practically living on the streets. But like I said, he's got the new wife and his finances have been looking up since that movie came out, he's finally getting some airplay, royalties and such. He's in his late fifties and word is, he's lost his teeth where murderous thoughts are concerned, but still has all that music inside his skull."

"Paul Dresden," Sadie said. "I saw him play a couple of times. It wasn't exactly pleasant, he seemed at war with himself, the piano, even the music. He used to have conductors walking off the stage, throwing fits. He played like he was trying to forge his body into a set of tools to hammer the music out."

"Yeah. He had a pretty unique approach. You know what? You and Ree could go to the Albert Hall, sit in the royal box to see him, be all swank—you made it all right, gave Ree a ticket to a class sort of world. I saw the man play every time I could, just couldn't admit it. Used to go in mufti—an overcoat and a suit, looked like any ugly little English clerk spending his shillings on great music. Thing about Dresden was, I wanted to learn what he had. How he made music as old and dried up as hell, so raw."

"Yes, I see—Brian Brain, leather creaking and boot chains clanking, not exactly a great career move letting your Visigoth fans know you were a lover of classical music. You used to always be sneaking off, never telling us where you were going. We all thought you were going off to screw someone's wife, of course. What else were you up to while we thought you were going at it like a monkey? Here, let's open some red, you do the honors and I'll get out the cheese and crackers."

"Oh, reading modern poetry and getting a degree in classics at Oxford. Got a third, didn't I? Better than a first they say, shows you can do the work but weren't no swot."

Sadie looked at him, the bottle of wine forgotten in her hand. She wasn't at all sure that he hadn't been reading poetry and the canons of literature. She turned to get the corkscrew and saw a face outside the window. It was sideways and smiling at her through the area railing. She'd forgotten to close the shutters and the kitchen was lit like a stage.

"Liall!" she called, opening the door. "Come in. Is everything all right? Does your mother know you're here?"

"I got a call from Hamish," Liall said. "He asked me. He said you said it was okay. I told my mama that too."

"Oi, kid," Brian said, getting up to clap him on the shoulder. "I forgot to tell Saids here the plan. See, I told Hames I'd give both lads a guitar lesson tonight," he explained to her. "Hames asked him to spend the night, as tomorrow's Saturday and his mum'll be here."

"Oh, that's great," Sadie said, smiling down at Liall. "Don't mind us crazy grown-ups—we can't get anything straight in this house. You go on up to Hamish's room. I'll call up the stairs when dinner's ready. Brian's cooking, so it'll be sure to be awful."

She watched him climb the stairs, a small blue knapsack in his hands. In her mind she saw his mother placing a clean pair of underwear, a toothbrush, and a shirt starched and folded to geometric precision in it.

***

And what of the Hollanders' new neighbor? Nearly two weeks had passed since Deen and Hamish had done their recon from the back fence. Their avid curiosity about the new owner had in no way diminished, but since that night, no fresh intel had been obtainable. The curtains in back had been closed the next morning. Faint, exceedingly faint, signs showed that someone lived there—the chimney pots gave out smoke, the carnation-cheeked cook could be seen busy in the basement kitchen. The garden gate on the west side of the house, the twin to their own, had been painted olive green, as had the railings. Several times they saw the blond lady let herself in the front door. Classical music could be heard playing within, but only by highly tuned ears. It was as if someone had arrived by night, been installed inside the house, and now wished to live there in utter secret.

***

Sadie heard the doorbell ring and went to open it. It was the lacquered blonde from next door.

"Hello," she said. "I'm so sorry, this is embarrassing. My name's Maureen de Angelo. My client's just moved in next door?"

"Oh, come in," Sadie said, opening the door wide. She hadn't particularly welcomed the interruption, but she loved her children and was going to pump this woman for all she was worth. "Would you like a cup of tea?"

"Most kind. I really shouldn't like to intrude but . . . oh, this is embarrassing."

"Really?" Sadie said. "Why? Oh, you don't know my name. I'm Sadie Hollander," she said, offering her hand. "That take care of your worries? Sit here, I'll go to the kitchen and make the tea. Back in a flash."

Sadie would have been quite interested to know that her guest, the moment she went out, slipped off her heels and paced the room, making notes in a green crocodile agenda, and taking measurements with a cotton tape measure. With a small camera she took several photos of the room and entryway, hiding it in her bag just before Sadie returned with the tea.

"There we are," Sadie said, setting a tray with the tea down and pouring two cups. She refrained from saying anything else, knowing that a good interrogator lets the subject feel they have to inject words into the silence.

"Thank you so much," the woman said. "What a charming room. Such an unusual color."

Sadie let that pass and the silence widened between them. She was warming to her task. She'd given the woman tea, now she could bloody well explain why she was there.

"It's rather awkward," Maureen said at last. "My client, who lives next door, well he asked me to find you a gift, that he could send with a note, to say hello with, if you see what I mean. I'm an interior designer and pride myself on knowing people's tastes. I wonder if I could ask you a favor?"

"Certainly," Sadie said, shrugging.

"Well, could you possibly think of anything in particular you might like? You see, I so want to choose something that would please you, but I really had no idea what that might be until I'd met you and seen your house. Clearly something stylish but not stuffy would be in order."

"Oh, really, just some flowers might be nice. Or a bottle of wine."

"My client is quite firm that it should be something nicer than that."

"Really? And what sort of person is he?"

"An older gentleman, who, believe me, can afford it."

"Well . . . I don't know. What about a nicer tea tray? This one's certainly seen better days, and we are great tea drinkers." They both looked down at the multitude of white rings on the plain wood tray.

"Just the thing. Thank you so much. Gosh, look at the time! I must dash, so very good of you to be so understanding and thank you most awfully for the tea . . ."

In a flurry of cream cashmeres, the blonde was gone. Game, set, and match, Sadie thought, sipping her now tepid tea. *Bloody woman learned far more than I got from her, I'd better not tell the children, they'd be furious with me. I wonder if it's going to be a luxurious, expensive tray? I could really use a thousand bucks. In cash. Who's her client? Evidently a sole and single person. The children say it lives behind closed curtains, it must like the dark. Just our sort of neighbor.*

7

Sadie kept her car in a lot by the river, a few blocks north. It was a battered Toyota wagon, its red paint faded to rusty tomato. She walked over to get it on Sunday morning, a pleasant walk on a breezy October day. They were all going up to Connecticut to see Gretchen.

"Hello, Mr. Palek," she said to the attendant at the lot. He was Indian and had been working at the lot many years, over which they'd developed a cordial relationship.

"Mrs. Hollander, by all pleasantries," he said. "This I knew to be a good, a fine and beautiful day but now it is more so. I shall fetch your car forthwith. These days they are kind to you? Your children, they are well?"

"Yes, very well, Mr. Palek. Except Gretchen, of course. We're going to visit her today. And your family is well?"

"They prosper. My daughter has been most joyfully accepted to the pharmacy school of the City College of New York."

"That little girl with the long braid? She's that grown up now?"

"I fear so. Is it not glorious? But I would go without a turban were it to bring your girl back home. It is a terrible thing, this sadness you have for her, and for her, to be so lost and lonely. Oh no, that was most infelicitous of me, I did not mean to speak of her being lonely, for surely she is in the hands of the best and kindest people. Oh, you are weeping, I could cut my tongue out, it is a viper that should die!"

"No, no—I'm so sorry, it's just that I do worry so that she *is* lost and lonely." Sadie bent her head and let out a ragged cry. She tried to crush the tears back into her eyes but they kept falling.

"Please, come sit in my office," he said gently, touching her elbow. "Please. I will brew some mint tea. Oh, if only my tongue had been cut out at birth."

He sounded, if anything, more unhappy than she, so she allowed herself to be led into the tiny cabin. He offered her his chair and Sadie sat, embarrassed by her sudden show of tears. He busied himself at the hot plate, his back to her. Eventually her tears stopped and she looked around her with interest—she'd looked through the window many times but had never been inside. It was as spic-and-span a miniature structure as she'd ever seen. The walls were gleaming white and a piece of electrician's tape held together a tear in the carpet. An exuberant display of scarlet plastic roses stood on the desk in a blue vase.

"Do you wash each petal?" she asked him.

"Yes, each midday, when there is little to occupy these evil hands. Now here is some tea."

She drank quietly; it really did make her feel much better. Mr. Palek drank silently too, then poured her more.

"What is it, this ailment that your daughter has?" he asked her.

"Well you see, she stopped talking about a year ago. Then she began cutting herself, her skin, in places where we couldn't see that she had. It got worse until she was doing herself real harm. I think sometimes that young people cross a line and think there's only farther to go."

"But she is still a good and gentle girl otherwise, as she always was?"

"Yes."

"Well, then it is quite clearly the work of a demon. One that has seized her. Such evil creatures roam the shadows, searching for ones with no cruelty in them, ones that they may frighten into doing their will."

"That may be so, but what should I do?"

"Your daughter must fight this demon. You must tell her this, that demons are simple, lonely creatures and by nature really quite weak. In fact, they are remarkably stupid. Like mice, they can be caught quite easily, in a jar filled with oil. Tell her to ask this demon a question of logic, regarding why it is there, and you shall see—it will flee, disgraced by its inability to answer."

Sadie laughed. "By God I will," she said. "That's just the ticket. Thank you, Mr. Palek. Thank you for the tea and your sound advice. I feel ever so much better."

* * *

Sadie never saw the innocuous sign that read ROLLINGBROOK, its black, pseudo-Colonial letters and scrolled top, without thinking, *Who in God's name thinks up these sorts of names?* So soothingly pastoral, so meaningless, so atomic-era conscious a denial of the Gothic reverberations of earlier names, Bedlam, Dragonwyk, the New York Home for the Insane. The sign could just as easily have been for a model dairy farm, where Belted Galloways grazed and the local amateur photographers snapped away, making statements about art with juxtapositions of clouds, black-and-white cows, and landscape.

The visitor's parking lot was not very full. Brian had taken ages to pry out of bed, then the children had insisted on stopping at a diner they'd grown inordinately fond of. By now, the usual Sunday visitor crowd had gone, most people preferring to get their weekly visit over with before lunch, so they could then toddle off to a couple of stiff drinks and some eggs Benedict, warmed by their sense of virtue at having spent an awkward hour with the poor looner.

Inside the entrance they were greeted by a rather sleepy girl at a desk, who gave them passes. Sadie led the way, down the long corridor of the old building then left, into the lounge. The more presentable of the guests, as they were called, were allowed to have visitors there, in its mock country house atmosphere.

Gretchen was at the far end, in a wheelchair. Gretchen did not need a wheelchair, was, in fact, perfectly fit, but they'd wheeled her in in one when she'd arrived, and since that moment she'd refused any other form of motion. Her long, pale blond hair spilled over her shoulders and her lovely face, with its blue-green eyes, was drawn.

Deen wanted to run up to her and kiss her, but at the same time wanted to turn and flee the building to hide in the woods and cry. Why did Gretchen have to be so crazy? Why couldn't she get up and walk out of here, say she was sorry she'd been difficult? She was always very quiet, it was true, but so good on the drums. And now she just did this one stupid drawing of that dog, over and over, when before she'd done perfect drawings of everything, of leaves and feathers and cigarette butts; small, delicate renderings that she made in the margins of her favorite books.

Everyone kissed her, Brian giving her a great smack. "Oi, kid, look at you—you're right mess, aren't you?" he said.

Sadie laughed. "Doesn't this place give you the creeps?" she asked him.

"Not half. Come on, this is bloody silly, us standing around Gretchen in a fucking wheelchair. God, look at them two over there. Oi you two, go stuff it!" he yelled across the room at a pair of men in bathrobes who were staring at him. "Come on, lass," he said, picking Gretchen up. "We'll all sit over here where we can have a proper conversation." He put her on a sofa and sat next to her. "God's truth and didn't our Edie end up in a joint like this?"

"I have to talk to her doctor," Sadie said. "You all have a good chat, after all, I saw her only a few days ago. Gretchen, I'll talk to you later, we'll have a natter about something Mr. Palek told me. You tell Brian everything. And you, Brian, don't steal her meds."

"Meds, Christ," Brian said to Gretchen when Sadie had left. "Don't you know that drugs are for recreational purposes? What're you doing in a place like this? You can't actually *like* being treated like a zombie. You should be running around in a scrap of a dress and doing drugs with boys in bathrooms, off the porcelain altar."

A nurse who'd been helping a patient nearby straightened up and stalked over to stand in front of Brian. "That sort of talk is no help at all," she said. "It's the sort of talk that gets them all confused, it's disgusting!" The righteous rage in her made her face scarlet.

"Them?" Brian said. "Who the fuck's *them*? And take a look at yourself, you're the one all fussed up and acting irrational. Our Gretchen here's enjoying herself." He waved his hand toward her and she did indeed have a small, sly smile on her face. "Get along with you, scat!" Brian said to the nurse, who attempted a dignified outrage as she turned and walked off. Brian made a cross with his fingers and aimed it at her back.

"That bitch tries anything on, you just tell Uncle Brian," he said to Gretchen. "Only supposing you could get your shit together and talk again. Don't you find talking useful? Miss it a bit? I know how silence is the best defense, but listen, lass, aren't you going a bit overboard?"

"I brought you a book," Deen said. Gretchen took it and touched its cover. "It's *Jane Eyre.* I just read it and got you a special copy. I mean, I didn't read this one—I got soup on some of the pages of mine. There isn't any soup on this one, I checked."

Hamish offered her a small drawing he'd labored over during the week. It was square, done in bright colors on hard, polished paper, of a foot in a night sky, and on each toe was a ring with an animal carved in semiprecious stones.

"It's a design for an album cover," he said. "The band would be you, me, and Liall, maybe Deen on the keyboards, with Uncle Brian producing. You haven't met Liall yet, he's cool. He has a fake leg and they ran out of black legs so they gave him a white one. I mean, it's really the color of a Band-Aid, nobody's color."

Gretchen smiled, touched one finger over the drawing, then put it inside the book. Her family sat, thinking, with varying degrees of articulateness, the same thing, how she hadn't simply stopped talking, she'd stopped participating. How she let things happen around her and was still sweet, but didn't seem to be part of it.

Outside the long bank of windows the sun shone obliquely across the endless meadow, tingeing the edges of the trees with red and making every leaf and blade stand out. Deen stared out at the Kodachrome landscape, wishing she were not there.

8

Deen's piano teacher, Elizabeth Schaper, was a very nice young woman who'd finished her master's degree at Juilliard three years earlier. She shared quarters with another young musician, a rather dirty girl named Fred, in a tiny apartment on Grand Street.

Nice is a damning word in many cases, but in this instance the most accurate way to describe Elizabeth's essential nature. Tall and narrow of shoulder, she had large brown eyes and always ascribed to people better motives than they actually had. In fact, because of her faith in people's goodness, she was often treated well by others, even loved, though rarely the love that a man feels toward a red and thriving woman. For her part, Elizabeth fell in love often and hard, staggering from one abyss of unrequited passion to another, spending many lonely nights in tears.

Deen did not love Elizabeth. She liked her well enough and sometimes was thrilled when she praised her work, but Deen had a tough little soul and instinctively knew that being nice wasn't enough to excite her respect. She privately thought that to be a great musician one needed many things, things like ruthlessness, intellect, and tenacity, and that being kind to people probably didn't rate very high on the list. Though of course you had to pretend to be kind to certain people, in order to get them to do what you wanted.

Fred she hated. Fred often banged in before the lesson was over, strutting about, her untidy little body made worse by sloppy gray corduroys and shapeless sweaters. Fred was a clarinetist and believed that classical music, social hierarchies, and capitalism were evils that must die, long live the avant-garde.

That afternoon, Fred made a great scraping of keys in the lock, then shoved the door open. She barreled in, tossing her clarinet case on a chair. Elizabeth and Deen were playing some Schubert pieces for four hands. They finished the final piece but without the same enjoyment, knowing that Fred was there, smirking at them.

"*Ooh,* lovely," Fred said as the last notes died. "Pretty-pretty, so dainty and tied up with pink bows. Music to soothe the rich, they clap, saying, aren't our lives just one big spun-sugar cake. God, what shit! What's *with* you people?"

She flung herself into a ratty armchair and lay back wearily. "Deen, what would your father think if he could see you sitting there like some little fucking Marie Antoinette, playing lovely little tinkling tunes? I bet he'd shit a brick."

"Stop it, Fred," Elizabeth said. "You know perfectly well he'd be thrilled his daughter was a musician, like him. And that was not a tinkling tune, that was Schubert. Here, I'll get you a cigarette. There, take a nice big puff, isn't that better? Really, don't you think Deen's playing has come along remarkably?"

"Yeah, great. Hey Deen—good thing your daddy made so much money, so you could carry on the capitalist fantasy that each generation aspires to greater culture. God, rich people!" She got up and went to her room, slamming the door.

"She's a bit on edge these days because she hasn't had many jobs lately," Elizabeth said as Deen prepared to leave. "She really likes you, just isn't very good at expressing it."

Huh, Deen thought as she went down the stairs. Huh and double huh. And why doesn't she clean her fingernails—it must gross people out, watching her play. I should've told that dirty little beast to go to hell. Pops would be *glad* I wanted to be a musician. And he'd probably find me a better teacher than Elizabeth. I've got to talk to Munster about that. What a dirty little sow Fred is. Always acts like I've done something bad just because we aren't poor. People like that always have no idea what they're talking about anyway, think everyone who has the taste not to wallow in vulgarity is rich. And Elizabeth's so dumb she can't see that that grubby little warthog's in love with her. Just acts like they're sisters or something. At least it's driving old Fred nuts.

Passing by hip little cafés with well-dressed, chattering young people, looking in at them as she trudged the sidewalks, Deen felt woefully outside of everything, like a ghost wandering unseen. A girl with dyed yellow hair wearing a striped coat with a high collar leaned across a table to kiss a man's cheek. Outside the café a dozen patrons smoked and talked into their cell phones. Deen wondered when she would ever be on the inside, laughing and flirting. God, being almost fourteen was about the worst thing that could happen to a person.

***

When she let herself in the front door she heard her mother's voice in the living room. Sadie was sitting on the sofa, serving tea to an old, fat man with a beard.

"Darling, this is Colonel Harrington," Sadie said. "Colonel, my daughter Deen."

"Delighted, my dear," he said, rising to bow to her. The effort made him grunt.

"Stay and have some tea," Sadie said, patting the cushion next to her. "Colonel Harrington's our new neighbor next door."

Deen had been about to make an excuse but when she heard that she sat down abruptly. Imagine Munster pulling this rabbit out of a hat. Sadie poured her a cup and handed it to her with a wink. Deen noticed she was using the new tray he'd sent a few days earlier, a splendid thing in lacquer with fritillaries that matched the color of the room, that had real silver handles.

"Yes, well, New York City, my word," the colonel said, obviously returning to what he'd been saying. "Quite a change for me, born and bred in the South as I was. Don't know quite how it came about but seemed like a voice rang out, said go to New York, my son. Sounded like the voice of a very old man I knew once, a man who'd been my grandfather's coachman. An authoritative voice, if you know what I mean. Had to listen, and here I am. Find New York a bit of a poser. Thought I might get to know my neighbors, old habits from the homeland and all that. Must say, the people on the other side seem far from friendly. Left my card there yesterday morning. No response whatsoever. She's a psychiatrist, I'm told. Pity, I have some interesting questions I should like to ask her."

As the old man rambled on, Deen stopped listening to observe him closely. He was old, he was fat, his beard and hair were white streaked with gray. His hair was rather long for an old man. She could see that Munster found him delightful—Munster loved eccentrics. Especially eccentrics with nice manners, which this one had in spades. He wore a real suit, the kind made with a waistcoat. A gold chain fell across his round stomach. He had very clean fingernails. Fred would go simply mad if she were here, Deen thought happily, get so incensed she'd lose it and bite him, sinking her teeth in. Then they'd call 911 and the police would have to shoot her.

"All been in storage for decades," he was saying, "while I roamed the world. Can't say exactly what I was seeking, never found it. Decided to make a home again, get all the family furniture out of mothballs. Naturally planned to live in the town where I was born, but then my grandaddy's coachman told me to come here. Must say, I find New York peculiar. Everything seems to be a matter of price. Found a wonderful woman to help me with the house, perhaps you've met her? Mrs. de Angelo. Wanted me to call her mizz but simply cannot, too damn old. Yes, thank you most kindly, I will take another cup of your excellent tea. I think you must've spent some time in England, Mrs. Hollander."

"Yes, my husband was English."

"Ah, a mystery unraveled. But you say was?"

"Yes, he died."

"I am most deeply sorry."

"That's all right—it's been over twelve years. Please go on about your house."

"Had an idea. To re-create my family home. Right here in New York City. Looked at a number of houses uptown—you see, I'm learning the lingo. Nothing suited me there, they somehow didn't feel like real houses. Now mine, I instantly recognized as a home, as I understand it. Do many New Yorkers live in their family houses?"

"No, not many. Most live in apartments, as a matter of fact."

"Really? Why is that?"

"Well, I suppose they can't afford it. Most of the old houses are broken up into apartments, some of them quite small."

"A pity. I can't quite see why. Still, it's a place I am a complete foreigner to. In any case, I asked Mrs. de Angelo to try to re-create the home I was raised in and she did a most admirable job. I have rarely been so pleased. I imagine that as an Eye-talian, she has a keen nose for the refinements of old families. Don't you find this is always so? They come to this country, observe our ways, and, in a flash, are better at them than we. Must say, this is a very fine room. The paintings are curious, are they African? I spent some years on the Dark Continent and formed a profound admiration for the boldness of their patterns."

He craned his neck and looked about the room, like a turtle peering from its shell. At that moment Hamish came skidding in, slid to a stop, and stared open-mouthed at the colonel.

"Who're you?" he said.

"This is my youngest, Hamish," Sadie said. "Hames, see if you can recall your manners and say hello to Colonel Harrington."

Hamish went over and put out his hand. "Glad to meet you, my boy," the colonel said. He fumbled about to reach Hamish's hand.

"He's the one who moved in next door," Deen hissed to him as he sat. Hamish responded with an amazed and gratified look.

"Are you really a colonel?" he asked.

"Not really."

"Deen wants to know what kind of piano you have" was his next question. "Do any other people live in the house with you? The last people who lived there called the cops once when Munster had a party. Munster says New Yorkers don't get to know their neighbors. She says they wait to get to know them in court."

"I fear your mother is correct, my boy. The piano is a Chickering. My cook Ettie lives in. Now, I must leave you. Mrs. Hollander, you've been wonderfully kind in breaking the rules and asking me to tea. Assure you I haven't had such excellent tea in a long while. Don't fear that I'll be bothering you often, one must be circumspect, but please call on me should you feel the wish to. At my age I am often at home."

With that the colonel heaved himself up, bowed to Sadie, and marched out with a curious gait, his steps precise but his feet staying close to the floor. Before they knew it he'd taken up his hat and let himself out.

"Well, if that don't beat all," Sadie said, sinking back into the sofa.

* * *

Sadie was walking across Washington Square Park a few days later, returning from a rather grisly session with her accountant. She passed the dry fountain filled with street performers shouting to the crowd. The park had its own peculiar population: druggies and pushers, stoners with masses of hair piled under knitted caps, old women getting exercise in ancient cloth coats buttoned to their chins, crazy people, bums, chess players, folk guitarists, and demonstrators. The same old crowd, many who spent each day there. Until they disappeared suddenly, jerked up on some invisible wire to meet their fate.

On a bench beneath the oak once used for hangings she saw a large figure strapped up in a sheepskin coat, his gray beard spread over its lapels.

She slowed and he looked up, smiling at her. "Good day to you, Miss," he said, taking off an imaginary cap.

"Excuse me, but are you . . . ?" Sadie couldn't say his name, what if the children had made it up? It was a most improbable name. "Do you possibly know my children? A boy and girl with caramel-colored hair?"

"Why yes, Deen and young master Hamish?"

"That's them. I'm their mother, Sadie Hollander," she said, offering her hand.

Corporal George Meens, late of the U.S. Army, rose. "Cap'n Meat," he said. "Very pleased to make your acquaintance. Would you like to sit?" he asked rather hesitantly. It had been a long while since a pretty woman had been civil to him.

"Thanks. My children seem to have taken a shine to you. They told me—they didn't want to but I wormed it out of them—that you chased away an older boy who'd been taunting them. They didn't want me to know that part, you see, they value their freedom to roam the neighborhood. I really appreciate your coming to their rescue."

"Oh, who wouldn't look out for such nice young ones? The boy was just being mean-spirited, taking it out on them for being white. I haven't seen him about since. It's a sad truth that simply by being large I carry a certain amount of threat. But I have to admit, it's a help on the streets."

"You don't have anywhere to stay?"

"Oh, I didn't mean that—of course I do," he lied. "I stay in a shelter at night. I merely meant that I'm on the streets until it opens. They go to great efforts to turn us out to seek work each morning."

"And do many?"

"Of course not," the Cap'n said.

"Well, that's a relief. I wouldn't want to think the do-gooders do *that* much good. The world would be terribly boring if everyone did what they were supposed to."

"Do you mind that I talk to your children? I've taken a bit of a shine to them myself. But if you'd prefer it, I could remain friendly but not chat with them."

Sadie was distressed. She wondered if he thought she'd stopped to warn him to stay away from Deen and Hamish. "Oh, no," she said. "I just wanted to meet you because the children had said such nice things about you. I'm very pleased that you're their friend."

"But you don't know if I'm safe for them to be around, what made me what I am."

"I think I know a little bit. And the person to be asked that question is called McNamara. You were probably a straight-arrow kid before you got drafted, weren't you? My father fought in World War Two, he thought it was the biggest lark of his life. He never understood that Vietnam was a mess."

"It's the smells that come back the strongest, the ones that came creeping in under the tent flap."

Sadie looked at him, at his crazy, still-black eyebrows over innocent gray eyes, and his broad, sandblasted face. It was a good face; it had grown into his character and represented his travails and his cheerfulness in spite of them. She'd think of a word to describe those crazy eyebrows, a word that she knew would come to her eventually.

"Listen," she said. "Would a twenty be a help?"

"Oh, that's far too much. I mean, I couldn't take anything, well, a ten wouldn't be refused."

"Consider it simply business, among friends," Sadie said, folding a note in her handbag and discreetly slipping it into his hand. "I hope we'll meet again. Are you often here?"

"Yes. It's become my bench, as it were. They say they used to hang people from this oak, back when hangings were a matter of public entertainment. I like to keep the tree company, see only what a fine old tree it is."

As Sadie walked away she reflected on yet another life broken on the merry carnival show of pop-up rhetoricians playing their fake battles with words and toilet plungers for lances, in that nest of liars in Washington.

Suddenly the word to describe Cap'n Meat's eyebrows came to her—*roadkill*.

9

Deen climbed the brownstone steps and read the names by the buzzers. The building was dark, soot-stained, and grim. A rusty perambulator was chained to the stunted tree in front. Above her, inside the building, she could hear an infant shrieking. Its cries were a piercing scream that didn't let up. She peered at the worn letters on the buzzer panel. There it was, DRESDEN, 1W. The baby's screams escalated as she pressed the bell. An even greater feeling of direness came over her as she realized the baby was in the apartment she was going to. She hadn't wanted to go at all, now this.

"Yes?" a voice rasped from the speaker.

"It's Deen Hollander. I'm supposed to see Paul?"

The only answer was the buzzing of the door. Deen pushed it open and entered an ochreous lobby with a marble floor and round fluorescent lights that made her hands look green. A door opened above and a voice called, "Up here." She climbed the littered marble stairs, grit under her shoes making scratching noises. The wainscoting was painted with a thick layer of chocolate enamel, the same color as her spirits. The stairwell echoed with the screams of the baby.

A thin, pale young woman stood holding the apartment door open with her hip, a crimson-faced infant in her arms. Its mouth was open wide, and its eyes screwed shut, tears of rage leaking from them. It had golden curls and was the fattest, strongest-looking baby Deen had ever seen. Deen did not like babies.

"I'm Kristen," the woman said, pushing a lock of tired brown hair from her cheek. Her face was anxious and timid, with rabbity teeth and olive stains beneath her eyes. "Paul's wife. And this is Rinaldo. Aren't you, my little genius?" She looked at her baby adoringly and tickled its chins. It stopped screaming and made a sucking noise.

Kristen motioned Deen inside. The door led directly into the kitchen, a room of remarkable squalor. Nappies hung everywhere from cotton lines, and chipped and dented baby paraphernalia covered the floor. The stove was caked in grease and the sink heaped with dirty crockery. A pine table painted blue sat in the center, covered by plastic dishes smeared with mush.

"I'll bring you to Paul in a minute," Kristen said. "He doesn't like visitors, so I'll let him get used to the idea first. I mean, he heard the buzzer, so he knows you're here. He hears *everything*," she added darkly.

The baby began grizzling and let out a cry. Deen flinched, praying it wasn't the prelude to another bout of shrieks. It stopped to paw a fat red fist at the gobbet of mucus dangling from its nose, then stared at her with round, unfriendly eyes. In fact, its expression was surprisingly malevolent, Deen thought.

Kristen swabbed its nose down with a Kleenex and held the baby toward Deen, its thick cotton diaper drooping from its barrel-like limbs. "You want to hold him?" she asked.

"God, no," Deen said. "I mean, uh . . ." She tried to think of a polite way to refuse. She was saved by a yell from the back of the apartment.

"Bring the bloody girl in, you cunt!"

Kristen's rabbit face twitched. "He's not at all happy about this," she whispered. "Straight through to the room with the curtains over the entrance. Go on," she said, giving Deen a shove.

Deen looked over her shoulder at the door, toward escape and freedom. She wished with all her might she had the nerve to make a run for it.

The hallway was dark, ending in an arch hung with faded red burlap curtains. Slipping through them, Deen entered a long room with a bay of tall windows at the end. Bookshelves lined the walls, filled with bound music folios, bundles of sheet music, and LPs. The only furniture in the room were a grand piano in the bay, a stereo cabinet, and an armchair facing it, halfway down the bare floorboards. Above its grimy yellow back she saw a man's head with tufts of dark hair standing up, seemingly at war with one another. A hand with long fingers moved through them, redefining their battle lines.

"Let's get this farce over with as quickly as we can," he said, still not turning to look at her. "Your mother is clearly a woman used to having her own way. Or, rather, getting it. One should be precise in these matters. Stand by the piano."

Deen walked to the piano and turned, facing him. She was miserable. This was all going to end badly, but at least soon, she hoped. A warming tingle of defiance stole into her being and she looked up, staring back at him.

He wore faded green canvas pants and shirt, like those of a boiler man's, work boots, and a tweed jacket so worn it was white around the lapels. His face was dark, with a beaky nose that twisted to starboard. His gray eyes had a mean little light in them and his cheeks were sunken. His hair was still dark but white whiskers glinted on his jaw. He was looking her up and down like a buyer at a cattle sale.

"Little girl, five foot three. Tawny hair, healthy, plenty of calcium. Fairly sturdy about the shoulders, but for the most part still an unformed blob. Say 'Polly want a cracker.' Go on, say it."

"Polly want a cracker," Deen said tonelessly.

"Not very much, apparently. Let me see your hands. No, closer—in front of me. Don't ever touch me. Hold them out. Now palms up."

Christ this is weird, Deen thought as he studied her hands. There was a purplish flap of skin on one of his eyelids. She hoped it was precancerous.

"Move your thumbs, no, you imbecile, the other way, as far back as they'll go. Now go away, sit at the piano."

He sank back in his chair and closed his eyes. Deen sat at the piano bench and looked out the windows. There wasn't much to see, some weedy-looking trees, trampled plots, a rusting barbecue.

"Your name," he said.

"Deen."

"I don't like it. How is it spelled?"

"D-e-e-n."

"That's not a real name. Try again."

"Ondine."

"Far better. No blobbishness to that. Play something cheap. Now."

"What do you mean, cheap?"

"Don't ask me questions! Cheap, something immortal, such as 'Send in the Clowns,' you know what I mean! Anything but whatever bloody so-called classical music you think you know."

Deen had in fact thought a good deal about what she'd play for him when he asked, as surely he would. She'd been rather proud of her choices, Bach's English Suite in G Minor, and Liszt's Transcendental Etude. She thought they'd display not only her skill but also a rarified taste. Now bitterness flowed in her soul, he was a lout and a lunatic, and she'd had just about as much as she could take of his crap.

She took a breath and launched into the Beatles' "Happy Birthday," not merely playing it, but vamping it, bringing every bit of loathing she'd harbored for years into the crude tune. She hoped he'd never heard anything so foul in his life. Her rage brought her to new heights of kitsch: she imagined she was playing it at a joint in Rockaway Beach, men pounding the tables and couples in mating colors singing along and hollering, their mouths wide with merriment.

When the last chords subsided to her pedal work she examined the piano with respect. It was a Steinway D, and it had a wonderful tone. She stroked its side, silently apologizing for playing something so unworthy of it. She didn't look at Paul. As the minutes passed she decided she'd never look at him, no matter what.

The silence stretched out, strung like a spider web between two buildings, a long, nearly invisible thread, with the strength of an armored division. In it Deen imagined every possible humiliation, every crack-brained, horrible thing he might say. Thirty minutes passed.

"Ah," he said finally. "The waiting was good for you and I needed the rest. Your mother is paying me by the hour, after all. Inside this room you will think of yourself, and be, Ondine. We will begin by putting your head in a vise and extracting everything you ever knew, or thought you knew, about classical music. I will exert a mesmeric power over you and you in turn will come to worship me. Until that day I expect the utmost obedience. You will also— Oh, bloody hell!"

The infant genius had begun shrieking again, its screams climbing to ear-piercing blasts. Paul clapped his hands over his ears then scrabbled for a cigar box under his chair. "Get out!" he said to Deen.

"Your mother called," Kristen said as Deen entered the kitchen. There seemed to be no other way out of the apartment. "She more or less told me to give you tea. Anyways, to keep you here a little while. She's hanging new curtains in your room and wants it to be a surprise. Oops, guess it won't be now. She's English, right? If I have to give you a cup of tea every time I'll have to talk to her about what my time's worth too. Paul's time's worth a fortune, everyone knows that, not like mine, but still. And just so you know, I don't do any fancy stuff with teapots and all that, a mug of Constant Comment's my brew. I drink it for my liver. Having a baby's hard on the organs, you know? *Did* Paul say for you to come back? He never takes students. Pupils, *he* told me to say, yelling it, like yelling's going to make me hear better. Uh, is this okay or could I like ask, how your mother's going to pay? Could you ask her if like, she could pay half check, half cash?"

Deen sat glumly at the blue table while Kristen made the tea. Next to the table, hunkered down in a netted crib, the baby slept, its wide bum in the air and its face resting on a meaty forearm. Suddenly it blinked open one eye and stared at her balefully. Deen stared back, thinking, you and me bud, someday, alone in an alley.

"So how'd it go?" Hamish asked her when she got home. "He attack you or anything? I heard he used a mallet on his last wife. And that conductor he attacked, he went for the head that time too. I checked him out on the Internet. He's got a classic sociopath's MO, just in case you're interested. Did hard time for the attack on his wife. Geeze, Munster can really pick them, can't she? Maybe she'll find a nice child molester for me to study with, alone. You really okay? Did he act fairly normal?"

"God, I don't know. I mean, he didn't really scare me. But I listened to a couple of his recordings and I think I have to go back. They have the most horrible baby. It's like a ball of stinky bodily fluids, you should see it."

"Geeze," Hamish said. "That's nasty. Tell you what, I'll get out my old lacrosse helmet for you to wear. And I'll program your cell phone to dial 911 first, then auto-dial me, okay? Just don't ever let on to either of them that you have a cell, keep it in your pocket when you're there, right where you can get at it."

10

Sadie was on her way home from a meeting with Ree's lawyer, a boring one regarding certain offers made by ad firms for a couple of Ree's songs. She found it amusing to think of his "Mayhem Monday," a song about the soul-destroying effects of commercialism, being used to flog SUVs. So much for the revolution.

It was just past six and not having wanted to fight the commuter crowds on the subway, she'd decided to walk from Chambers Street. But now she was growing tired and longing for that first drink. She trudged on. A MILLER LITE sign winked at her from a tavern window: Hello darlin', it said. In an instant she was slipping off her peacoat and ordering a Ketel One, rocks, and lime please. *Ahhh.*

"Just the thing, huh?" the bartender said, putting a fresh bowl of pretzels out for her. He was an old-fashioned bartender, one who liked to see his customers take a healthy interest in their booze.

Sadie looked around her, taking note of the joint. It was her kind of bar, no swank to it, a serious-minded establishment with a long mahogany bar, black vinyl stools, and old photographs and memorabilia on the walls. It was getting depressingly difficult to find a bar of this sort left in Manhattan.

She debated with herself whether to order another. Oh, what the hell, why not? Brian had gone back to London the day before and one more would take the gloominess off letting herself into the house and hearing its echoes. Not that she missed Brian a bit, of course. That's what she told herself anyway, hoping she might eventually believe it. She nodded to the bartender, who'd been keeping an eye on her; he came over and poured her another.

"Hi. I see you every morning, when I'm getting equipment out of my truck," a young blond man said, coming over to stand next to her. He set his bottle of Heineken down and smiled.

Sadie looked at him, her eyebrows knit in concentration. Gawd, it was that good-looking stone mason.

"Oh, you're doing work at number seventeen," she said.

"Yeah, more stonework for the rich people. Some of the people in this town, they've got so much money they have gold bars for eyeballs. I usually do jobs in Connecticut. Live there. Those people at seventeen, they got a place there and another place here. You know that site down in the Yucatán? Chicken-something? Where the stones are as tall as men, all perfectly fitted together? Now every asswipe with dough wants to be a Mayan king. I get to do some interesting stuff, but the clients are freakin' assholes. This one guy wanted me to go to Maine and dig up some rock formation on a hilltop. To put in his yard in Greenwich. As a 'focus point' for the landscaping, he called it. I took one look at the photo and told the guy fucking NASA couldn't shift that rock. Let me buy you one, okay?"

***

A few days later, on a bright Saturday in early November, Hamish and Liall were practicing guitar in the garden, working on a Guns N' Roses song they were reshaping quite radically. Above them, in the living room, Deen was studying a score. The French doors to the balcony were open.

"Put that egghead stuff away and do keyboards for us," Hames called up to her.

"Huh," she said, not looking up. "What I play is *real* music, not King Crimson."

Liall looked intrigued. "You mean, she could just pick up and play whatever we were playing? I mean, if she wanted to?" he asked Hames.

"Sure. She can play anything if she hears a few chords. She's got an amazing ear."

"I'm gonna be able to play like that someday. Be able to pick up a guitar and play *anything*. Hey, your mother really just show up at breakfast this morning with her new guy? Say like, hi, this is Steve?"

"Yeah. She does that once in a while. They're usually idiots. But they don't last long."

"Brian gets rid of them," Deen said from above.

"How's he do that?"

"Oh, I don't know, he just sort of makes them fade away. I think he makes Munster embarrassed about them. They *are* usually almost criminally stupid."

"That one's showing off, with that tight shirt of his," Liall said.

"I know, disgusting, isn't it? Wants everyone to know he's got a six-pack."

"Oh, gross," Hamish moaned.

Just then an object came sailing over the garden fence and landed with a plop near the boys' feet. It was a large man's handkerchief tied into a hobo's knot. Hamish knelt to untie it. A piece of writing paper was folded inside. Opening it, he drew out four guitar picks and read what was written on it in large, shaky letters that sloped uphill at a gallop. "Tea, children? This Afternoon? Your mother too."

Deen came down the iron steps to look. "These are real tortoise-shell," she said, holding a pick up to inspect it. "They're supposed to be the best but you can't get them anymore. I think Colonel Harrington likes hearing you play."

"That's the old guy next door?" Liall asked. "He wants us to come to tea? What's the deal with that—he one of them, or what?"

"You mean, a pervert?" Hamish said. "I don't think so."

"Well, he asks you to get something just don't bend over with your back to him, okay?"

The three children marched over to the colonel's at four o'clock. Deen had asserted that tea was always at four, saying this in such a lofty manner that the two younger boys could not argue with her.

The door was opened by the carnation-cheeked cook, who smiled delightedly at them. "It's so good you children come," she said, leading them to the back parlor. Deen snuck a look at the grand piano in the front room as they passed the door.

Colonel Harrington was sitting in a tapestry-work armchair by the fireplace, in which several logs burned. Several other armchairs made up a circle around the fire, each with a small stand next to it. In the middle a mahogany trolley held silver trays of tiny sandwiches, next to a low table with a teapot, cups, lemon wedges, and sugar. Hard by the colonel's side, a tiered cake stand was filled with powdered cakes and cookies. A flowered china bowl brimming with Pringles was perched on the mantelpiece.

"Ah my dears, what a pleasure," he said, beaming rather vaguely at them. "A fine treat, to see you here, in my little nest."

"This is Liall MacFarland," Hamish said. "The other guitarist."

"A great pleasure, my boy," the colonel said, offering his hand. "A fine Scottish name. I have always been partial to the Scottish peoples. You of course are Presbyterian, I am sure. Of a stern nature? Yes, of course, thought as much. Ach and have some tea noo, will ye me lad."

Hamish, Deen, and Liall looked at each other and mentally shrugged, whatever. They sat, wiggling to install themselves in the overstuffed chairs. Everywhere they looked around the room there was some fascinating object. Deen was especially taken by a large glass dome containing a dozen or so stuffed hummingbirds on a branch. Hamish looked goggle-eyed at the food. He had just lately begun to grow and was finding his mother's lackadaisical approach to food an agony.

"Deen, my dear, would you do the honors and pour the tea? I'm so old and fat I spill it over everything. Thank you, yes, sugar and lemon. I'm firmly of the more is better school, as you can see." The colonel waved his hand about the room. "Now you young ones tuck in."

"Did the lady who let us in *make* these?" Hamish asked, picking up a lemon madeleine and sniffing it with a look of rapture.

"She did."

"And these?" he asked, holding up one of the tiny sandwiches. "All of it?"

"Yes."

"Wow."

* * *

As the children were politely stuffing themselves, their mother arrived home to find Brenda muttering over a table she was polishing.

"I can't do nothing about cigarette burns," she was saying. "About the follies of mankind when they're drunk. . . ."

"Brenda, what's the matter?" Sadie said.

"Nothing. Those came for you." She pointed to a bunch of cream roses, dozens of them in a ring of fern, and bound into a white lace paper cone.

Sadie picked it up. "Gawd, I feel like a virgin. Look, it's from that wonderful old lunatic next door. I'm invited to tea. Where are the children?"

"With that lunatic. And my boy, Liall, too. You're just fooling, right, that old man's not really a lunatic?"

"Of course not. I use it as a term of endearment."

"Well, it's nearly time for me and Liall to go home. And as far as special projects go, today I took some elbow grease to the washer and drier and all, back of the kitchen. Somebody spilled an awful lot of detergent around those things, then let it build up into a sort of cement. But what am I going to do, go over there and say, my boy Liall's got to go home now?"

"You could let him spend the night with us. I'll bring him home in the car tomorrow morning."

"That's just one more bother to you."

"Not a bit of it. Someday I'll tell you all about Gretchen, and then you'll understand why it's so nice to see those two boys doing normal things like playing guitar and having tea with old lunatics."

"I already think I know a bit."

"You probably know it all, Brenda."

"Yes, and it's a world of trouble we're born into. Sometimes I think we took to Jesus dying on a cross because we all do, a little bit every day, and that's a fact. And I can't do nothing with these cigarette burns. Some real nice furniture and someone set a cigarette down on it and just walked away. It's a wonder you and your family weren't burnt to a crisp."

Still muttering about the slow crucifixion of mankind on this earth, Brenda went downstairs to get her coat. She hadn't really expected to hear herself say yes to Liall's staying over, but thought herself a better judge of character than most people, and though Sadie liked to pretend to be a holy terror and drank like a fish, she was awfully good to the children.

Sadie dashed on a bit of lipstick in front of the hall mirror then went to the colonel's. "Hello, Ettie," she said to the woman who opened the door. "Are my children eating everything in sight?"

Ettie and Sadie had become acquainted some days earlier, when Sadie had introduced herself. Ettie had been struggling to move a heavy box down the area steps to her kitchen. Sadie had found the sight of a diminutive woman wrestling with a box larger and heavier than herself appalling. *Bloody deliverymen,* she'd thought, grabbing one end.

She'd made a friend for life, something not difficult to do in the lexicon of Ettie Salvatore, for Ettie loved people. And she knew so few. She needed to love many more, and so she cut pictures from magazines of people with faces she liked, nice people, and hoarded them, to keep and run a touch over their nice faces. Ettie had been watching the Hollanders for weeks and had entirely embraced them in her mind. Sadie she particularly respected for being a widow true to her dead husband, one who'd never remarried and who, one could see, put her children first, a fine boy and girl, and the other one who was a ghost. So what if she spent a night or two with that young blondie? Her heart, when it came to her one true love, the father of her children, it still had cords and chains all around it. With the sacred lamp ever burning in the center. And you could tell she wasn't one of those landowner sorts who never saw anyone beneath them, no, she was a true lady, she helped people struggling with boxes.

Thankfully, all these thoughts had already been through Ettie's mind and there is no reason to suppose that the two stood in the colonel's doorway while they passed. Instead, Ettie said, "Mees, the little ones are in back. I show you."

"My dear, now my cup truly runneth over. I've saved the chair next to mine for you, while I've been interrogating the youngsters." The colonel patted the arm of the chair. "They've been most fascinating company. Would you be so kind and pour now, Deen's been an awfully good sport about it, but we've all been awaiting your deft touch.

"How especially fetching you look today, in that color. And I must say, your children are charming company. Their Scottish friend I think wise beyond his years. Do have some tiny cakes, and some of Ettie's famous sandwiches."

"My God," Sadie said, looking over the food, "fit for a bloody great country house tea. Say, Colonel, does your largesse run to a slug of something in my tea?"

"How thoughtless of me. As the widow of a fallen idol of the stage, you must, of course, um . . . please, dear lady, tell me your preferred drink."

"Vodka, but it doesn't go with tea. So a dollop of scotch if you have some?"

"Would Oban do?"

"Would it. I'm beginning to like you, Colonel."

The colonel rang for Ettie and said, "Ettie, would you be so kind as to unlock the sideboard and get out a bottle called Oban? O-B-A-N. And a bottle of my bourbon, please." He took a key from his waistcoat pocket and gave it to her.

The colonel was not unaware that the party had taken on a decidedly grown-up flavor and that children are restless creatures, especially when grown-ups get to drinking and nattering. "Perhaps Deen, you'd like to try the piano?" he said. "And would you young fellows like to explore the garden, or visit Ettie in the kitchen?" They were all off in a flash.

"Ah," the colonel sighed as Ettie put the two bottles on the table. When Sadie had adjusted their cups of tea to something with more kick in them he sat back. "Simply grand. Wonderful to hear the clock chime five and sit back in good company with a slug of whiskey.

"I was educated at Harvard. All we Harringtons were; it was our custom to go north, study with our Yankee brethren. Of course, there were occasionally certain sons who were not quite Harvard material, in that case a younger son or even a cousin, went in his place. I decided I should like to become a doctor and took the necessary courses in the hard sciences. I hoped one day to be a very much wiser man than I am now, to perhaps devote my life to the suffering of the poor in other countries. I fear I did not carry on with my medical studies. I did though, eventually become acquainted with the work of Mr. C. G. Jung, made quite a study of his ideas. Must admit though, I frittered my life away, drinking whiskey and ruminating on the protomythian, the nature of dreams and the collective unconscious."

"Did you ever go through a Jungian analysis?" Sadie asked. "Figure out your anima and animus?"

"Yes, my greatest years were spent with Herr Schafflin. I had a fascination with attics, in fact thought I was imprisoned in one for a long time. I could describe it now in great detail. With him I explored the entire cast of characters that had shaped me, and yes, the male and female elements of my being. My fixation with the towering carved bed I was born in, became, if not understood, at least realized.

"I never married. Knew just what sort of girl I admired and even later why, but it never came to pass. Do have some more, my dear, let's switch to straight whiskey and skip the tea, shall we? Thank you. Cheers. The carved bed was swagged in chains of roses. Inside the curled petals of each rose was a face, that of a monkey. I don't think the bed actually exists, though I have looked for it. I long to see it though, because I've an idea that the monkey's face is actually that of God's."

***

Hey, got a light?" Steve asked Sadie in bed a few nights later. He sat back on the pillows and took a long hit off a joint, then passed it to her.

"That was pretty fucking amazing," he said.

Sadie, already stoned as hell, heard his words clanging on and on in her head, beneath them another voice of her own chanted, *Does he really have to say such awful things?* Shit, she thought, I hate it when that basso profundo voice weighs in.

"You know," Steve said, wrapping his arms up over the back of the pillow, the joint in his mouth. "The stone business sucks these days. You got all these little guys from South America standing at intersections, willing to do stone work for eight bucks an hour. And they've like, lived and breathed rocks for twenty generations. Gotta give the fuckers their due, they know their rocks. And strong? I saw this one shrimp pick up a rock that stood to his knees and just walk it across a yard like it was a baby. But they're too fucking cheap! Hey, got any more of that red wine?"

Sadie stroked his chest, only half listening. She reached out and poured herself a vodka. She'd brought up a glass with lots of ice in it, rather craftily, she thought. It was the third time she'd spent a night with Steve and she found that she needed it—he was one of those people that got garrulous while high, even after sex. *In fact,* the bass voice said in her head, *he's a bloody chatterbox.* She took another sip of vodka.

"The thing is," he went on relentlessly, "the housewives don't like being left alone in their eighty-five-hundred-square-foot houses, with these Marielitos churning up the soil outside their windows and leering at them. Fuck straight, if I were a dame, I wouldn't either. Those little guys, all they can think about is popping some blond American pussy. Here, put this in the ashtray, I'll roll a new one. You know what's funny? It's this, it's all a matter of like, the food chain. It makes me laugh. Half the time I'm out there sweating, moving stones around and the same housewives are coming out every fifteen minutes, you want some iced tea and lemonade? You want a cold towel? You want me to run your clothes through the washer? While

I suck you off? They're so fucking horny. And so obvious. Married to some fat dickwad who waddles off to the eight fifteen every morning, bye, honey. I feel like a piece of fucking meat when their eyes slather all over me. And I got some pride you know, never bang 'em."

Sadie waved her hand, saying no thanks to another hit. "I think the Marielitos were Cuban, actually. But you're right about the food chain part," she said. "I used to be the young woman in one of the snarlier, bloodier parts of it. Though all I did was see teeth gnashing shut around me, Ree made sure of that."

"He screw around on you?"

"Oh, I suppose a bit, nothing serious."

"But expected you to keep clean, right? Hey, you ever meet Alice Cooper? Really? He's my hero. Do you know why he called himself Alice? That's always bugged me like hell. Was he a fag?"

"If I were a tall, hairy guy and had a voice like a bucket of live coals, I'd call myself Alice," Sadie said, dreamily.

"You want some more vodka?"

"Please. I'm not quite drunk enough yet to fall asleep."

"You call that sleep? I call it passed out. You got to be careful about never smoking in bed, okay? At least, if I'm not here. It's one thing if you fry yourself to a crisp, but it's those kids of yours I'm thinking about. Teenagers sleep hard too, like drunks. I tell you what, I'm going to install hard-wired smoke detectors in this place for you. It'll cost you a couple hundred but I'll do the work for free. I'll use hotel-grade ones. Hotels hate to have their guests burn up."

11

Hamish was beginning to grow and was very often ravenously hungry. His mother's nonchalant attitude toward food meant there was usually little for him to eat in the fridge, though he opened the door often, staring hopelessly at its contents and sighing.

His weekly allowance, a sum adequate for his needs but in no way princely, gave him just enough for a hot dog here and there, which he'd wolf down, longing for five more.

Being an intelligent boy, he decided he'd become quite fond of Ettie, and began watching her movements with a lively interest. It's not that he stalked her exactly, but he did become familiar with her routine. Two days after the tea at the colonel's he saw his chance and struck. Ettie was leaving Balducci's, her cart full and a bulging shopping bag in one hand. He offered to carry the bag for her, which she handed him, blushing with pleasure.

Since that day bliss had come into Hamish's life. In the form of leftover fried chicken, beef bourguignon, oyster stew, ginger cookies, and Ettie's specialty, grilled cheese sandwiches. These were not any grilled cheese sandwiches, these were thick slices of sourdough bread with Gruyère and tomato, browned in clarified butter. She'd make two for him while she got the colonel's dinner ready, her heart full to have his company as she worked. They talked as Ettie cooked and Hamish ate, both of them highly interested in the workings of their respective households.

One day Hamish told Ettie about the old bum who'd done him a kindness. "Munster gives him money regular," he explained. "And we do too, I mean a little bit. But I saw him yesterday and I had only a dollar. He looked kind of hungry. He's pretty fat, so his stomach must ache and ache when its empty. And then there's his cat, Titus, he's got to feed him too."

Ettie took this very much to heart. Upstairs that night in her top-floor room, watching a video her sister had sent from Guatemala, she could barely concentrate on who was in love with who. She felt it a terrible thing that a kind man was hungry, for he must be very kind and good if the boy liked him so, such a good boy as Jaimes. Switching off the set she sat in her armchair and squeezed her eyes shut to think. Yes, she would ask the colonel. He would know what to do. But you can't just ask him to feed every bum in the city, especially some bum she'd never seen. No, it was clear, she must go and find this bum and speak to him herself first.

So the next afternoon, after the colonel's lunch, she set out for the park. She had a five-dollar bill in her coat pocket and a shopping bag with some sandwiches she'd prepared. And in another packet, a mash of chicken and rice, for his cat. She'd thought carefully and had decided that pure meat might be too much for the stomach of a city cat, one owned by a bum. It might gobble it down, then throw it right up.

That evening, when Ettie put out the colonel's drink tray before dinner, the hour when he was most receptive to requests, she'd discovered, she said, "Um?"

"Yes, my dear? I know what your 'ums' signify. What is it? You need to order a side of beef for that boy? Go right ahead, it gives me such pleasure to hear what he packs away each afternoon."

"Well, he knows this old man. A good man, who has no home. One time, this old man was very good to Jaimes and Miss Deen, he scared away a bad man who was trying to hurt them. This is brave I think. This old man, he has a good and clean cat he keeps in his coat pocket, it's a very big pocket, but he has to hide his cat because there are so many bad people in this world. I say, Ettie, go see this man and talk with him, so I do, today. Then ask the colonel what to do."

"Hmm. Describe his face to me," the colonel said, refilling his glass.

"Big, like old stone that's been out in the weather, long gray hair. With old blue eyes and face hairs, like his cat's. He looked at me like a boy whose mother comes to pat his head, when I gave him food."

"Oh," the colonel said. "And was he very hungry?"

"Yes."

"Well, let me think about it a bit, will you?"

In the end, the colonel called in Mrs. de Angelo. Now there was a woman, he thought, who could solve any problem. He explained to her that he had a rather special project that needed her delicacy and intellect, and that she should bill him for whatever fee she thought appropriate.

Mrs. de Angelo arrived the next afternoon, listened carefully to what the colonel had to say, then ate several tea sandwiches while she thought.

"Well, you already have me on retainer to oversee things," she said at last. "So I'll just bill you for the extra hours, and perhaps a fee for the design work. First thing is, a place to leave him food. The difficulty is that a bum can't be seen loitering, or worse, possibly intent to B and E."

"A term whose origins I do not understand, dear lady."

"Breaking and entering."

"Ah."

"So what we've got to do is devise a place to stash the food that looks so ordinary that everyone passes it by without a thought, but that your bum can open without attracting suspicion. It'll have to be something at waist height. . . . Hmm, the front steps and area railing don't really have any places that're right . . . but the garden gate's inset from the building. We could build the fence to the left of it out with a false front, make a hatch with a secret spring, your bum could look like he was just stopping to get his breath, and away he goes. And a hatch from the garden side, for Ettie to place the food in. I'll have my carpenter over tomorrow to do the job. And tell Ettie to place the food in a shopping bag, ready to go."

"Most remarkable," the colonel said. "Conceived, and sure to be executed, with military precision. Wish we'd had you in the war, would've gone a damn sight smoother. Now that our business is so admirably concluded, may I offer you a drink?"

"No thanks, I never drink."

"Really? Not ever?"

"It's hell on the skin for a woman my age. I'll have a sparkling water, though."

The colonel rang for Ettie rather sadly.

Three days after Mrs. D's visit to the colonel, her carpenter showed Ettie how the secret hatch in the false garden wall worked. Intrigued by the project, he went so far as to pretend several times to be a bum, walking down Tenth Street and drawing out a bag they'd placed in it.

For her part, Ettie was ecstatic. She'd already planned a series of wholesome foods to give to the Cap'n and his cat. Things that would keep but still provide extra nourishment. The carpenter had even insulated and wired a heat pad to the base of the hatch, saying, "It's gonna be no good to the old guy if it's frozen." Ettie had been so impressed by this foresight that she'd made him an apple cake to take home to his wife. One of her extra special ones with the burned sugar.

The next afternoon she went to tell the Cap'n the news. He was not in the park. She made a sweep of the surrounding streets, but he was nowhere to be found. The next day she tried again. He wasn't there. The following day she asked the colonel's permission to take Jaimes along with her to search for him, leaving the colonel a cold dinner while they walked the streets into the now quick-fading light. She began to cry, as finally, she and Hamish gave up.

"He's just off on a toot, Munster says," Hamish told her, patting her arm. "He'll be back in his spot in the park any day now, you'll see. Please, you have to come home now, it's no use you getting sick worrying about him, then you wouldn't be able to cook him something when he does show up. Come on, the colonel needs you too, you know."

"Oh, one time I can do something good. The colonel, he say, feed that man. And his cat too. I've seen too many hungry people not to care this one time, just to feed one old man, only one, a poor man and his cat. Poor Titus."

"Come away, Ettie. I'll ask the guys I play basketball with to keep an eye out for him, we'll find him."

But the days passed and no one had news of the Cap'n. His broad bulk was never seen on his bench in Washington Square Park. Miss Lily worried about him also, he never came around anymore. And sometimes, in those hours that seem to be no part of the real world, the predawn hours of night's wakefulness and worry, she woke and saw his figure, willing it to come back to her.

***

As threatened, Paul Dresden had made Deen play elementary-level tunes day after day. He told her he was emptying her of all the wrong music inside her head and her fingers. The program also included scales, which he demanded she play endlessly, basic technique, he said, stripped of content and especially emotion. He'd told her something she'd found interesting, that she should play the same way she'd eat—correctly, efficiently, and with savor. "And forget the fucking manners," he added. "No pinkies raised, no flourishes!"

Four afternoons a week Deen toiled with him in his studio. Sometimes she played two-voiced Scarlatti sonatas the entire session while Paul appeared to sleep.

Now they were gradually progressing to slightly more difficult pieces. Paul's method of teaching was a negative one, involving shouts of derision, stinging criticism and sarcasm. Deen was beginning to rather like him.

Kristen continued to greet Deen at the door with her baby, presenting the stolid infant as if bestowing a royal favor, a part of the routine Deen had grown to loathe. Kristen also acted the role of keeper of the gate, making Deen wait in her noxious kitchen until she deemed the Great One sufficiently prepared to receive her.

For the infant Rinaldo's part, it had taken as great a dislike to Deen as she to it. It opened its mouth wide and let out a scream each time it saw her.

Today, Deen had been invited to stay for dinner after the lesson, although children are not so much invited to do things as told to do them. Kristen had called Sadie to suggest it, saying they should all get to know each other better. She had in fact made the suggestion only in the hopes that Sadie would come, but her plan had backfired and Sadie had eluded her net. Sadie accepted for her daughter, making it rather too plain that she never for a moment considered going herself.

Deen had been dreading it for days. The lesson finished, Paul told her to go sit with Kristen, as he had some work to do.

"He's composing a symphony," Kristen said as Deen came in. "And I'm never to disturb him before dinnertime. I even take the phone off the hook. Not that anyone ever calls us."

Kristen sat the baby in its high chair, carefully feeding its elephantine legs through the seat. "There now. I thought we could have a nice chat and a cup of tea. And after, you can help me give him his bath."

Deen could think of no greater treat. She sidled around the table, hoping it wouldn't notice her, but it looked up and its eyes went round and it began to shriek. Deen wished she could throw a blanket over its face, which had turned the color of raw beefsteak, with a stream of ochre snot dangling from its nose. A gob of the stuff went into its mouth. It gave a gulp then went silent, beating its fists on the tray. Kristen ran to it, her face white with fear as she tipped its head back. It fought off her hands with surprisingly loud smacks of flesh on flesh. Deen supposed she oughtn't hope it choked to death. Finally it gave a great, slurping gulp and opened its mouth to howl again.

Lived to howl another day, Deen thought sourly. She dreaded what was going to be served for dinner, hoping that smell in the steamy kitchen wasn't it. It smelled like scorched balsa wood.

When the delightful task of helping to bathe the infant was offered to Deen she demurred, saying that Paul had told her she mustn't do any work with her hands. Kristen said nothing, just made a suffering face.

"Well, well," Paul said, when at last he came in. "What a charming scene of domesticity. Sweetheart, do we have any of that cooking sherry left? I rather feel like a drink. Yes, a drinkie, let's all have a slug of awful sherry. We so rarely have a guest, perhaps because we're so damn poor we can barely feed ourselves, eh, my love? Ondine, I assume your mother lets you have a tiny glass now and then?"

"Yes, wine and sherry."

"Ah, splendid. What care we for our great white leader's so-called family values? Though they haven't quite foisted him on us as our next president yet. What a farce of an election."

Kristen went to the cupboard and poured him a glass of sherry, wiping the glass surreptitiously with the hem of her sweater first.

She brought it to Paul, who sat at the table looking around him as if he'd never seen any of these people before, and found them comical.

"And how is this great and thriving creature?" he said, looking at his son, who stared back at him with a crafty expression. "Fattening him up, I take it? Cells multiplying daily on a diet of milk and pureed carrots? Were there any giants in your family, perhaps an uncle with the circus, my pet? Kristen, our guest has not been given a glass of sherry, please correct that. There, Ondine, to your health."

He raised his glass and drained it. "My, that was disgusting." He stared at Kristen, who was still standing. "Sit down, for Christ's sake!" he suddenly roared. "Can't we even *pretend* to be civilized, just this once? Have a fucking glass of sherry and some interesting conversation, speak of greater things than nappies and washing powders? Are we but beasts to mill and constantly low? Put your withered ass in a chair, woman, at least try to act like the lady of the house."

Kristen scuttled into her chair and put on a bright look. "Deen, I've been dying to ask you," she said, her gaiety rather hectic, "what was your father really like? I had such a crush on him when I was younger. He was so beautiful, whirling onstage, all that long hair flying around him."

"Ignore her," Paul said. "That kind of codswollop you'll do best to ignore as a matter of principle. All right, we've had our sham adult drink, made a stab at making it look like we don't live in the most abject squalor and poverty, let's move on. Get some dinner on the table, woman. I've been praying it doesn't taste as foul as it smells, but so few prayers are answered. Do you pray, Ondine? To God?"

"Not much."

"Nor do I. Aha, proof that there is no God," he said as Kristen put plates on the table. "That bad smell *is* dinner. Even I, a disbeliever, hoped that it might just be a nappy crisis, but no, 'tis our daily bread. For which I am decidedly ungrateful. And God*damn* it!" he shouted, crashing his fist on the table. "Must we have spaghetti Bolognese *every* night? Only varied by the degree to which it is ill-prepared or burnt? You *cunt*! Can't you learn to cook anything else?"

Deen had never had a father, neither one who was sweet to her nor one who roared. She'd never experienced that grace note of family life, the enraged breadwinner at the dinner table. She wished the floor would dissolve and swallow her up. It didn't occur to her that what she was seeing was anything less catastrophic than a total breakdown of a marriage. She tried to think of what to say to get herself out the door, but just then Paul put his head down and began to eat. Kristen also seemed unperturbed. She was carefully cutting hanks of spaghetti into tiny bits and feeding them into her son's mouth. Her rabbity face shone with adoration as the baby gummed down the food from a plastic spoon, making quacking sounds between each spoonful.

Paul slumped back in his chair. "You should see him eat a banana," he said. "It cures you of any love you might still have for the human race."

12

Gene's Restaurant on Eleventh near the corner of Sixth Avenue was a haven to those who yearned for the vanished glories of the Village. Descend five red-painted steps from the sidewalk to a door with an ironwork grille and enter a dreamworld, an Italian joint that hadn't changed since the fifties. A coat-check girl leans over the half door of her cubicle, her face slack with boredom. Across from her, Jimmy the barman stands, wide and genial in an ochre monkey suit, behind his polished mahogany bar. Beyond them the dining room is carpeted in a swirly pattern reminiscent of first-class railway cars. Waiters in monkey suits heft trays piled high, conversing with each other in Spanish and Albanian.

The diners are straight from a Max Beckmann painting—raddled old dames in orange wigs, fat men smoking cigars and ordering double brandies, cadaverous poets with long manes of white hair. Most of them are regulars who've aged right along with the establishment, neither the clientele nor the owner exactly embracing change. It was the kind of place where a wineglass is set before a teenage grandchild in a party, nothing said. It had held on to its ideas and ways, and its pride in being slightly raffish.

George arrived at the bar each night around nine, slipping onto his stool at the corner, which Jimmy saved for him if he could, using many of the subtle arts of the good bartender to do so.

George was a writer. He wrote about New York. He'd had pieces in all the more serious publications, though if asked, would freely admit that it'd been some time since he'd had anything new published.

He delighted in listening to conversations, to the authentic. In his seat beneath the window facing the street at Gene's he could hear and see almost everyone at the pocket-size bar. He sat there rapt, a knowing look on his face, gradually getting stewed until Jimmy, by certain coded signals, made it known that it was time for George to quit.

George followed the conversations around him with a look on his face so engaging and complicit that hardly anyone got annoyed. His face seemed to say, Do go on, this is most enjoyable, don't mind me.

He was into his fourth Johnnie Black and completely at ease in his soul. His torso wafted slightly, as though fanned by gentle breezes. He smiled at a man who caught his eye. He leaned forward to listen to the couple around the corner. In their mid-sixties, he thought, and decided they must be in publishing, for the man wore a bow tie and a gray flannel suit, and the woman a stylish wool sheath and oversize round tortoiseshell glasses. He longed to ask her where she'd bought them, or if they were old and treasured, repaired numerous times. His mind wandered down a path, bordered by lustrous blooms, in which he'd write a piece about New York literary types and their eyewear. Yes, yes, it would be a wonderful piece, he'd interview that man at Dell & Myrowitz. . . .

He was so excited he longed to rush home, start right on it. But first he'd have just one more; the couple's conversation was getting interesting.

"I suppose he thought he was doing her a favor," the man said.

"Some favor!" the woman snorted. "Her next book hit the remainder bins before it'd even been reviewed."

They were both drinking rye and ginger ale. Behind them Marissa, the coat-check girl, was helping a tiny old woman into a vast mink, patting it into place around her shriveled body.

Rye and ginger; even the drinks here clung to the old ways, George reflected. Jimmy suffered agonies when some newcomer ordered a modish drink, though he, of course, made it with the blandest professionalism. Jimmy's compendium of recipes was like a great leather-bound bible, filled with Gibsons, Manhattans, and whiskey sours. George rocked lightly on his anchor, recalling a pretty young woman who'd come in with her father some weeks back. She'd asked for a sidecar. Jimmy's face had lit up like a blazing sunset showing between the clouds over Bayonne.

Ah, that'd been a rare, tender moment, George thought, smiling. He nodded yes to Jimmy's, "One more, Mr. George?"

Right, he became *Mr.* George when Jimmy decided it would be his last drink, let the ritual begin. He watched admiringly as Jimmy selected a fresh glass from the mirrored shelf, placed it just so, then held the bottle of Johnnie aloft, timing the pour to meet exactly as a double. He carried it on the palm of his left hand, his right held slightly out, as if to say, Thus I come to greet my people, I your lord, of the House of Walker. A fresh cocktail napkin bearing the arms of Gene appeared magically from his fingers, upon which the sacred glass was set down. In his head, George could hear the muffled drum roll, and was stirred by it.

As usual he acquitted himself well, sat up straight, drank his scotch, and said good night politely to all. Then he took his cloak and strode up the five red-painted steps, his back straight.

A man at the other end of the bar, who was unknown to Jimmy, said, "That guy some kind of stone drunk? Sits there every night, ogling everyone and getting shitfaced?"

Jimmy's face clanged down like a security grille, but as always, he was polite. "The gentleman is a writer, sir," he said.

***

Sadie, of course, was no great dotter of *i*'s and crosser of *t*'s when it came to finances. Some years back she'd made an attempt to actually figure out her annual income and expenses but all she'd been able to determine was that it seemed a bloody miracle they weren't all in the poorhouse. Since then she just handed a bulging file to an accountant she'd heard of who had a reputation for being artist-friendly. Who then pushed and cajoled the figures to suit her client's needs, and the need to keep the law at bay.

Sadie was Ree's sole heir and executor and as such owned all his music rights and royalties. As he'd written most of the Royhatten Transference's songs with Brian as cowriter, it was fairly straightforward and was handled by an entertainment lawyer they both used to save unnecessary costs. That part of her income was unfudgeable.

Income from record sales, videos, and recording rights had held fairly steady over the years, though CD sales were declining. The lawyer blamed emerging software for file sharing, and the Internet. Sadie put the blame squarely on the greed of the record companies. CDs had been a unique opportunity for them to lower the price of music, but instead they'd seen it as yet another chance to jack them up. So it was no wonder the kids were finding ways to get around forking out twenty bucks for a CD.

What hadn't held steady was the cost of life in the Big Ampule. Sadie felt she hardly splashed money around, but was appalled by her monthly bills.

While Sadie was no financial whiz, she did have a certain crusty New

England grip on what a dollar was worth. She'd never gone in for the stock market; it was all too confusing and filled with men with hyena faces and sporty suspenders. What she had done was realize she had a unique trove—a bank vault filled with reel-to-reel recordings of the RT. She'd fancied herself the archivist of the band and had either recorded many herself or kept copies of others. It was the basis of what she called her "dead man's souk." For years she'd been selling recordings to an ex-industry guy, for cash. Fortunately there seemed to be no limit to the market for bootlegs of the band. She'd offered to give Brian half, but he'd just laughed, saying, "You get what you can for them love, Ree'd kill me if he thought I were taking anything from you." The cash had been a huge help; with it she floated most of their everyday expenses.

But this year, with Gretchen in that filthily expensive place, she was feeling about as skint as she had back in the early days with Ree. She'd just gotten another bill from Rollingbrook and didn't know how the hell she was going to pay it. That night she drank her fears away but then woke sometime around two, knowing she was going to fret for hours.

At least Steve wasn't there nattering at her. She adored his white middle-class rage, but he was getting to be a bit of a bore. And he was starting to give her tender looks. The problem with men was they were so unused to having sex and being treated pleasantly by a woman who didn't give a shit about love or sharing or commitment that it made them restless, leading them toward the very trap they'd been avoiding most of their lives.

None of these thoughts is going to help me come up with fifteen grand, she chided herself. Gretchen *was* getting better, but it didn't seem wise to spring her before some concrete progress was made, much as she longed to have her home. Oh, what had made Gretchen lose it like that? She'd always been such an easy child, not a big talker of course, a bit odd, in fact, but who with even a jot of imagination wasn't?

An image from a 16 mm film she'd made flashed into her mind—

seven-year-old Gretchen having a doll's tea, her father sitting meekly on one of the tiny Mexican chairs while she gravely handed around cups. Ree had looked so incongruous, and yet not, with his long hair. The two humans were the long, fair-haired dolls, the other occupants of the table were toy animals—Gretchen had always hated dolls, had found them frightening.

What was plucking at her memory? Oh yes, Hames asking her to buy him a new computer. Well, that was out of the question. But what had he said? That he could add on equipment to be able to burn CDs from LPs, and then film to DVD. Boys, they could never get their hands on enough bloody equipment.

It had never occurred to her that there was money to be made from all the films she'd shot of Ree and the band, not unless she sold it all to someone for a documentary, and that wouldn't bring in much . . . but they were good, she knew that, had been the one thing in her life she'd showed some talent for. And she had reels of the stuff, all carefully stored in a separate vault at the bank. She got out of bed and tied the sash of her bathrobe.

"Hey, kid, wakey, wakey."

"Munster! What time's it?"

"Time to log on."

"Wha?"

"Come on, kid—I'll buy you that new computer you've been after me for if this works."

Hamish got up blearily in his cotton pj's and sat at his desk. "So, log on to what?" he said.

"Type in your father's name. What're you doing?"

"Googling. Everything else sucks."

"What's this?" she asked.

"It means it's logging through the files, it takes a few minutes. Here it is, okay, three hundred and thirty-seven thousand matches. What're you looking for?"

"Bootleg recordings."

"Okay, let me define the search."

"How do you do that?"

"It's too boring to explain to someone like you, okay?"

"Need the Vulcan mind meld, huh?"

"Yeah. Hang on, here's some. Lots of them. Look at this, geeze, Pops live, on tape and video, trading for twenty-four bucks!"

"Kid, I can't look at this shit on the screen, it all makes me feel hypnotized. How about I hire you for a job? I mean it, I'll make it right to you, okay? Like real business. If you can track down a single name, the most frequent one in this bootleg stuff, either a company or a person, give me a list."

"Okay," Hamish said. "But we might have to discuss a cut of the profits. But could I please get some sleep before I do this?"

"Report on my desk at twenty-one hundred tonight," Sadie said, as she closed the door.

***

The result of their efforts was a rail-thin young man named Ira Salter. Sadie met him in a café. He ordered tea, she asked for a vodka rocks. She presented him with his crimes and held a threat over his head, saying, "You ever read that FBI warning they make us suckers sit through in the beginning of a video?"

"I think I'm usually firing up the popcorn maker at that moment," he said.

"The Rutledge Recording Company could, if it wanted to, skin you alive. I as executor, could cry for your head. Thing about *sales* on the Internet, is they leave a paper trail. Or so my twelve-year-old son tells me. You can run, but you can only hide for a month or so. I have no interest in stopping your sales."

"No?"

"No. I would like to increase them. I think I'll have another drink."

She held an arm up and the waiter came back. "Hit me again," Sadie said. "And get this boy some booze, for Christ's sake. What is it you will drink?"

"I'll have an Irish coffee."

"Gawd."

"Do you actually have something to say to me, besides making fun of me?"

"Okay, here, this is all the business we're going to do at this meeting."

She took a Polaroid out of her pocketbook and held it in front of him, keeping her fingers on it. It was a photo of a bank vault, one that opened out to reveal rows of shelves. On them were tapes and films in deep yellow boxes, dates and titles written in Magic Marker on their sides.

"I was a multi-media sort when I was young," she said. "Fancied myself a filmmaker."

"I'm interested," Ira said.

"Think cash."

"I live cash."

"So maybe you're not such a wuss after all, even if you do drink Irish coffee," Sadie said, hitting his glass with hers.

The next time she met him in the same café and handed him a reel of film, duped from the original, and he handed her six grand; she took a quick drink, counted the bills under the table, and left. She stood on the wide avenue, holding her arm up for a cab. One pulled up almost immediately. "Driver, take me to a furrier," she said.

13

A great lumpy figure in a sheepskin coat belted and tied with twine made its way up Eighth Avenue at the dim and gloomy end of a November afternoon. The old khaki pack on his back made him a towering hunchback and the cat in his pocket gave him a crooked gait.

Cap'n Meat was on the run. He knew that the little world he inhabited was fragile, but not how fragile until a boot had come splintering through its paper walls. Some days ago he'd crept back to his underpass in Central Park after dark, to lay himself down to sleep. Someone had been there, some malignant being. Bags of reeking garbage had been kicked open and strewn over the ground. The Cap'n, thinking it was kids at first, shone his flashlight over the scene. Where he normally slept, over by one curving wall, an area of trash had been cleared in the shape of a man's body. Where his heart would be, a razor blade was jammed into the soil, its edge pointing up. Above it, on the stone, an eye had been painted, by a finger dipped in red paint.

Thoroughly spooked, he turned and made quick progress toward the nearest place with people and light. He had no way of knowing if he was being followed by whoever had put this curse on his shelter, so he zigged and zagged, hoping to get away. That night he wandered Times Square, feeling safer there, but not enough to find a shadowed place to lie down in.

For days, too afraid to return to any of his regular haunts, he stole about the city, seeking places that had never known him and keeping his face averted from the world. He had almost no money and was feeling too low to panhandle. The nights were getting cold, especially so in those friendless hours before dawn. He knew of a number of tunnels he could go to, but he'd lost the nerve it took to go in among the other bums and look tough enough not to be attacked and robbed of everything. He dreamed of a box car somewhere way up north that he could crawl into and sleep. He scratched around for leavings of meat to feed to Titus, who ate them but seemed to have caught his owner's lowness of soul, for the cat merely sat in his pocket, hardly moving. The Cap'n himself lost interest in food, the iron talons of despondency that gripped his being causing him to forget everything else.

One night he lined up for a shelter, but when it came to his turn the people at the desk recognized him. The young guy, the one with the hole for a mouth, hit the side of the Cap'n's coat hard, making Titus rise up and screech.

"Get out of here!" he yelled at the Cap'n. "You know the rules about pets, get that filthy animal out of here! Bum's can't have cats, can't you get that through that fat old head of yours?"

Desperate, he sneaked and edged his way toward his old bench in Washington Square Park the next morning. He'd found some trash bags and covered his coat with them, trying to disguise himself. He looked around: there didn't seem anything out of place. Gingerly he sat, gradually easing back, a faint thread of hope snaking into his insides. Maybe Sadie would come by and give him some money. Maybe he'd get his courage back if something good like that happened, get some food and the strength to return to his old routine. A flash of sun came as it rose above a rooftop and he leaned back, sighing. Above him, on the limb of the old oak, a red eye stared down at him.

He did go north then, in search of his boxcar. Dogs barked at him as he picked through trash cans, their yaps and howls echoing down the empty night streets. Titus growled inside his pocket. He'd find something for them both to eat then head west, find the railroad tracks.

He was stumbling over a tract of broken land spotted with refuse and the drying husks of milkweeds when a cruiser came bounding over the terrain, fixing him in its lights and whoop-whooping its siren.

The Cap'n sank to his knees and cried out to the sky. This was the end. They might only book him for vagrancy, that wasn't what mattered, but what they would do was take Titus away and give him to the Animal Control. In his grief at the cat's certain abandonment he spoke softly to it, trying to explain, ignoring the policeman approaching him.

"What're you saying, old man?"

"How can I ever explain to him that I didn't abandon him," the Cap'n cried.

"Who, sir?"

"My poor cat."

The Cap'n looked up, he couldn't see the cop, only a tall black figure outlined by the headlights. But the cop hadn't kicked him, or made any move. His partner was standing to one side, lighting a cigarette.

"All right, what gives here?"

"I've got a cat in my pocket, a friend. If you take me in, you'll take him away from me, give him to the Animal Control."

"Hey, Tommy," the first cop said to the other. "You see me takin' in some old vagrant, kickin' the shit outta him, then takin' his cat away?"

"Nope," Tommy said.

"Hey fella, just tell me it's really some cat, not some old lady's head you got in your pocket, okay?"

The Cap'n undid the flap on Titus's pocket. Titus stuck his head out and blinked at the headlights, then ducked back in.

"I tried to get them out of the swamp, but they died," the Cap'n said. "But it was long ago, and I never felt they hated me because of it."

"Oh yeah, where was that?"

"It was called Pyong."

"Oh yeah. You get hit too?"

"Just in the leg. I tried, you see, to get them all out of there, but then the radioman got hit."

"Hey, Tommy—we got any of that chicken left?"

"Yeah, and some slaw."

"Listen, old man. There's an old railway depot right over there. I cleared a coupla winos outta there last week. I ain't sayin' it's perfect or nuthin', but at least you can kip down there tonight. Here, Tommy, hand me that chicken. Now, no fires, I'll come back and roust you out of there if you make any fires, got that? And here's ten bucks, nah, I was in the forces too. Come on, Tommy, we gotta go."

* * *

What had become of that little boy in a sun suit, with his tin truck zooming across the dirt? Of days of jam and motes of grain dust suspended in a shaft of light in the barn. His mother sighing over a picture magazine, tracing her finger over the silhouette of a cocktail dress.

The road between there and here seemed impossible to map, the Cap'n thought. A cartographer would look at it and say it couldn't be done.

They'd dubbed him Captain Meat that day in the saw grass and the mud filled with live, squirming creatures, some of them human. The chain of command eaten and shot and blasted away until he was the only one left to command. His one idea to get them the fuck out of there.

He'd dragged two injured friends but they'd gotten shot again, so there was no point in dragging them any farther. Then their radioman got shot, geeze, Ma, they got me right in the gut! Inappropriate laughter, they called it.

Five of them had made it to the rendezvous, one screaming. The other men sat there, giving him the look, not because they thought he'd done any worse a job than any other poor sucker, but because he'd become a commanding officer, become the real enemy.

He'd never seen any reason not to call himself what they'd named him that day, why pretend to wash away something you were never going to get off your skin? He didn't recognize any part of what he'd once been, so they'd done him a favor giving him a new name.

14

In no time at all the Hollander children were spending nearly as much time in the colonel's house as in their own. Hamish ate leftovers and helped Ettie in the kitchen, and Deen practiced on the colonel's Chickering. The colonel had consulted with Sadie before inviting Deen to use the piano whenever she liked, to make sure she approved of the idea.

Sadie had. It was her opinion that adults had to be somewhat cautious in making friendships, but that children had diplomatic immunity and were not expected by the adults who befriended them to do much beyond receive their offerings politely.

Deen had leaped at the chance. The colonel's piano was far superior to their own cranky Steinway baby grand, and it was wonderful to practice in a room where no boys clumped in and out.

Colonel Harrington let out a fat man's sigh of contentment from his chair by the fire. Deen was playing Brahms and he had a glass of bourbon in his hand. There was no more a man could wish for. True, the house was a bit chilly, it seemed the furnace had broken down, but Mrs. de Angelo had been called and she'd be sure to sort the problem out.

Basking like an old bull sea lion in the heat from the fire, he listened to Deen's playing. A great admirer of classical music and quite knowledgeable on the subject, he'd recognized in Deen a serious talent from the first. In fact, he'd spent many hours listening to her play through the open window by his chair. He was intrigued by what this new fellow was setting her to do lately. Strange as it seemed, he thought it was showing results, that Deen's playing had a new maturity and assurance.

Ettie came in quietly. "Colonel, the man who Meez D call, he look at the furnace and say he got to talk to you. Meez D coming too, any minute."

"Hey man? Hi. Name's Robert," the plumber said, coming into the room. "Fact is, we got to talk about your entire system down there."

The colonel offered his hand. "Sit down, sir. May I offer you a drink?"

"Well, say, it is kind of late, and I ain't union, so sure, I'll take a drink. Thank you kindly."

The colonel leaned over and handed him the bottle. "Everything you need's there," he said, indicating the drink tray. "There's no ice though, would you like some?"

"Natural be just fine for this here," Robert said, taking a sip. "Just fine."

"Ah, and here is Mrs. de Angelo. Sit down, dear lady, have a drink. This is Robert, who has kindly answered your summons and has much to say about the heating plant."

"I came as soon as I could," she said. With an air of having far more important things to do, she shook Robert's offered hand. "How bad is it?" she asked him.

"Bad."

"Oh crap, maybe I will have that drink." She poured herself a bourbon and took a slug. "Okay, give it to me straight."

"Whole shebang's got to be replaced. Some fool put in pipes all the wrong gauge. Boiler's not what it says it is either, somebody took some leedle teeny screws and stuck on the name of a respectable manufacturer, got full price for it too, no doubt. Probably some union dudes, those guys know every scam in the book. Boiler's just plumb too small for this here house anyways, even if it weren't a hunk of Chinese junk. They go and stick this thing in and for a few years it looks all right, even gives out some heat, but now she's all burned out."

"Colonel, I want you to know that I had a contractor look over the place from top to bottom before you signed the contract. He never said anything about this. And the listing said the boiler had been replaced three years ago."

"Three years, that's just about what I'd figure that piece of junk would last," Robert said. "Say, Colonel, you mind if I have some more of that sippin' whiskey?"

"Please, go right ahead. Well, well, Mrs. de Angelo, don't fret, these things happen. The question is, Robert, can you fix it?"

"Nope. I mean, I can get you all fixed up and install a proper system, but I can't fix that old gal. I can even give you some heat while I'm doing it. It'll take a little longer that way but I don't charge union wages. And I don't do union work neither—I do the job right."

"How much?" Mrs. D asked.

"About sixteen grand. That's for as sweet a boiler you ever seen included, and all the fittings. And all I charge is ten percent over cost for the materials. I don't have my hand down everyone's pockets, not like them union bosses with their diamond pinkie rings and their shivery smiles, all teeth."

"When can you start?" Mrs. D asked.

"Tomorrow."

"Excellent!" the colonel said. "Let's all have another drink. My, think of how toasty we'll be this winter. It almost makes me feel guilty, when so many people haven't even a home to go to."

"Now, now, Colonel," Mrs. D said. "You pay me to manage the household for you and I'm not going to let you turn it into a shelter. Speaking of which, Ettie find her bum yet?"

"No, I fear something may have happened to the poor fellow. Listen, hush everyone, my girl's playing one of her favorites."

They sat in silence, drinking whiskey and listening to Deen play a rousing gavotte. A few minutes after she'd finished they heard her call out "Good night, Colonel!" then let herself out the front door.

"That's some flying fingers on the eighty-eights," Robert said. "How old's that kid?"

"Fourteen, I believe. Rather remarkable, isn't she?"

"A goddamn genius," Mrs. D said.

"You said a mouthful, Mrs. D," Robert laughed. "Say, let's all have another drink. I'm starting to like this here job."

"What the hell have I gotten into?" Mrs. D asked, looking at her refilled glass.

"Some mighty good sippin' whiskey, I'd say," Robert told her.

The colonel leaned back. Ah, life was good. He'd dreamed for so long of a life like this, of sitting by a fire, drinking whiskey and talking, it was such a fine thing to have friends gathered at his hearth. Yes, a fine thing, something a man could spend his entire life seeking and never find.

***

I never thought Paul would take a pupil," Kristen said to Sadie. She'd called the day before and more or less blackmailed Sadie into coming to tea. "But he seems really taken with Deen."

Sadie thought that while the sentiment was irreproachable, there was something unsettling in the woman's smile, or was it a leer?

"Deen's so pretty, isn't she, with all that hair, just like her father's." Kristen got up as the kettle whistled.

Sadie took a look around the kitchen with distaste. It wasn't so much the griminess, there were plenty of places she'd been that were dirtier, but it was just grim, no life or personality to it. Unknown to her, poor Kristen had been scrubbing it all day, cramming nappies into cupboards and hiding certain of Rinaldo's less presentable toys.

Sadie also looked with disfavor at the infant sprawled in its pen. Rinaldo, what a peculiarly horrid name, she thought, and so perfectly suited to it.

"Here we are," Kristen said, bringing a tray to the table. In deference to her guest's English associations she'd bought real tea, was in fact afraid to serve Sadie her usual Constant Comment. She'd also tried to assemble something like a proper tea set, washing each piece with care, even the undersides, where hosts of smears and dried egg yolk lurked. A plate of sugar cookies from a packet completed her supreme effort. "Do you take milk?" she asked, pleased by how British it sounded.

"No thanks. So, you said there was something you wanted to talk to me about?"

"Oh, let's have our tea first, enjoy ourselves. I hardly ever have people over. Such a treat. Mmm," Kristen said, biting down on a cookie and taking a dainty sip of tea.

"Why's that?" Sadie asked her, beginning to feel annoyed.

"Oh well, Paul doesn't really like people around, says they stare at him. Being a genius he's different, you know what I mean. He needs a lot of time by himself. He's composing a *symphony*."

"Really. And does the genius hide back there all day long?" Sadie nodded her head in the direction of Paul's studio.

"He doesn't *hide*—you really shouldn't say things like that. He's just not like other people, because he's working on works of pure genius in his sanctum sanctorum. Oh, you were just teasing, weren't you? That's probably your famous English humor." She let out a little laugh. "We don't really get it, us Americans."

"I was born and raised in Tilbury, Vermont."

"Gee, really?"

"Yes, really. Now, you insisted I come over here to talk to you about something. What is it?"

Kristen's face began working, her eyes darting around, looking for help. It came as the baby let out a snort, flopped over, then let out an ear-piercing shriek. It brought its fists up to its head and beat them against its skull, screaming louder.

Kristen flew to him, emitting a small grunt as she picked him up. "There's Mommy, there, there," she said, kissing its yellow curls. "Who's my little genius, who's Daddy's special baby genius? Such a big-strong baby pudding." She put it over her shoulder, her back to Sadie.

It made a wet, bubbling sound and stared at Sadie. Then opened wide, preparing to scream again.

Sadie saw her chance and gave it the Look. The Look was something you didn't chance letting loving parents see, but the coast was clear. It was a look that bored into the other person's eyes, said yeah, you. Now, see what my eyes are saying? I'm memorizing yours, and I'll hunt you down to the ends of the earth and kill you, if you don't stop it at once.

The infant snapped its mouth shut and crawled down its mother's bosom, whimpering.

Kristen laid it back in its pen tenderly, pulling a blanket over its thick limbs.

"Isn't he the most beautiful baby?" she whispered. She sat back down at the table. "When I first held him, in the hospital, I had a mystical experience. I knew what life was all about all of a sudden, what it means."

"And what is that?"

"Oh, *you* know, of course you do."

Sadie wanted to throw a sugar cookie right at the woman's forehead.

"The thing is," Kristen began. "Well, I've been reading this stuff about how the maestro, that's what Paul is, is a kind of god to his pupil. Like Deen is. I mean, there's nothing *wrong*, nothing's happened, that goes without saying. It's just that I was sort of thinking, well, what if once in a while you came and sat in on their lesson, brought some knitting or something. See, Paul won't let me in there, not ever. I mean, I spy on him, that's how I know there's nothing wrong, but I also know that a relationship between a maestro and his pupil can get very, uh, strong."

Sadie looked at Kristen, appalled. She was so angry that she waited for a minute, needing her words to be clear. "I don't care what sorts of peculiar fantasies you drag in and let fester in your mind," she said, "but leave my daughter out of them. And I *don't* knit."

"But I was just trying to be, like, another mom to Deen!" Kristen wailed as Sadie left. The door clanked shut.

***

Deen, I want to talk to you about your situation over at the Dresden's," Sadie said to her in the kitchen before dinner. "Kristen shanghaied me into having tea with her today and suggested the stupidest thing, she thinks you and Paul are going to fall in love with each other."

Deen looked at her mother, her mouth open. She couldn't believe what she was hearing.

Sadie thought, gawd, that was such an idiotic way of putting it, *fall in love*? The tiniest giggle rose to her throat.

Deen let out a snort. Sadie's mouth twitched. Then Deen gave an involuntary gurgle, and before they knew it they were laughing, rocking back and forth, hooting with laughter.

"It was pretty damn funny, really," Sadie said, wiping her eyes. "She's such a busybody, isn't she? And that *baby*, Christ, Deen, I'd no idea what you've been through. Just for the record, all three of you were *nothing* like that, that grotesque beast. But really, do you like your lessons with Paul enough to run that gauntlet each time? We could work something else out, really darling."

"I didn't want to go there ever in the beginning," Deen said. "And I know this sounds kind of weird, but Kristen's not that bad, if you stop and think how she has to put up with Paul, who I think probably is a great pianist. Elizabeth was fine, but really Munster, even I was starting to see her limitations. She'll probably end up taking pupils more than anything, and then playing in some quartet out on Martha's Vineyard every summer or something. I don't want to end up like that."

"Well, if you say you can put up with that gargoyle of a baby, you must really feel the lessons are worth it."

"Haven't you noticed that my playing's changed?"

"Oh, Deen—you know I don't know jack about music."

"Sure you do, Munster. You just think you don't."

* * *

While these pleasant times were occurring in the pair of row houses on Tenth Street, other, less pleasant things were stirring and rustling in the neighborhood. An angry bum, his hood covering his eyes, stalked the nighttime streets, muttering and cursing. Holding his head up, sniffing, where was that fat old man, where were him and his fat, petted cat?

"Motherfucking cat sits there mee-owing, says love me, Mr. Fat Old Bum, love me everybody. And what do they do? Why they love even a *cat*. Some fuckin animal, just a shitbag covered in fur, that don't know how to spell or write or even say it's own *name*!

"He'll come creepin back, my little boy, the one with them sunny curls once, all kissed and washed and tucked in every night, he'll come roving back, creeping back to his old haunts. Can't never stay away, them that has their old haunts, always lookin' for Mamma in a tree branch, a patch of sidewalk, like they was back on that farm they was raised on, with the rows of beans and that nail that always stuck outta that step on the vee-ran-da. Oh yeah."

A mayonnaise jar is unsealed. A finger with a long, crooked nail dips into the red paint inside it. Stirs it around, once, twice. Then points at the place it will mark, throttles, makes a long, low arch. The finger dips again, into the sanguine paint. Comes out, a drop hovering from it, makes another inverted curve below, then stabs back into the crimson, rushes out and defines a small loop. I'm lookin' at you, from *everywhere*.

15

Gretchen sat in her wheelchair, in her usual corner of the lounge, lurking behind the potted plants. She was reading the part of *Jane Eyre* where she's gone away from Mr. Rochester, then hears his voice calling to her in the night. She knew that that could happen, that a person could call out to some one far away, in another part of England.

She heard footsteps coming toward her. She stopped reading, not looking up.

"Naughty again, I see. Well, Miss Jane Eyre, you won't catch me getting you anything from the kitchen just because you've missed dinner once more."

Nurse Peterson moved closer, leaning over Gretchen. Gretchen wanted to move away from her, but gave no sign that she knew she was there.

"What's this?" a male voice said.

"She pretends to read," Nurse Peterson told him.

"You're sure she doesn't actually read?" the doctor said.

"Quite sure, doctor. She never turns a page."

"Gretchen, you seem to have a special liking for this book," the doctor said, moving closer to look at it. "Why don't you show me which part you like best? You could show me the page and I could read that part. Then we'd have something we could talk about to-morrow."

"She doesn't read it, doctor. But try taking it away from her. She goes wild. We had to have an orderly restrain her."

"When did this happen? And why would you want to take it away from her?"

"Yesterday. Just look at the marks on my arms."

"Again, why did you try to take it from her?"

"Well, we can't just have the patients ordering us around, can we? I told her to give it to me so I could put her to bed but she wouldn't. Just ignored me, like she always does, so I took it. She attacked me, like I said. I had to explain to my kids why I had scratches all over my arm."

"Don't ever take any item I approve her having again, do you un-derstand? Gretchen, I'll see you tomorrow. Don't worry about your book, it's yours to do what you like with. Mrs. Peterson, we'll discuss this further in the morning."

Gretchen heard his footsteps move away.

The nurse waited till he was gone, then leaned over to whisper in Gretchen's ear: "Now you've really gone and done it. Made me have to stand here and listen to that doctor tell me off, you sly little thing, when you're the one who should be punished for attacking me. But just remember, your boyfriend there, the doctor, he isn't here all the time. Sometimes *I'm* in charge."

* * *

Robert Jeffries surveyed the boiler with sorrow. It was some piece of hundred percent union bullshit for sure. He took a socket wrench and began the pleasurable business of dismantling it. The new boiler hummed by his side, feeding the temporary connecting pipes he'd rigged. When he finished the job an honest boiler would sit on the block, every pipe the proper dimension and every solder a neat, non-union job. He'd even make it pretty too, and it would cost that old man upstairs less to run. He always took pride in doing good work, in proving you didn't have to have some fancy card with a number on it, from the Brotherhood of Jackasses or whatever. But for this here job he took a special pleasure in doing it right, because how many home-owners understood the innate need of a man working with pipes all day long, and provided them with a tot of sippin' whiskey at the end of the day? Good sippin' whiskey too.

Ettie came in at noon with a tray. "Meester ask me to bring you lunch," she said.

"S'okay, I brought my own."

"In that bag?" Ettie said, looking at a brown paper bag with its top neatly folded. "Not enough for a cat in there. This better." She took the linen towel off the tray and showed him. "The colonel, he say he think you a southern man too, he say Ettie, make southern lunch."

"Man, oh man," Robert said. "Fried chicken, collards, succotash, coleslaw, what don't you got here, woman? Pone, where's the pone? Shit, here she is, hiding her lights behind this here mountain of rice. Man, sure I'll eat it."

"He say too, you come for tea when you finish, that tea's word for something else. Okay?"

"A-OK. Say, you cooked all this?"

"Yes."

"You married?"

"Nope."

"Maybe we ought to talk some. You ever been married?"

"Yes, a very long time once. He's dead."

"He ever belong to a union?"

"No, he cut cane. The rebels killed him."

"Damn, that's not right. You like movies?"

"Julia Roberts, yes! I love Julia Roberts, any movie, I see it four, five times. So romantic, always with the shining eyes."

"You know they got a body double for those leg shots in *Pretty Woman*, but yeah, I like her fine."

"You eat, maybe we talk tomorrow."

"You okay with a black man asking you out?" he said, looking at her seriously.

"It's nice," she said, moving out the door.

"Ettie, Ettie," he said, taking up a fork to eat her cooking. "You make an old man cry for his past."

***

Sadie erased the phone message from Steve, the third one in two days. Oh crap, why did they always have to start acting like it was love? It was especially idiotic in this instance, he must be at least fifteen years her junior. And why did she always grow tired of them after a week or so? Because she was a bloody-minded bitch and simply using them, that's why. Was it her indifference that made them want to woo her? What a laugh. Aw, it was all so fucked up, and she didn't want to hurt Steve, but she was going to.

She'd call him back tomorrow. Tell him the truth, that she didn't want to continue. Or lie, make some lame excuse, see if he'd be a good boy and simply fade away. Then she'd feel guilty, and then she'd get drunk, and then she'd wonder why the hell she'd been fool enough to give up some guy who was funny, had muscles like that, and loved to screw. . . . Oh, damn it all, there was no solution.

Sipping her vodka she stared at Brian's cell number on the chalkboard. Funny, he hadn't dropped in on them in a while. He usually popped in every two or three weeks. And over the years, invariably showed up during the few times she had a new guy. It never failed. Until now. Steve was the only one, Sadie realized, who'd never come down to the kitchen one morning to find a bleary Englishman smoking and staring at him.

Oh well, if Brian wasn't going to come stomping in in his boots to get rid of this one, she'd just have to do it herself.

***

If you were to navigate the Cap'n's bloodstream, become an Argonaut small enough to slip inside a human vein, you'd see the molecules inside him growing grumpy, forming cliques, dysplasias. Little weird noodles attacking some big old cell, sticking themselves into it. The endless, wearisome mutations of age. Trek through his aorta, feel with your own fingers the layer of fatty deposits hanging down like greasy confetti.

The outside of the Cap'n lay on his blanket inside the decommissioned railroad depot, feverish and low in spirits for days. Titus prowled around his supine form and the broken ground outside, killing rats and mice and eating them with wondrous relish, then laying himself down to sleep next to the fat, beached form that he knew and trusted. In his lowest moments the Cap'n reached out and stroked Titus's fur, thanking the gods that this one creature was still with him. Titus let out a purr that shook and trembled his insides, then lay back, in the comfortable sprawl of a carnivore with a stomach full of raw flesh. Thus the old captain and his cat shared hours of sleep in the dusty, strewn depot, two more objects among the broken furniture.

16

Kristen stood at the sink. She was shaking. Her pale cheeks were mottled and red. She hit the counter with the flat of her hand. Why couldn't Deen understand that she was just trying to help? It was important, a duty, for grown women to offer guidance to girls on the brink of maturity. Just like her aunt Natalie had when she'd been growing up, though sometimes the hugs got a bit messy, with all the tears and lipstick and stuff, and Aunt Natalie, well, they'd had to put her in a home.

Kristen, in all truth, lied to herself mightily with her next thought. She thought how much she liked Sadie. She was so bohemian, such a character, and hadn't she stayed unmarried since Ree (Ooh, Kristen thought, Ree . . . it's almost like I knew him) had passed away? That's the term Kristen invariably used for death.

Yes, she really liked Sadie. And Deen, she almost felt like her older sister or something. Maybe one day Deen would be famous too, and say how this wonderful woman had a big influence on her. *Yes, the wife of my great teacher, a wonderful woman named Kristen.*

But so far Deen didn't see what a good friend Kristen was to her. She would eventually, but first she had to be led with loving patience. But still, why did Deen have to be so mean? Say that awful thing? Actually *laughing* as she told her, "I don't think my mother was that keen on your plan, whatever it was—she didn't tell me."

Tears welled in Kristen's eyes. Either Sadie was so plum fucked-up, no, I mean wacky, bohemian but essentially nice, that she sort of forgot what they'd talked about, or, or, that little brat was lying her head off.

* * *

She at you again? In her beastly kitchen?" Paul asked Deen. "Oh come on, Ondine, there's no use covering up for the sow, her and her ghastly ways. She tried something on with your mother the other day, sipping her tea and pretending to be ladylike, but it didn't work. God, she's so *female*! Such a full-blooded member of her tribe. Do you know how females work? They burrow up from below, attacking the foundation. Weave and nibble to the tune of their own discontent.

"Today we will make music in extremis. I will make sounds and you will repeat them to me on the piano." With that he stood, leaped onto his chair, then flew off it, letting out a series of caws that beat the air like metal.

Deen played three triads with dissonant notes.

"Jesus! No, not that bloody fucking way! Like it sounds!" he screamed. "Here, maybe this will help." He took off his scarf and tied it around her eyes. It smelled of sweat and lighter fluid.

"Fat-assed bitch!" he yelled.

Fat-assed bitch, Deen played, making the final chord explosive.

"Damn, that's nice!"

Mozart's "Damn that's Nice," a light, frolicking air.

Next she heard the sound of water falling into a porcelain basin. "The Piss Song." A progression that started in a minor key, plopped, then ran up to a drizzle.

"Good," he said eventually. "You can take that ridiculous headgear off. We are going to proceed to Liszt this week. Perhaps you think this is a step up. It's not. Liszt is for idiots. You will assuredly think you already know the piece—you do not. I will give you my own transcription of it. You will study it and learn it before you even think of playing it, analyzing its structure. It's fucking hard to play, even if it is for idiots. Here is the score. Many people think of this piece as kitsch, which has always endeared it to me. Now go, and give my regards to that hellhag out there."

* * *

Sadie stood in her kitchen, a much nicer kitchen than Kristen's. Barefoot and wearing torn jeans and a striped silk shirt with some unknown man's monogram on its pocket, she was, rather typically, staring vaguely at the fridge and wondering what the hell to cook for dinner. Why did each day have to have a bloody dinner, she wondered.

After some minutes sipping a drink and mulling the contents of the fridge, she decided on Savoy cabbage and a rather suspect steak—she'd just make sure it was thoroughly cooked. The area door opened and Deen came down the steps.

"How's the wunderkind Rinaldo?" Sadie asked her.

"Just as awful as ever. She was changing its diaper when I got there, it kind of peeled off in a sheet of yellow crap. You never smelled such a stench."

"Lovely. Lessons going okay?"

"Sure. I had to play blindfolded today. It's always interesting at least. Munster, you think he ever leaves that apartment?"

"An agoraphobe? I hadn't thought of that. But yes, quite possibly. Maybe that's why he married that stooge—to guard the gate."

"God, Munster, any normal parent would never let their child go near there."

Sadie laughed. "Well, thank God we're not normal, what an unpleasant thought."

Hamish came clattering down the stairs, sounding like an army.

"What, tore yourself away from the delights of Ettie's kitchen?" his mother asked him.

"She makes me go home for dinner," he said sadly. "It's a rotten shame. She was making chicken pot pie with leeks, and she makes her own pastry for it. And she makes all the stocks from scratch. What's *that*?"

"A steak, what the hell does it look like?"

"Like the sole of some old wino's boot. Hey Munster—Ettie's all upset about the Cap'n disappearing. I am too. Is there any way to call the cops or something, see if he's okay?"

"I don't know, darling. Bums do that you know, go off on toots. But I'll talk to a cop I know at the station tomorrow, all right?"

"Thanks. And Munster? Ettie's showing me how to cook some stuff, maybe I'll make dinner tomorrow, if you'll buy the ingredients. It couldn't be any worse than this."

Sadie raised her eyes and offered a silent hallelujah to the gods.

***

Robert crept up the stairs from the basement. The girl, Deen, was playing some Liszt. The colonel always went upstairs for his nap round about this time of day and Ettie was out doing the shopping. He tiptoed down the hall, drawn to the way the girl was making the keys sing. When she'd finished the piece he stuck his head round the door.

"S'okay if I talk to you about piano music?" he asked her.

Deen looked at him, at his long face and prominent nose, and the way his eyes stared longingly at the keyboard. "Sure," she said.

"I'm Robert, the one that's doing the boiler work."

"I know. You stay and drink with the colonel. He likes you."

"Thing is," Robert said. "Damn, but I got to get this right. The thing is, this tune you're playing? I want to show you something about this tune. It's all nice and just like the doctor ordered, that's good. But you ever fiddle with a tune, make it so people want to jump up and stomp around some? Mind if I sit?"

Robert slid onto the bench next to Deen. "Here look, this gizmo in the tune here? Nice, real nice. But you put your left hand to doing this and roll the notes around and all of a sudden you got something. Go ahead, you try it, now fly it up another key. That's right. Now watch this, fill in a spin here, put some funk behind it, like this. See, the left hand's spinning the rhythm, now the right's adding some too. Yeah, like that! You know how to play 'The Pig Knuckle Waltz'? Well, that ain't so surprising, I wrote it myself. I'll show you, it's just these here three thumps, and a little bit of razzling around like this, you can play it all sorts of ways after you get it into your fingers. Go ahead, we can play it together."

Deen let out a laugh as she watched Robert's fingers walking up and down the keys and followed them. As she became used to the tempo and notes she started adding riffs, as he did, they bounced them back and forth, sometimes joining together in a rousing stomp. She was having such a good time she didn't want to stop, but all tunes must end, and at last they jangled their way to a spanking finish.

"Amen, sister," Robert said. "I been listening to you play and admiring how you can fly on a keyboard but saying to myself, where's the fun in that old longhair stuff, where's the fun for a kid?"

"You play really well," Deen said. "You ever play classical music?"

"Some, what I picked up here and there. I can't read music, don't know anything about that. And to tell you the truth, whatever I played, the thump was always in it. It ain't none of my business, but I thought you needed to know what puts the honk in the honkytonk. Besides, you don't make it as a classical pianist, you can always earn a few dollars in a barroom now. Here, I'll show you another one, it's called 'Take It Round Back.' It starts out like this."

* * *

The next afternoon, Deen, thinking herself alone in the house, couldn't help playing "The Pig Knuckle Waltz." First for the pleasure of it, but also for the question that was growing in her mind, which was, why didn't anyone get up and dance when classical music was played? And then a truly revolutionary idea, what if *real* musicians played living music?

"The fuck's that?" Liall asked Hamish in the kitchen.

"I dunno. Yes, I do—it's Deen's fingering, but . . ."

"But she's playing more like dance music. It's *good*, it's like all complicated still but it's got some kick to it."

"Let's sneak up on her, okay?"

Deen was enjoying what she'd done with the ending, realizing she'd let her breathing go to shit in her excitement. Oh no, Hames had heard everything, and Liall, who followed him in. Damn, busted.

Hames leaned on the end of the piano lid. " 'Free your mind, and your behind will follow,' " he said. "That's what Bootsy said. You going to play some rock with us now?"

"I might," Deen said. "But there's no future in it—you two bozos can't even read music."

"Actually, we can," Hamish informed her. "Liall got it right away, then he showed me. Look," he said, pulling a grubby sheaf of paper from his pocket, "we wrote these songs. Ourselves." He held the sheets out to Deen.

Deen looked at the scrawls on them. "What's this symbol mean?" she asked, pointing to a figure like an eight, but wavier.

"That's when we go into a jam. And the drummer lights up. We're waiting for Gretchen to come home for that part. But see there, Liall sketched out a keyboard accompaniment and everything."

"What would I play?"

"Pop's Farfisa. Munster put a bedspread over it but I checked it out, it's all in working order. Come on Deen, don't you ever get the urge to play some real music, instead of all that classical crap?"

And so a loud wailing and thumping came from the top floor of the old brick row house. Anyone passing by might have thought they could see the very bricks shudder, as the children, in what is only normal for the young, turned their amps up to full volume.

17

Cap'n Meat rolled over and groaned. He wasn't feeling any too good but then again, he wasn't feeling nearly so bad as he had the last few days. Titus was curled up next to him on a bit of sacking.

I must be feeling better, he thought, because I'm hungry. The big bottle of water the cop had given him still had a few sips left in it; he drank what was left. "Come on, Titus," he said. "Time to get a grip on things." With an effort, he stood and tidied himself as best he could.

He walked south, buying a bagel and a cup of coffee, looking for a bus stop for Manhattan. Titus didn't like the subway. Bus drivers didn't like bums, but he had a Metrocard, same as any citizen.

It was early afternoon by the time man and cat arrived in Midtown. The Cap'n was still feeling weak and woozy, so he bought some hot dogs and water and headed to a place he knew in the rail yards.

It wasn't ideal but he could probably rest there safely at least till midnight. He laid out his bag and set his pack behind him, then fed Titus one of the hot dogs and gave him some water. As he settled in he arranged Titus's feet in his pocket. "Just in case," he whispered to the cat. "And if we have to cut and run I'll get you in my pocket first, grab my pack last, that's a promise." Then, his limbs aching, he fell asleep.

Bad men came at him with sticks late in the night. Two of them. So desperate they'd roll him for the few dollars in his pocket, his pack, and his sleeping bag. And his cat, which they'd roast on a spit if their need were great enough. Real family men.

The Cap'n put his arms up to shield his head, then lashed out with a boot, getting one on the kneecap. Then he jumped up and tore the stick from the other. He checked: Titus was in his pocket. They hadn't figured on him being so big when they attacked him, now they backed off. But then, the blood in them for harm rose and they came at him again. The Cap'n hit the first on the side of the head; he fell to the ground. He ran toward the other, his fist raised. The smaller man turned and fled.

Losing no time, the Cap'n climbed the steep steps cut into the towering stone wall of the rail yard. The other might return with a posse, there was no going back to that place. A blow he'd taken to his scalp was leaking blood and he was limping from others that had landed on his legs.

Shaken and sore, he limped around the edges of the Village the rest of the night and all the next day. His head felt muddled and he barely saw what was around him, but he was still afraid of whoever had made the red eyes, afraid to go back to his regular spots.

By the end of the afternoon though, he was past caring. He felt he couldn't go on any longer and wanted to sit on his bench under the oak tree once more. He sank down on it and put his hand on Titus's head. The leaves had fallen from the trees and they drifted and clattered across the walkways. The sky was a dark, faraway blue. The Cap'n stared up at it, his mind empty.

"Hey, isn't that that old bum?" Liall asked Hamish.

"Where?"

"There, on his bench."

Hamish stared, then broke into a sprint. "Cap'n Meat! Are you okay? Cap'n, it's me, Hamish, can you hear me? What's wrong?"

"Somebody beat the crap out of him," Liall said. "Look at his face."

"Cap'n Meat, say something."

"Oh, I thought it was a dream. There you are, dear boy. Friends. Not many. Mustn't worry, I'll be fine. Would you, would you take Titus? I can't keep him."

"What'll we do?" Liall asked.

Hamish ran over to the curb and flagged down a cab, opening its door. "I'll be right back," he told the driver. "Come on, help me get him up," Hamish told Liall.

* * *

He needs a doctor," Sadie said as they pushed and tugged the Cap'n down the area steps. "Hames, quick, call Dr. Ed."

She got him onto his back on the kitchen floor with help from Liall and Deen. "Deen, get a glass of milk and stir in three big tablespoons of brown sugar." Sadie pushed her hair back and looked at the nearly dead bum on the floor. Christ, why me? she thought. "You get a hold of Ed?" she called to Hamish.

"He wants to talk to you," he said, handing her the phone.

"Ed, hello, yes, we have a problem here, could you come round? Uh, a guest, who's staying with us. Yes, come in the kitchen door."

Sadie went upstairs and got a futon, which she laid out in the back of the kitchen. "Deen, run upstairs and get the blankets I left out on the landing, and grab a pillow."

Sadie knelt and looked at the wound on the Cap'n's head. The Cap'n opened his eyes and smiled faintly at her, then tried to speak. "Just keep quiet," Sadie said. "Everything'll be okay."

"Where's Titus?" Deen cried.

The Cap'n brought his fingers to his pocket. Deen gently opened it. "Come on out, Titus, please." The cat poked his head out and let out a yowl. Deen stroked it and it crept out onto her lap, trying to hide under her arm.

"Oh shit, where's that milk and sugar? Hames bring it to me. Liall, you hold his head up a bit, that's right." Sadie brought the glass to the Cap'n's mouth and he took a sip, then another. The next try the milk rolled down his beard, so she pinched his nose and tilted another swallow into his mouth. "Well, we'll give him some more in a bit. Now you boys help me pick him up and get him on the futon. You take his feet and I'll take his head. Now lift." They got him an inch or two off the floor then set him down. "Gawd," Sadie said, "we can't even pick him up and the futon's a bloody mile away."

"The incapacitated are *rolled,*" a precise voice with a Harvard Yard accent said behind them. "You bring the bed to the patient, *roll* him onto it, which even a child could do, provided they had the wits. *Then* the futon is dragged to wherever you desire it. Though of course it's usually a gurney and somewhat more hygienic than a futon dragged across a dirty kitchen floor."

"Hey, Dr. Ed," Hamish said. "He always knows everything," he whispered to Liall. The two boys brought the futon over, then Ed and Sadie rolled the Cap'n onto it. Sadie got the boys to take the basket chairs in the back of the kitchen upstairs, clearing an area to make a sickroom for the Cap'n. They tugged him over to it on the futon and Sadie put a pillow under his head.

Dr. Ed took off his black cashmere coat, laid it over a chair, then knelt by his new patient, placing his Gladstone bag by his right side. He held a hand up, one that commanded the rest of the party to leave him to do his job. They slunk away on tiptoe, easing chairs out from the table so they wouldn't squeak, then sat around the pine table. Titus stayed with Deen, curled up on her lap.

They snuck glances at what Ed was doing. Dr. Ed scared the Hollanders a little bit, or rather, quite a bit when it came to the children, somewhat less so in the case of Sadie. Edward Portman was a tall, gaunt figure who wore bow ties and a long black coat that made one think of Count Dracula. He was a research doctor at the cancer center at Sloane-Kettering, a chess master, and one of that rare type of epicurean who are not visited in the flesh by the signs of their pleasure.

If he had a soft spot it was for Sadie. All his caustic, finicky ways, well, they didn't go away like *pff* when he was around Sadie, but they were softened by a smile of amusement that played somewhere around his lips when he talked to her. And Sadie, who was no stupe when it came to seeing the advantage of things, had made him into their family GP. What sort of lunatic would she have to be, she'd explained to him, to go to some moron MD, when she happened to have one of the best medical minds of the city just crazy about her? Ed had found this reasoning irreproachable.

Ed put his stethoscope back in his bag and snapped it shut.

"Played the fiddle," Cap'n Meat said, his voice sounding as if it were coming from the bottom of a well. "Music that made the very gnats minuet. On a candy purple wind."

Ed sat down at the table, lighting a cigarette with a silver lighter that shot a pointed blue flame up with a hiss. *Snap*, he shut its cover. They waited as he drew the drug in, knowing from experience he'd talk only when he'd finished his first cigarette and lit another. Sadie got up and poured him a glass of the wine she'd gotten out. Ed scoffed at such meaningless matters as fees for attending the Hollander household, but never turned down a good bottle of French wine. Actually, he was horribly expert in red Burgundies and clarets, so Sadie, in her cunning way, had confessed the whole story one day to the owner of Garnet, who made up cases as needed for her now of hideously expensive wines. Still, it was far cheaper than paying some hack to diagnose tonsillitis for meningitis.

Ed took a sip and moved the wine over his tongue before swallowing it. Sadie took a big slug. "Your *guest* needs a complete workup," he said. "I'd suggest calling an ambulance and having him taken to Bellevue."

"I've always thought that that's such a pretty word, *Bellevue*," Sadie said. "Redolent of some grand estate on a hilltop. And yet one that strikes terror into the heart of every New Yorker. So Tennessee Williams, don't you think?"

"Perhaps. I'll leave the creative side to you. Meanwhile, your honored guest there needs blood work, cancer screening, a full psychological evaluation, and, most certainly, a bath."

"Oh, Ed, don't be such a stuffed shirt. Surely you could test his blood yourself. If we send that guy into the state hospital system, on the state's dime, he'll never get out, and you know it."

"And Titus would be heartbroken if they got split up," Deen said.

"Who's Titus?"

Deen leaned back and showed him the cat on her lap.

"Well, you children have always wanted a cat," Ed said. "You could always assuage your guilt by taking far better care of the pet than the human. I believe that's how most people do things."

"I know the Cap'n needs a bath now, but he told me he likes to keep himself neat and clean," Liall said. "He told me there are lots of places you can wash up in the city if you want to."

"Yes, quite possibly so. But he's a bum, and bums are crazy. You see, the one state follows as a result of the other."

"That's just a gross generalization," Hamish said. "I know they mostly are crazy, but the Cap'n isn't. He's as sane as any of us." Realizing that the Hollander family wasn't exactly a paragon of sanity, he turned red and ducked his head.

Ed fired up another cigarette from his rocket-powered lighter and smiled at Hamish; it wasn't a pretty smile. "Your loyalty to your friend is commendable. But what's the realistic outcome? That you'll have a large, elderly bum living in your kitchen, taking sponge baths and drinking the vintage Burgundies? His pals drifting in to see him, drinking sterno from socks and playing tunes on the banjo?"

"Really, Ed, don't be such an ass," Sadie said. "All I'm proposing is that we let him rest up here a few days until you get the tests done, and you do something about that gash on his head and pump whatever into him. Really, you are the attending physician now, what state is your conscience in? You're really willing to send him into the maw of the dependent medical system?"

"Well, since he seems a particular friend of yours . . . but if I decide he needs hospitalization that's exactly where he's going, no arguments. Hamish, come hold a light for me so I can suture the wound."

"I'll give him a bit of a sponging, when you're done," Sadie said, rather faintly.

"No you won't, Hamish and I will, won't we my boy?" He clapped a hand on Hamish's shoulder and grinned down at him ghoulishly. "Splendid opportunity for a young man to learn what poor diet and hygiene can do to the human body. What you can do, Sadie, since I'm clearly going to forfeit my dinner reservation, is cook one of your ghastly dinners, for my sins."

Hamish started to speak but just then caught Sadie's eye as he looked back. She put a finger over her lips and winked.

***

Yes, thank you," Ed said later when Deen offered him more bread. He used it to mop up the last speck of sauce on his plate. Then he leaned back to light a cigarette.

"It would be grotesque to even suppose for a moment that you cooked that dinner, Sadie. Is anyone going to let me in on the joke?"

"I cooked it," Hamish said. "Munster just heated it up."

"Really."

"Ettie's been teaching me how to cook."

"And who is this wondrous creature?"

When Ed ate, he ate, and when he wished to talk, he drank claret. Sadie refilled his glass as the children launched into the story of Ettie, the colonel, Robert the boiler man, and the plan to put out food for the Cap'n.

Ed's long, sardonic face showed what passed for pleasure, his dark brows twisting and his mouth turning down to show yellow eyeteeth. For a splinter of time he imagined that this was his house, and these people his family around him, then quickly dismissed such foolishness.

18

Ettie smiled, yes, here was Jaimes to tell her of his dinner, such a good boy to come to tell her right away the next morning. "Your family, yes they were surprised?" she asked him.

"Oh," Hamish said, stopping. "Yes, everyone really liked it. And a friend of Munster's was there too, and he's this really cranky doctor who goes to all the fancy restaurants alone because he says talking spoils a good dinner. He had seconds of everything."

"This is true? A *doctor*?"

"Yes, and Ettie? I have really good news, we found the Cap'n. That's why the doctor was there, the Cap'n's sick. He's sleeping in the kitchen and Dr. Ed's going to fix him all up."

Ettie sat down on her chair with a bump. She stared, her mouth agape, then put her face in her hands and cried.

"Hey, Ettie, he'll be okay," Hamish said, wishing she wouldn't cry.

"I cry like an old grandmother," she laughed, wiping her eyes. "Quick, I must talk to your mother, okay? I made breakfast for you just like the colonel's, it's in the oven. You eat, yes?"

Hamish didn't answer. He'd opened the oven door and was too deeply absorbed in the wonders before him. A stack of toasted sourdough bread soaked with butter. A heap of bacon, thick and browned. Shirred eggs with cheese, their mound dusted with pepper and paprika. Grated potato pancakes. Muffins. He never even heard the door close as Ettie went out.

***

Mees?" Ettie said, tapping on the area door. She stuck her head around as Sadie waved her in. *Sshh,* Sadie hissed to her, pointing to the back, where the Cap'n lay sleeping.

Sadie beckoned Ettie in and made her way quietly to the espresso machine, pouring Ettie a cup. "He could probably sleep through a nuclear attack at the moment," she said. "But I'm keeping that end of the kitchen a low noise area. Here, sit down." Sadie was still in her peacock silk dressing gown, her hair a tangled bird's nest. She picked up her coffee and took a long sip.

Then she looked up, startled, at Ettie. "Gawd, that dinner! Ettie, Hames can *cook*. I mean, I'm sure you ever so tactfully coached him every step of the way, but he told me that he really stood at the stove and did the cooking. You're an angel to spend so much time with him, I'm sure he must bore you to death and get muddy footprints all over your kitchen and wolf down everything in sight. But I think you've given him something really important."

"It's good he's still only twelve," Ettie said. "When he's older, not so easy. Now, he likes me and I can talk to him. Show him things."

"Do you have family here?"

"A cousin. She's got two boys and they don't listen to me ever. They want me to bring them videos and games, always these kinds of toys.

Mees, I cook all day for one old man. This is good, I love my job. But I got plenty of time to cook for other people too. Him over there, I could do all the cooking for him too. Soups and things, baby foods. Tell me, Yes, Ettie, you may do this?"

Sadie looked at Ettie's face for a moment. She must be only in her mid-thirties, she thought. With a face like a girl from the mountaintops, one made for hardship and thinner air, with wide, blooming cheeks. And a heart like a quivering satin valentine, beating on her sleeve.

"He'll think he's died and gone to heaven," she warned her.

***

Dr. Ed, punctilious in all medical matters, whether a bum on a futon or a double-blind study, arrived at the end of the day. He nodded to Sadie then went to the Cap'n, waking him up by shaking his shoulder.

"Hello," Ed said.

"'Lo," the Cap'n said.

Ed took his pulse "Feeling better? You have diabetes. Entirely treatable. Presently we'll discuss treatment, but for now I'm going to give you this." He drew a hypodermic from his bag, filled it from a vial and injected the Cap'n's arm. "Feel you could get up to use the facilities?"

"Yes."

"Good man. We'll put this on you, I'll hold it up, mustn't shock the ladies." Ed held out a brown wool bathrobe he'd brought, screening the half-clad Cap'n, then helped him put it on. He held his arm as the Cap'n walked to the bathroom door. "I brought you these too, you could put them on in there," he said, handing him a pair of cotton pajamas.

When the Cap'n came out, he helped him back into bed and straightened the covers over him. The Cap'n looked up at him, his eyes puzzled. "I shouldn't be here," he said.

Titus lay quietly in his basket by the Cap'n's head, his eyes also watching Ed's every move.

"Well, you are here. May I?" Ed asked the Cap'n, touching the cat's head. The Cap'n nodded. Ed patted the cat, giving him a thorough physical exam. "A fine, strong fellow," he said when he'd finished. "Sleep as much as you can, in a couple of days we'll have a chat about your treatment."

Ed strode to the kitchen sink and washed his hands. Sadie handed him a clean tea towel. She'd already uncorked one of his reserved bottles, an '85 Mercury. They sat down at the table.

"Your friend there is in surprisingly good health, overall. A spot of type 2 diabetes is all. Otherwise commendably robust. I'd hazard he'd been through a rough patch, and that, combined with a lack of insulin, brought him low, then some less than friendly type gave him a beating, of course. I'll leave you some pills for him, and of course you know how to give injections. Hamish home this evening?"

"He is, but I'm afraid he didn't do any cooking, he and Deen spent all morning getting the Cap'n settled in."

"Hmm, pity."

A finger tapped at the area door. It was Ettie, holding a large pot in one arm and a cooler in the other. Sadie took the cooler and said, "Ettie, this is Ed Portman, the doctor who's taking care of the Cap'n. Ed, this is Ettie Salvatore, the one who's teaching Hames to cook."

Ed rose and bowed over her hand. "I'm honored," he said.

"A *doctor*," Ettie breathed. Then she fled, her cheeks flamingo red. "Mees, this pot is duck broth with lots of vegetables. And here are carrots in wine with onions, rice with herbs, duck cutlets with sauce, spinach with cheese, some little cakes. Everything to heat up in the stove, I marked the numbers, temperature, and minutes on each." Then she turned around to look once more at the doctor, fascinated. Ed grinned at her, at which she grabbed the empty cooler and ran, taking one last amazed, terrified look at him before she went out the door.

Ed rubbed his hands together. "I'm beginning to rather like this case," he said. "There are certain possibilities to it."

* * *

Brenda, when she arrived the next morning, was not entranced to find an old, fat bum ensconced on a mattress in her kitchen. Sadie had explained the situation to her. Well, she'd listened hadn't she? Never said a word.

"Bad enough I got to slave like this for my boy," she muttered as she gathered her arsenal of rags, Windex, and sponges. "But now I got to sweep around that old barge?" She flapped a rag at the Cap'n, who put his hands together and bowed his head to her.

"Sure, go on, act like you're all nice as pie. Act like the king of Egyptland if you want to. It don't fool me. You're nothing but what the cat dragged in, and you're clogging up my floor."

When she stumped upstairs, Sadie was standing at the French doors, looking out at the garden. "The leaves are all gone," she said.

"Well, sometimes it's a good thing when things are gone. Why you want some old bum clogging up your floor down there, Sadie? I know those children of yours can wrap you around their little fingers like wire, but that old man's just trouble. Why don't you send him to the state hospital, where he belongs? And how am I supposed to clean that floor with him lying on it?"

"Brenda, you know that kitchen floor hadn't been cleaned and waxed for years until you arrived, it was an absolute disgrace. I'm sure it'll survive just this once without a mopping. I'm sorry, I know it's a bit odd to have a bum down there, but if a man stumbles onto a porch, sick and injured, would you send him away?"

"You're talking country matters. I don't see any porches around here."

"Just my point."

"Well, it's your kitchen I guess. He able to get up and use the john?"

"He is. Ah, now I see—Brenda, I promise you, I would never ask you to clean up after him. Leave the kitchen loo to me, banish it from your mind."

"I will not," Brenda said, standing taller. "I clean this house, don't I? Even that old bum's bathroom."

"Funny how we all think of him as old," Sadie said, speaking more to herself. "I imagine he's not much older than me. In any case, let's compromise, Brenda, have the children clean it. They brought him here and he's their friend. That's fair, don't you think?"

"Yes, it might be just the thing. Show those youngsters the errors of their ways. That it's one thing to ask everybody over, another thing to clean up after them. And I did poke my head around the door, just to make sure, and he seems neat around his person. And that cat of his? That's one of the cleanest, shiniest cats I ever did see. Kind of homey to look at, the way it lies there, never leaving his side."

Oh, you old fraud, Sadie thought as Brenda went upstairs. *That cat's gotten to you too, hasn't it?*

***

Hamish and Deen tidied up the Cap'n's bed and saw to his needs, giving him what food he could take at first, and telling him how they'd all looked and looked for him. As his strength returned Deen gave him some shampoo and he got up shakily to give his hair and beard a good wash. When he got back into bed he thanked Deen and said he felt much better. But he was dispirited. He felt he had no right to be in such a fine house, troubling so many people.

"Munster's reading to him," Deen told the colonel. They were sitting by the fire and eating tea sandwiches rather thoughtfully. Deen had fallen into the habit of sharing tea with the colonel most afternoons, before she practiced. It was getting dark well before six now and nowhere seemed to ward off the onset of winter more than the colonel's back parlor. And he didn't seem to mind at all if they fell into long silences, was more comfortable a person to be around than anyone.

"Is she? And what book did she choose?"

"*David Copperfield*. She reads that to everyone when they're sick."

"Ah, very sensible. Imagine she reads well?"

"Well, she does actually. Gives the characters sort of special voices."

"Your wandering friend must think he's been transported to Eden."

Deen took another chicken salad sandwich and bit into it. She liked all the others but the chicken salad ones were the best. "You see, he does and still, he keeps saying he's got to leave, that it's wrong of him to be bothering us. He used to always have a big smile and so we didn't worry about him, but well . . . he was crying. He turned his back, but I'm sure he was. Colonel, isn't there a place he could go, have to himself and a windowsill for Titus to sit in? I don't think he *wants* to wander anymore."

The colonel sighed. "I don't know. But tell you what, I'll ask the inestimable Mrs. de Angelo to look into the matter. Yes, we'll sic her on the answer. A most remarkable woman. Why, she'll have it all sorted out in no time."

Deen, glad to dispense with gloomy thoughts, turned to a happier one. "How do you happen to have a concert piano?" she said. "Hardly anyone does."

"No, and it was the wonder of the entire county. Belonged to my aunt Belinda. Conventional opinion was that she was a dreadful show-off for having it. Still, it was far and away her greatest pleasure. She played well, might've been even better, but from time to time a true musician made their way to her drawing room. You see, she had it so that she could hear it played, not out of vainglory at all. She was the only woman in my family who was ever kind to me, so when I decided to settle down I had it gone over, in the hopes that I, too, might some day have a real musician come to visit. Never knew I'd land slap up against a talent such as yours, my dear. Fact is, I never knew such happiness." The colonel reached out and patted the arm of Deen's chair, missing her hand.

***

The Angry One ran helter from one street corner, skelter to the next. Where was his fat old Thanksgiving turkey? The one he ached and whistled to carve? Him and his damn tabby cat?

Angry Ones don't have homes or snapshots. Rage is their memento. They aren't asked to share a drop of wine and tell stories round the fire. They don't have stories. They are humans stripped of flesh. They aren't real to themselves, the places they walk are perpetually strange to them. They hide among us, for we choose not to see them. They hide under a child's bed holding their breath, waiting to poke a skinny arm out to grab a tiny ankle.

The Angry One had been circling the city for days, throwing his head back and sniffing the air. He'd put the red eye on his quarry and flushed him from his hidey-holes. Now he *will* come to my arms.

But he didn't, and the Angry One got his paws on some hooch and poured his rage into the sky.

"He will come unto me!" he shouted into the night. "As the little *children* also shall, so I sayeth. Man, what you lookin' at? Go home and do what you do with your mamma. And yea, as I was sayin'— now I said get the *hell* outta here asshole, go home, take off your nine-hundred-dollar coat, hang it up all nice and neat, *then* go fuck your mother!

"And lo, the house of Nem was lone and mournful. Yes, like a *pimp* with no *bitches*. That kind of house, women keenin' and cryin', swords lyin' rusty all over the yard. Then a holy man with a crown of fire comes walkin' up to the gate, says, why are all your swords rusty? Why are your women cryin'? What the *fuck's* goin' on here?"

He lit a page of the *Post* he scooped from the sidewalk, blew on it, and sent it aloft. It rose then wafted over the avenue, moving delicately in the currents.

"I don't *know* why ruin must come to some houses! But I *suspect* that someone there did some wrong. And then, *everybody* pays. But I *do* know, and say thus unto all you motherfuckers, when I come ridin' in your yard wearing a crown of *flames*, you honkies better scatter, run for some hole to hide in. Then I'll sniff every last one of you out, dig you out with my fingernails!"

As he walked up the wide avenue, his long coat stalking his heels, his face hooded, the other pedestrians subtly parted to leave him alone. Certainly none dared to look at him, or wished to see his face. Distance and unknowing were their prophylactic. If he hadn't hated them all so much he might've cried, begged that someone, just once, look at him like he was their friend.

19

Ettie announced, "Meez D to see you," to the colonel, who as usual was ensconced in his armchair by the fire. He'd been listening to Scarlatti.

"Ah, my dear Mrs. de Angelo," he said, aiming the remote at the CD player to turn it off. "Impeccable timing, as always. Do sit down, have a drink."

"No thanks. I had to go right to bed that last time, and the next day was a total write-off. I needed a steam bath, a massage, and a facial before I could even face going out that evening."

"My dear, I am so sorry. I had no intention of making you unwell. You must forgive an old southerner his antiquated ways. Do tuck the costs of the beauticians into the accounts."

"It's all right. I hadn't taken a day off since God knows when. Now, I've just had a word with Robert and seen the new heating system, it all looks fine. He says he has a few details to finish but otherwise the job's done. I've paid half his bill from your household account and will send him the other half next week. We have to be quite sure it's working before we pay the rest. I explained that to him and he agreed. I'll tell him to clean up and let himself out, shall I?"

"Well," the colonel said, "fact is, Robert and I have become quite chummy. You wouldn't deny an old man some amusing company, would you? Thing is, he usually comes up for a drink about this time of day."

"It's your house."

"I can see you don't approve," the colonel said sadly. "You won't approve of my next project either, I'm afraid. Hesitate to ask, but might you accept another little commission from me? Think you'll find it amusing, though I'm afraid you won't think it a good idea at all."

"For what you pay me, I'm hardly likely to turn it down."

"You don't take on these projects for even a tiny bit of liking?"

"Oh, you are a terrible old charmer. Christ, give me a damn drink. I can't stand sitting here watching you relish that bourbon, with that little smile on your face. And if your next project's as mad as it sounds, I'll need a drink just to hear about it."

"We'll speak of it later," the colonel said, hearing Robert's tread in the hall.

"Okeydoke, now that's as sweet a boiler as I've ever done," Robert said, coming in. "Hiya Mrs. D, how's tricks? I'm here to swear before you, Colonel sir, that that system down there doesn't have one single corner cut, is no union labor job spilling with sloppy work and miscalculations. Thanks, I will have a drink. Santé.

"And just in time, you hear that wind, trying to tear the roof off? That one's coming straight down from the Arctic Circle, tomorrow the Eskimos would feel right at home in this town. It sure is a night to be indoors, with some fine central heating and a glass of good sippin' whiskey."

"Well, let's have a refill and toast the completion of the project. To a most nonunion job!" the colonel said, raising his glass.

"To hell with the pipefitters local number nothing!" Robert said.

"Here's to Botox," Mrs. D said.

"Ah," the colonel sighed, taking a mighty sip. "Things could not be better. Still, there is, as there almost inevitably is, a sad element to the completion of things. I shall no longer have your company, Robert, of an evening."

"And I'll bet you a bushelful of hundred dollar bills there won't be any sippin' whiskey on my next job. But say, Colonel? I got an idea. I kind of promised that kid next door I'd show her some more moves on the keys. But maybe you don't think I should be messing with her training and all, that might be right. Though it just seems to me that she's got a right to know what puts the jangle into the music. So I was thinking, maybe I could come over Thursdays, spend some time with that kid at the piano, then sort of stop in and pay my respects to you, like."

"I didn't realize you were a pianist as well as a plumber," Mrs. D said. Her tone conveyed a certain amount of skepticism.

"Well I ain't, and that's a fact. Never was a pianist, and no pretty colors can paint it that I ever could read music or was going to play on some big stage. I played in barrooms and such. Juke joints. I was near to living in barrooms, couldn't think but for the songs rolling through my head. Then I met a woman and married her, and well, I loved her enough to give up the barrooms and juke joints and get a trade, some steady work. She died, a long while ago, well, there you go. And now I'm too old for that kind of life. But there was this old man who taught me, see, he knew things about the piano. He's been dead a long long time and it seemed to me I might pass on some of those things he showed me along to that young girl Deen."

Mrs. D was not so crisply businesslike that she'd entirely lost sight of her human soul. So she poured herself another slug of bourbon and expelled a breath from her chest. Thought, in fact, that it might be a kind of paradise here, by a wood fire, with an old madman and a plumber who drank music in his hidden heart. That she must be going mad to start liking her clients, and worse, caring about them.

Thus was what the Hollander children later dubbed the Thursday Night Imbibers Club born. Without exactly planning it, Robert and Mrs. D forgathered by the colonel's hearth each Thursday evening that winter, to drink and plot, talk of ways to improve the lot of the people in the twinned town houses, one of which the colonel had landed in as though a pod falling from a far planet. They ate Ettie's sandwiches, sometimes holding one up to look at it in sheer wonder before they took another bite. They were the best and oddest of company, three people who on the surface had almost nothing in common.

They always broke up early, at the reasonable hour of eight, when Robert would go out to stand at the corner of Bleecker to whistle up a taxi for Mrs. D. He'd jog back, hand her into it, then go back to sit with Ettie, doing whatever heavy work she had to get the colonel's dinner ready and served. He sometimes, no, he often, felt hopeless, about how much older he was than Ettie, but she seemed to favor him, they went to four P.M. matinees of movies together and lately she'd let him hold her hand.

Oh Ettie, oh Ettie, Robert thought as he trudged to the subway and his Brooklyn home. I'd like to know you well enough to touch my hand to your pretty pink cheek. I'd like to lean down to you and tell you this is the first anniversary of this day, and that day, and that time you rubbed my hands 'cause I was cold.

Sitting at the yellow Formica table at home, he'd make himself stop having such thoughts, promise himself to stop making up such foolishness. He was resolute in his mind, but that other part of him was already lost.

***

Sadie, visited by a rare interest in dinner, had made roast duck, a confit of onions and leeks in red wine, whipped potatoes and carrots, and pears poached with cinnamon and ginger for dessert. She'd gone over to tell Ettie of this sudden inspiration, and that Ettie needn't bring them dinner. Ettie had looked somewhat disappointed, so Sadie explained that the cold temperatures made her long to cook a fall meal. In this she was being truthful, but so often truths have several layers. The layer below her first truth was that she was getting a bit miffed at being labeled a monstrously lousy cook. Or even a drunken slattern who swore and muttered to herself as she stirred a pot of foul gummage. And beneath that, like the butter that lines a cake pan, she was just a tiny bit jealous of Ettie.

The dinner was a success. The pears were perhaps too well poached, in fact a touch burned, but that was simply due to the fact that Sadie, by then, was not very sober, as a result she didn't care much about bloody pears. Hamish rescued them, adding a bit of water to the pan and serving them over vanilla ice cream.

Deen had brought a tray with dinner for the Cap'n in his little encampment at the back of the kitchen, then stayed to chat with him as Sadie and Hames put the food on the table. She stroked Titus, who'd grown partial to letting Deen pick him up, swinging his orange-and-white-striped tail like a clock pendulum, and oozing over her shoulder.

"He behaved terribly well when I brought him to meet the colonel," she told him. "The colonel got the idea in his head that he wanted to meet Titus, and well, it had to happen, didn't it? I guess rich old people are like that." She mimicked the colonel's accent and tone: "I say, what a very fine fellow. What color would you say he is? Marmalade? Yes, yes, a marmalade cat, I can just see the sun beams through the orange pulp in the jar."

"He asked if I'd let him sit on his lap. You won't mind if I tell you Titus did, actually sort of *sprawled* on the colonel's lap? He got fur all over his suit."

"Did he now?" the Cap'n said, smiling. "That cat really knows a right'un from a wrong'un. That's the smartest cat that ever lived."

"Let's see if he likes odds and sods of duck meat," Sadie said, putting a saucer down by Titus's water bowl.

They watched as Titus marched around it, then poked at it with a paw. Satisfied it wouldn't leap up to bite him, he neatly scarfed down the lot.

After dinner Deen and Hamish helped Sadie up the stairs, pulling as needed, or shoving at her from behind. She swayed before her bed then flopped down on it. They covered her with the eiderdown, making sure her bare feet were under the covers, then snuck out.

Hames clomped down to the kitchen to put the lights out. "Good night, Cap'n," he called.

"Eh, my dears, sleep well." He sounded very nearly asleep.

His voice had that chewy sound, Hamish thought, as he tried to make less noise with his feet going upstairs. He wasn't very successful.

***

The Cap'n woke just as a faint smudge of charcoal light came through the windows. For a few minutes he lingered in the bed, in the shelter of a house. Then he got up, willing his mind to regain the ability to do things for himself. He took a leak, then brushed his teeth and washed. He carefully rinsed the suds from the sink. He stowed his few things in his backpack and dressed.

He surveyed the sauce-coated pots on the stove and the dishes on the table. First he stacked what he could in the dishwasher then set to scrubbing the rest. He wiped down the counters and table.

He folded the blankets and sheets from his bed, piling them in a neat stack. He swept the floor and primed the coffeemaker. He found the things they liked for breakfast in the cupboards and set them out on a tray, with cups and plates. He put on his coat, bound up its straps, put Titus in his pocket, and let himself out into the area, where he climbed the steps to the street. Ah, the smell of the city at dawn, when the cold air captured pockets of diesel fumes. He walked away, turning once to salute the house and its occupants.

20

They say that beauty is not easily defined or agreed on, and that it is changeable according to fashion. But then again, there may be other possibilities. It might be that ever since man walked upright we have recognized certain elements of harmony, fitness, and grace in each other's physiognomies that are universal and unchanging.

Some say we define beauty through an innate instinct to choose the most profitable sets of genes and thereby further our species, but if that were so, why wouldn't we find someone with large, curving teeth or webbed feet or a fine pair of hairy buttocks the more desirable mate?

While our perception of beauty is both practical, in that we look for signs of health, strength, and sexual suitability, we also wish to distance ourselves from our common ancestors, that we exalt in those among us who look least like the wild creatures we once competed with for food. That there are no practical benefits in a graceful foot, calligraphic eyebrows, or hair the color of sunlight on a copse of beeches. Yet we weep over these things.

True beauties, those rare creatures among us, are gaped at on the street. They are sidled up to, squawked at, and fought over. Their seduction is a prize, a leopard pelt to be worn as a boast. And they sometimes don't have a very easy time of it. Some of them know their beauty and openly court these attentions, practicing gestures and striking poses, while others don't particularly know or care.

Gretchen was of the latter type. She honestly didn't know why people stared at her and often wished they wouldn't. But she looked just as one would imagine a fair princess in an old tale, an English beauty of slender delicacy with wide eyes the blue-green of a hidden pool. Her silvery blond hair flowed down her back, tucked behind the prettiest pair of ears one could hope to see, and her chin was ever so slightly pointed. Ree had called her Mab. It was his own name for her and he hadn't liked anyone else to use it.

Gretchen's malaise had dampened her beauty, making her skin duller and putting shadows around her eyes, but at twenty-one there was nearly nothing that could hide her looks—she only appeared both downcast and achingly lovely. Because of this there were many people who were fonder of her and treated her with greater care than they might a plain girl. And then there were a few others who were maddened by it, finding reasons to dislike her, even if they had to make them up out of whole cloth.

There are certain women with a malignancy of the soul, women who hate others of their sex because they are attractive. Nurse Peterson was of this unlovely tribe. Nurse Peterson and a band of lesser harpies she led secretly tormented Gretchen. Their crimes were made even more horrible by the fact that they knew Gretchen couldn't speak of them.

It was late, in that deep hour of the night when the day seems most remote. Gretchen lay in her bed, tense with fear. It was Mrs. Peterson's night on duty, the night of pain. She heard sinister footsteps creaking, rubber on linoleum, and knew that pain was near.

Peterson, who shall not be graced with a Christian name, looked around her before entering Gretchen's room. She was excited, hoping she'd catch Gretchen doing something she wasn't supposed to. Peterson liked to have an excuse, a jumping off point as it were, for torturing the girl. Since Gretchen didn't speak and was generally a good girl, Peterson was often frustrated.

But tonight Gretchen presented her with a veritable Christmas feast of wrongdoing, and her eyes grew wide as she took in its potential, not merely for an outburst of indignation and pinching right now, but wonderfully, for a full-blown hullabaloo in the morning. *Gretchen had drawn on the wall.* On the pristine white wall. One of those damn dogs, in shades of green. A trail of purple tears ran from its left eye.

"Oh criminy, are you going to catch hell in the morning," she hissed, leaning over Gretchen. "It's going to be a real scene. Antisocial behavior, destruction of property, criminal mischief. And you *had* to do that disgusting dog. That hairy mutt. Even your doctor boyfriends won't be able to help you this time."

She began pinching Gretchen hard, with every intent to cause as much pain as possible. But sneakily, in places where the girl had hurt her own flesh, leaving scars and discoloration. Gretchen lay utterly still, making no sound. When the dreadful woman had satisfied, or at least as much as she thought prudent to, her foul urges, she crept away.

There is no question, even for one moment, that what the nurse did was anything less than unconscionably wrong. But the world is a strange place and sometimes good comes of evil. This continued mistreatment of Gretchen had created a new force inside her, in a place called the will, and in it she hated Peterson with a potent fervor. She thought about getting well so that she could kill the vicious besom, or at least bite off one of her red, ugly ears. In its odd way, life had placed Gretchen smack in the sights of a sadist, but a petty one, a nickel-and-dimer on the scale of human evil, who hurt her flesh just enough to cure her of wishing to hurt it herself.

But still, lying there alone, with tears running down her face, Gretchen spent a terrible night. She cried for her mother, and for her sister and brother, and for her father, who she'd loved very much.

Her tears fed on themselves, overwhelming her. She cried for her own fear and pain, then for the unhappiness everyone bears, feeling the weight of all that unhappiness welling up inside her. Each tear she cried was merely one of millions, a sea of tears, each drop the despair of another living soul. She cried in agony, her heart torn to shreds as the weight of so much sorrow overcame her. A cry burst ragged from her lips and she pressed her hands over them.

***

Mrs. D had a sense of style bordering on great, and could have been a legendary tastemaker if she weren't stymied by a secret fear that she was not sufficiently well-bred. All her life this fear had perched on her shoulder, whispering at her and keeping her bound to the conventional.

But lately she'd discovered a hidden insouciance. Her divorce, which had gone thermonuclear, thank you very much, was now five years past. And having taken up drinking for the first time in her life, she was finding that a hangover brought out a certain roguishness in her. A kind of what-the-hell zest for things. The fact that she'd turned fifty-five the month before had also made her realize that while she'd always look smart, her days as a gladiator in the arena of sex were nearly over. Surprisingly, this realization made her feel cockier, and far better disposed to her fellow man.

So when her latest commission from that mad old so-called colonel was made known to her, she took to it with glee. She was to assemble and arrange for whatever she deemed necessary for a rustic life in the garden shed, for a bum. Said bum was to be provided with the tools and materials to personalize and finish the arrangements inside, Mrs. D to think of everything needed for said bum's homely comforts. No expense need be spared, but it mustn't look as if it had cost much at all.

So Mrs. D had planned out the shed and set two carpenters to work, then gone shopping at the flea markets and antiques shops. The Twenty-sixth Street market had yielded just the right shabby things, then she'd fallen for a lot of eighteenth-century wainscoting at a fancy-ass antiques dealer's uptown.

"So unutterably chic," the dealer purred. "Enough to create the most divine, *intime* room. The paint, you know, is original, made from buttermilk, the pigments dug from the earth. So chalky, such a yellow of nature."

"Nature my aunt Sally," Mrs. D said. "Listen, how much do you want for me to take this load of old boards off your hands?"

"Three thousand?"

"Three thousand *what*?"

The dealer, a younger French woman with black hair drawn back in a chignon and a ballerina's goddamn perfect posture, made a face. "Perhaps we are not trading in dollars today?" she said.

"Nope, we're not. Let's deal in French francs today, since you speak that language. What did they last trade at, about four to the dollar?"

"But that would make, oh I don't know, but an impossible price!"

"Seven hundred and fifty."

"Twelve hundred, and for that I do not touch them once after taking your filthy money, you must arrange for the delivery yourself. And the check must be made out to cash."

The lucre changed hands and a flatbed truck brought the boards to Tenth Street, where Mrs. D conferred with the carpenters about their placement.

When the job was finished she lit a cigarette, another thing she'd lately said to hell with about, and looked around her. The wainscoting covered the now insulated walls horizontally, as well as the ceiling, which rose to a peak. Three windows had been put in, old ones with new double glazing, one to the right of the door and the other two facing each other on the side walls, one for morning light and one for evening. Said bum's bed folded out from the wall to the left of the door, the east window just beyond its foot.

A pot-bellied stove sat on a brick platform on the back wall, a coal and wood bin on one side, and a rough kitchen counter on the other. A two-ring gas burner sat on top of it. The floor had been insulated below the structure, which sat on posts, then decked over inside with plywood and a layer of thick linoleum of mulberry red. Four kerosene lanterns hung from brackets on the walls. A small pine table sat beside the west window, a sturdy ladder-back chair next to it. An armchair covered in a faded Brunscwig Indienne took up the corner opposite the bed. A tiny porch had been built onto the front, replacing the steps. It had white balustrades and its boards were painted sky blue, as were those beneath its roof. It was made entirely of salvaged parts from nineteenth-century houses. The white paint on the balustrades and railing had been left in a state of nature.

Next to the shed, between it and the fence, a stack of tools, nails, lumber, and sawhorses sat with boxes containing a tea kettle, sauce pans, jelly jars, muffin tins, a small mirror, coffee cups, plates, soup bowls, mixing bowls, a Staffordshire milk pitcher with a bucolic scene in blue, candlesticks, candles, silverware, cooking implements, pot holders, tea towels, three flashlights, kitchen matches, a set of cast-iron frying pans, a broom, cleaning items, two tin buckets, a plastic washbasin, bath towels, a box of Pears soap, a percolator, balls of twine, a cat litter box, writing paper and envelopes, a needlepoint rug, two faded red quilts, a sewing kit, a pair of men's slippers in Black Watch tartan, and a complete set of Dickens.

Behind the pile of stuff was Mrs. D's triumph, a completely, flagrantly illegal defiance of every city code, a glorious structure known as a two-holer. There had been enough of that damn Frenchwoman's yellow boards to finish the inside, the door had the traditional crescent moon cut in the top and its roof was hidden from spying neighbors beneath a pergola. In the spring, if said bum hadn't fried himself to a crisp with the kerosene lanterns, she'd have a wisteria vine planted to train over it.

21

Kristen walked determinedly up Greenwich Avenue, headed for the Hollander house. Her thin legs trembled as she shoved Rinaldo's stroller. The corner of her mouth jerked as she practiced what to say. *Oh, hi! I was right here and thought I'd just stop in to say hello. . . .*

She stopped to blow her nose, then shoved the tired Kleenex back in her pocket. She was chaining the stroller to the tree in front of the Hollander's when she stopped, straightening up to listen. Someone inside the house was playing the piano. And if it was Deen it would cause a certain someone to have a heart attack, because it was a hell-for-leather barroom version of some Mozart variations. As music went, it was pure sacrilege.

Kristen snuck up the sandstone steps, Rinaldo in her arms. Her sharp nose, reddened by the cold, sniffed, drinking in the implications. She knew it was Deen, knew the way her fingers made notes. Oh boy, this was good—the little brat would never want Paul to know that she took the music he taught her and turned it into crude honky-tonk. She waited until the song ended, then rang the buzzer.

Deen opened the door. "Oh, hi," she said, not very enthusiastically.

"Hi, Deen. Your mom at home?"

"Nope."

"Are you going to ask me in?"

"Sure, I guess."

Kristen looked down at Deen, a bright smile on her lips. "So, this is where you live. What a fabulous house!" She peeled off her coat and walked into the living room. "Your mom bought it for like nothing in the eighties, right?"

"Did you want to see her?" Deen asked, showing some spirit. "Because she won't be home for a long time. I'll tell her you came by."

"Let's you and me talk for a minute, Deen," Kristen said, sitting on the sofa and patting the cushion next to her. Deen crouched miserably on the ottoman nearby.

"I think we have something we need to get clear, don't you? Hmm, Deen?"

"Like what?"

"Like, what Paul would say if he found out about your *other* music."

Deen didn't ask how she'd found out, grown-ups just did find stuff out, and she hung her head, worried.

Children are perpetually being told not to do certain things, and of course are always trying to find out why. They must, if they are going to grow up and learn anything about the world, must always be pushing at the walls that surround them. Even the dullest children experiment with chewing gum, or what happens when you light a certain toy on fire. Imaginative children lead lives riddled with worry, and have many secrets they need to keep.

Adults look back and think such fears negligible, but to a child they are real. They are not so much afraid of punishment as being shown, once again, proof of the cruel truth that they are silly, inconsiderate, naughty *children*, who at this rate may never graduate to that shimmering city called adult freedom.

So Deen hung her head and mumbled something, while Kristen looked down at her, triumph an ugly gleam in her eyes.

The front door opened and Sadie rushed in. She threw her cell phone onto a chair, saying: "Miserable piece of shit!" to it, then went to the telephone.

"Deen, darling, Uncle Brian's been in an accident. No, no—he'll be all right, really," she added, seeing her daughter's face.

"Kristen, what're you doing here? Hang on a sec," Sadie waved her hand for silence. "Trace, what's the news?" Sadie listened, saying, uh-huh, uh-huh, uh-huh. "Can you book me on the next flight to Heathrow? Really? That's great. I'll be ready. Yeah, I'll tell him."

She put the receiver down. "They're sending a car for me, the flight's in two hours. Shit!" Sadie rubbed her hand over her eyes. "I have to get this all together quick. Deen, I have to go to London, Brian was on his stupid motorcycle, the bloody idiot. He has some quite serious injuries. He'd put me down as his next of kin, or whatever. Where's Hames? Oh lord, what'm I going to do about you two? I really need to pack. . . . Deen, any friends you could stay with?"

"You know I don't have any friends, Munster."

"Well, yes you do," Kristen said sweetly. "She could stay with us, Sadie. We'd love to have her."

"Oh, well, you sure?" Sadie asked. "At least it's somewhere. And Hames can stay at the Fieldings, I'll call Rachel right now."

Rachel Fielding agreed and the deal was done. Deen looked at her mother like a person who'd been wrongly sentenced to death might look at the judge. She opened her mouth to protest, then caught a look from Kristen. Better not, the look said.

Sadie moved toward the stairs. "Oh Christ, I know it'll be a bit hellish, darling. Still, it'll be convenient for your lessons. I'll make it up to you, promise. Meanwhile, I must fly." With that she ran up the stairs. She knew she was making a mistake, should probably arrange for Deen to stay at the colonel's, but it was all such a muddle. Brian was much more badly injured than she'd let on and she was desperately worried about him. Perhaps she'd sort it all out by phone in a day or two.

Kristen looked away, pretending not to understand how grossly she'd been insulted. She buried the thought and smiled stickily at Deen. "Don't worry, honey," she said. "Your Uncle Brian'll be okay and while your mom's away I'll be like a substitute mom to you. We'll have a real nice time."

Deen felt anything but reassured. A half hour later Sadie kissed her and got into a black town car.

Deen packed some clothes in her a knapsack, then followed Kristen through the streets to her lair. She walked several steps behind, dragging her feet, at each step feeling the bite of the shackles. It struck her that the terrible Rinaldo had been noiseless for the first time, as if somehow its mother had *willed* it to be. As if it were she who told it when to be quiet and when to shriek. She was filled with dread at the idea of living in that squalid hole, with those two crazy people and their offspring.

***

I've got to get out of here," she whispered into her cell phone later that evening. "Hames, really, I've got to. No, I can't just take it for a few days, I'm telling you! *Sshh,* here she comes.

"Hi, it's me again. I don't care! You have no idea what it's like here. She served the most horrible spag bog for dinner. And Paul acted like he's not sure who I am. And that baby? It screams nonstop when I just look at it. I thought about killing it. Yeah, but I'm under eighteen. What do you mean, they waive that for killing a baby? Okay, I know, yeah I know, it'd make that place Gretchen's in look like a spa. I won't. But I have to get out of here. Just somewhere. How do you know? The DHS can't just . . . really? Shit, Hames, you have to help me. Oh, fuck, she's banging on the door."

"Deen? Everything all right?" Kristen called through the door. "My, you are a one for cleanliness, you must've used up half the hot water in the building. Come on, honey, hop into your bed and I'll give you a kiss good night."

Deen emerged, allowed herself to be pecked on the head, then went to her cubbyhole across the hall, where Kristen had put out a futon. She cried for a while silently into the yellowish, coverless kapok-filled pillow, her tears describing new rings in its stains. The effort of crying and making no sound wore her out eventually, her silent heaves began to mingle with hypnagogic imagery, and at last she fell asleep.

22

Brian had been taken to St. Elfreda's Hospital, on the edge of Richmond Park. Once the park had been a forest, where the kings of England hunted; now the deer that grazed there were nearly tame.

Brian's neck was broken, he had multiple broken bones, and an arm so badly scraped it would require grafts. He was braced and pinned into his bed, and doped into a coma while the doctors studied the injuries to his spine.

The Rutledge Recording Company, Ree's old label, had arranged for Sadie to be met at Heathrow. The chief himself, Sir Trevor Bagshaw, had offered to perform this courtesy. He'd known Sadie long ago, when he'd been a sound mixer for the company, a lowly technician, unnoticed and unloved as he watched the band, envying their sleek antics.

As he sat in the back of his Bentley, waiting for his driver to find Sadie, he wondered if she'd recognize him. It had been a long time. He was proud of his beautifully cut hair and his beautifully cut suit, but not quite as proud of his new paunch. He sucked it in, sitting up straighter.

"Good Christ, Trevor?" Sadie said, getting in. "You're looking very prosperous."

"Sadie, how good to see you again. I sent word you were to be VIP'd through the formalities—I hope that was the case?"

"Sure, Trev. Some functionary whisked me right past all the proles. Who would've guessed it? You having me VIP'd, a loathsome verb I'm unfamiliar with, but is sadly all too clear, this Nazi staff car of yours, bespoke suits, what next? I'm afraid we must be getting terribly old."

Trevor nodded to the driver and they moved away from the curb. He longed to be able to think of a way of introducing the subject of his recent knighthood, but was afraid of Sadie's jibes. He wasn't at all sure that meeting her had been such a good idea.

"How's Brian?" she asked him.

"Well, there's hope." He filled her in on the little he knew, then sighed. "It's been good for his press though. Interest in Brian's doings had rather fallen off of late. He'd get a kick out of how much his near death has excited the public. The papers are all over the story."

"Always keeping an eye on the residuals, eh Trev?"

Sarcastic bitch, Trevor thought. *Always did think she was above the common herd, prancing around like the queen of bloody Siam with the band, them and their long hair and golden looks.*

Sadie stopped paying attention to old Trev, tuning out his not-so-subtle tootings of his own horn. Looking out the window at the misted, dank winter air, moisture dripping down the noisome brickwork and gloomy evergreens of suburban London, she thought, *Plus ça* bloody *change.* . . . The dankness grew and formed horizontal streaks on the car window. She'd gazed out a thousand such windows, at the endless damp of London winters. It was fitting to return here now, in this season, to the London of memory. But it was not an auspicious time for healing.

Ree, she thought, you died at this time of year. In the port of Amsterdam. The Dutch, in their thoroughness, had taken you to the hospital, but you were gone. They performed their humanitarian rites over your body, to no avail. Then they wrapped you in a spotless winding-sheet. Your hair still shone, I touched your cheek. They'd washed you, you smelled of chamomile.

Afterward they offered me a veritable United Nations of grief-women, of every known cult, from starched Catholics to earth-worshipping priestesses. But you were dead, so I had no use for their words.

She traced a shape, a bird's head with a long beak, on the window, then rubbed it out. Trevor was still nattering on; she had no idea about what and didn't care. She hadn't been called to Ree's side as he lay dying, no one had.

Brian was the last of them. Giff had died soon after Ree in what was described as a boating accident, and Evan, the bass player, a few years later, of an overdose as well. The dear old sixties had demanded many sacrifices.

If Brian lived long enough he might someday be an old man. She tried to picture it. He'd be a bit crooked, and his hair a white brush. His nose would become rather remarkable, a gargoyle's. But she could picture him hopping about like a gnome, talking about his latest project, a wizened thing with still the remains of the sinew needed to haul ass on a heavy guitar.

Perhaps, she thought, I'll be in time to help him. Because he was the last, it didn't bear thinking about losing him. She made a vow to do everything she could. It would mean staying here for as long as it takes, a voice in her head said. Well then, I will, she answered.

The car passed a stand of great elms, the winter morning cupping them in an amphitheater of mist. Their branches were bare, exposing the nests of a colony of rooks, ragged bolls of leaves clogging the tree limbs. A shaft of lemonish light fell from between the clouds and the rooks rose, circling their territory, their cries stamped into her memory: *Ra-cah, ra-cah, ra-coah-cah.*

***

Trevor had cannily let the press know when Sadie would be arriving at St. Elfreda's, where they thronged the front entrance, cameras ready. As Sadie got out their voices rose in a gabble; theresheis, oi Saids, give us a pose, oi, over here, be a dear and give us a quote, Brian and you getting hitched? Secret love, is it? future Mrs. Brain, eh, show us a bit of leg, got any news of the lad? He wake up yet then? Still carrying a torch for Ree? The kids comin' to join you, love?

Sadie was much bigger news in the United Kingdom than in New York. She'd been a bit of a rock princess here, in her youth. She pushed her way through the crowd, kicking a shin where needed, and pushing off a fat reporter who wouldn't move out of the way. When she reached the top step she turned and gave them a crooked smile, letting them snap away. She'd learned long before that the press was like a caged beast, that you had to be its master, but that if you didn't toss it some meat once in a while it would devour you.

Outside Brian's room the specialist in charge waited for her gravely, a chart in his hand. As Sadie walked toward him down the corridor she began planning. She would play the grieving female, but not Brian's female. More the widow of the great Ree, chaste and untouched since Ree's death. The doctor was in his late fifties, she guessed, and she'd use everything in her bag of tricks to get him on her side. Make him win the first tremulous smile from her, all the usual rot.

As she drew close enough and he put out his hand, she read two things in his face—that he was pleased by her associated fame with the band, and that he was afraid to tell her what he knew. Her left foot came down wrong and she put a hand out to the wall.

The next thing she knew, she was lying on a hospital bed. A nurse was staring at her, from behind the doctor, who was taking her pulse.

"Mrs. Hollander, I'm Mr. Mendelsen. Brian's surgeon. You fainted, probably due to the flight and the stress over your friend's condition. You're in the extra bed in Brian's room. We'll let you lie here for a bit, shall we? Yes, until you feel better. Nurse, will you get Mrs. Hollander some orange juice, please?"

"I'm awfully sorry I fainted," Sadie said.

"Well, well. Now, I think you should try to sleep after you've had the orange juice. Then later we can talk about Brian's condition and what you can do to help him."

"He's there?" Sadie said, nodding her head toward a curtain around the other bed.

"Yes. You mustn't talk to him just yet, I'll want to be there when you do, to determine if there are any signs of response, all right? Good, good. Ah, here's the nurse with the orange juice."

As soon as they had gone, Sadie sprang up and slipped through the curtain surrounding Brian's bed. Geeze, he looked like something the cat had dragged in. He was strapped and trussed into a number of pale plastic armatures, his head surrounded by something like a cross between a helmet and the stand for a Christmas tree. Like a knight in plastic armor, on a plastic tomb.

"Listen, you cocksucking piece of shit," she said to him. "What in the bloody hell were you thinking, acting the lad, doing stupid tricks on your motorcycle? For Christ's sake, Brian. And why the hell didn't you ever get married, have some weepy, impossibly young bride here, instead of *me*? You asshole! I had to leave my children with who knows who, rushed off with the *oddest* assortment of clothes. And Gretchen will be wondering why I don't visit. It's a disaster, and it's all your bloody fault. So you owe me. You get your ass in gear and get us out of this, hear me? Just fucking pull yourself together."

Brian's face grew pinker and he let out a *phff* of air with his lips.

23

The first morning of Deen's enforced sojourn *chez* Dresden, she was woken before dawn by the baby's cries. Kristen came out of the bedroom, the creature clutched to her bosom. Deen pulled the nylon quilt she'd been issued over her head and went back to sleep, in spite of the grizzlings and bangs coming from the kitchen.

Later, waiting till Paul could safely be assumed to be dressed, she darted across to the bathroom, locking the door firmly.

"Goddamn it," she heard Paul saying, as he passed by. "I don't want to hear another word on the subject! Send Ondine in to me for her lesson at two, until then, shut your fucking piehole!"

Deen tiptoed out and straightened her futon, then went to get her keys and cell phone. They weren't where she thought she'd left them, nor were they in her coat pockets. Her suspicions grew as she methodically searched the bed, then the few possessions she'd brought.

"What've you done with my cell phone and my keys?" she yelled at Kristen, who sat placidly feeding bits of fried egg into her infant's mouth.

"Your mom asked me to take care of you," Kristen said. "She called me a blessing and asked me to take you under my wing, remember? So all I want to do is like, do a really good job, be your substitute mom while she's gone. I don't think a girl your age should have a cell phone. I don't have one. And I never would've dreamed of screeching at my mom like that when I was your age. I was told to mind my *p*'s and *q*'s, and I did, didn't have all sorts of fancy stuff and privileges like you, with your la-di-dah house and a maid to clean it. *I* didn't grow up with all sorts of temptations to lead me to the devil."

Deen stared at her. She grew up a great deal in that long instant. She came to the knowledge that life is a battle. She saw that victory went to the more resourceful, and that the woman in front of her was probably insane.

"Well, I need my keys so I can get my books and things for my lessons," she said.

"Oh, that's okay, your mom gave me your schedule with all your teacher's names and numbers, so I called them all while you were sleeping and said there'd been an emergency and your mom had left me in charge. I told them I'd let them know when you can start your lessons again.

"It'll be okay, honey—one thing I always knew about myself was, I was born to raise kids."

"You call that screaming, snot-manufacturing, foul dwarf of yours a *kid*?" Deen cried. "The Centers for Disease Control in Atlanta ought to send a team up in space suits to *dispose* of it!"

"Now, that's just because you're a tad jealous, isn't it? I know I give my punkin pudding more attention than you, but it's okay honey, I love you too. But I won't have you talking about him like that, understood? Look, let's get something straight—I'm in charge here, and you're a kid and you're going to do as I say. For starters you're going to help me out around here, learn some real things instead of poetry and ballet and whatever. It'll be real good for you to live a bit less swanky for a while. When your mom gets back I'm going to give her a daughter she can be proud of, one who knows how to clean and care for a home, someone who'll be fit to marry a man someday and keep him happy."

***

The next day, with no piano lesson with Paul, Deen was in Kristen's loving care every moment. For Deen, the day passed with agonizing slowness.

Kristen had called sweetly for her to get up and have some breakfast, she always put on an act of being nice as pie when Paul was around. Paul stood by the window, eating his cornflakes and staring outside, where it was sleeting. He put the bowl down and stalked off to his studio. He wouldn't reappear until dinnertime.

Impossible as it seems, Kristen spent a good part of each day engaged in housework. The rest she spent in the feeding and appeasement of that drooling idol, her baby. The few times she went out it was only to shop at a dingy market on Ninth Avenue, or to choose which twenty-nine-cent bootlaces to buy for Paul at a penny emporium.

Getting the evil gargantuan ready to go out was an ordeal of minute agonies, each a nail driven into the cross anew. The stroller was dirty, wash it down, no, use Lysol. Oops, punkin threw up some of his breakfast, change his coat, put this one to soak in the sink. It fought the putting on of mittens and booties like a virgin fighting off a rapist. Often it would propel so much fluid from its eyes, mouth, and nose while screaming during the process, that its coat would have to come off again and its top changed, as baby mustn't go out in the cold with anything damp near its dear little throat. Deen thought she would like to place something damp around its throat—her own reddened hands, soaked with water and Ivory liquid.

When things are dire they can always get direr. There's always room for one more grain of misery. Kristen had read somewhere that fresh chicken livers were a super-nutrient, that a small portion each day from an early age would build a body like Hercules's.

The gorged idol apparently agreed. It couldn't get enough of them. And with the cunning of all simple life-forms it had developed a foolproof method for getting more. It would begin by making a wet, sucking noise. Then hold its hands out and twist them, as though turning a pair of knobs. Next it opened its mouth wide and let out a shriek. But not its regular shriek, the ear-piercer, this was a new shriek, more like a roar. It would sustain it until it heard the refrigerator door open, then die down to whimpers.

Kristen tried to cut it down on this new drug, looking rather frightened, but it was not to be refused.

Having eaten close to half a pound of sautéed liver at lunch, it now snored in its crib in its favorite position, head resting on meaty arms and fat bum high in the air. From time to time it let out a moist fart.

Deen was drying dishes when suddenly Kristen let out an enraged howl. Leaping back from the cupboard below the sink she held up a rag covered in what looked like chocolate sprinkles.

"Just look at this! Mice!" Flinging it away from her she took the phone receiver from her cardigan pocket. She kept it there so that Deen couldn't make any calls.

"Yes, this is Mrs. Paul Dresden in 1W. We have mice. What do you mean, so does everyone, lady? It's an outrage! I want you to do something about it. Mice are filthy. My baby could get hantavirus! Yes, first thing tomorrow, or else."

She scooped up the baby and inspected its thick limbs for signs of bites. Then glared at Deen. "From now on, he doesn't go anywhere near the floor, got it? Punkin dum wanna hab hantavirub," she crooned to it. It rolled over sleepily in her arms and let out a drilling fart in the key of C.

* * *

Darkness falls, the sleet continues to come down outside the windows. Soundlessly, Paul enters the kitchen. His hair sticks up all over the place but his face is still. His son, the inflated idol, looks up at him, his mouth agape. It's dark in the humid, dirty kitchen, a lamp by the door the only illumination.

"Let us now pray," Paul said, dropping his head. "Our father, who hath gathered this feast of burnt offerings and foul essences, yea, unto the perpetual spaghetti Bolognese. Oh please, not again."

The infant stole a hand into its diaper and lay back in its high chair.

Paul raised his head and looked around, seeming unsure where he was. His gaze stopped on Deen. "What is this child of a noble house doing here?" he asked Kristen. "Hast thou stolen her? Menaced her with evil threats, made her a hostage in your eternal feud with your betters? Her father, the duke, and her brothers, warriors all, shall not rest until we hang from gibbets, and our house is razed. And what's that foul brat up to *now*? Christ, woman, can't you teach him not to frig himself at the dinner table?"

"Paul, I have to talk to you. We have mice. I called the super but he could care less. You have to do something. Our baby could get hantavirus!"

"The worries of an inane woman," Paul said to Deen, sighing. "Who spends her days occupied in mindless matters. Such women invent plagues, sorcery with yarn, idiotic tales and color periodicals filled with calumny. Personally, I'd worry more about the poor mouse. Rinaldo would probably roll over and crush the life out of it. God, look at him, he's huge, as if he's been fed on kryptonite. What've you been feeding him, woman? Come on, out with it."

Kristen shook, not daring to tell him. She pulled the cardigan closer around her thin floral-print dress and stared down at her plate.

"Ondine, pray tell me, what has she been feeding him?"

"It's gotten a taste for sautéed chicken livers."

"Really. Why do you call it it?"

"Well, you can hardly call a thing like that a person."

"And why not?"

"Because it's an it! You're all sick, all of you! She cleans the place all day and just gets crap smeared over it worse, and lectures me about being Miss Fancypants. It's completely psycho to slave away for nothing, and end up with a shithole like this! And that *thing* there, you could sell it to the circus!"

Deen got up and ran to her cubbyhole, throwing herself down on the slippery quilt, too stunned with pity for herself to even cry. She was sure her mother had died in a plane crash and that Uncle Brian was also dead and she'd never, ever get out of this hell.

"My, even by your standards, that was a particularly horrid meal," Paul remarked to his wife. "Any hope for a bit of dessert?"

***

That very same evening, uptown and a few blocks east, the colonel, Robert and Mrs. D were having a serious discussion in the colonel's back parlor. Not surprisingly, they were also drinking neat whiskey.

Their faces, though, were anything but jovial. Deen had not appeared for her piano session with Robert, and Ettie had burst into tears as she brought in the tea sandwiches, saying she hadn't seen Jaimes in three days.

Mrs. D went next door to peer in the windows. "The place has that feel," she reported, when she came back. "An empty house. Houses breathe when they're inhabited, I'd say no one's been there in days. I don't know what to think."

"Come, come, Mrs. D, that's not your usual style," the colonel said. He'd lately begun calling her Mrs. D too, and in so doing become a tiny bit less a southerner and that much more a New Yorker, though he still stuck out like a sore thumb.

"Something must've happened to make them up sticks and go," Robert said. "Must've been something that came on real sudden, didn't leave any of them time to tell no one nothing."

Mrs. D smacked her hand down on the arm of her chair. "Colonel, do have today's paper? No, of course you don't. Do you think Ettie has a *Post*?"

Ettie was summoned, yes, she said, she had a copy. She ran to get it. When she returned she asked Mrs. D anxiously; "Is there something about the family? They were in accident? I *know* something wrong. Tell me."

"They're fine, I'm sure Ettie, but I think they've gone off somewhere. . . . Here it is. I saw the piece this morning but didn't make the connection." Mrs. D snapped the paper smartly and read the article aloud. '"ROCKER IN COMA. Sixties rocker Brian Brain, of the Royhatten Transference, remains in serious condition after a motorcycle accident in London. An unnamed source at the hospital has been quoted as saying he may never be able to walk again.'"

"Dear me," the colonel said.

"Aha—here it is. 'Sadie Hollander, the widow of legendary rocker Ree Hollander, and a close friend of Brian's, arrived Tuesday to be by his side. The British tabloids have been filled with the story, a number of headlines suggesting the two may be linked by more than just friendship.' Oh, really," Mrs. D said, adding her own commentary.

The three people sat in silence for a moment, thinking through the possibilities.

"So she lit right out of town, *whoosh,* to be by her friend," Robert said. "That's what a real friend does do. *Whoosh*. I don't know anything about what them tabloids are saying about that other thing. So she lights out, but where are the children?"

"I can't believe I didn't get all their cell numbers," Mrs. D said. "I could kick myself."

"Perhaps she sent them off to their relatives," the colonel said.

"She no *familia*," Ettie said, beginning to cry and her English breaking down. "And Colonel? Those children, they call to say hi Ettie, I here, if they can." She broke into Spanish to complete her thoughts, her fears communicating themselves to the others.

"We got to call the cops," Robert said. "Right now."

"I can't *believe* I didn't get their cell numbers," Mrs. D moaned.

Just then the bell rang at the front door. Ettie ran for it, Robert and Mrs. D following. It was Hamish. Ettie grabbed him, holding the boy as she wailed her happiness to see him. Then she grabbed his coat sleeve and dragged him to the colonel's parlor.

"It's Deen," he said, looking around at the adults. "Munster left her with the Dresdens. You know, Deen's piano teacher and his wife. I'm staying at the Fieldings. I stay there once in a while and it's pretty decent.

"Deen called the first night, said it was horrible, but I just figured she was being dramatic. I mean, she goes there every other day for her lessons, for hours. But since then she doesn't answer her cell phone. I tried calling their apartment but the phone just rings and rings, they don't even have an answering machine. That's weird. Munster called twice and I lied, said Deen was okay, I mean, she's all the way over in London, so what can she do? I just didn't want her all worried. I was going to ask the Fieldings to help, but then I remembered you all get together to drink on Thursday nights."

Mrs. D was already rifling the pages of her Filofax. "What's the Dresden's address?" she asked Hamish. "And give me your cell numbers, your mother's and Deen's too." She noted them down. "Colonel, I think I should go over there right now."

"Yes, I think that would be best."

"He's attacked people with a hammer," Hamish said.

"Who?" they all cried.

"Paul. But it was a while ago."

Robert's face hardened. "Mrs. D, I was going to go with you anyways, but now I think I better go armed. Colonel, you got a baseball bat?"

"No, but naturally I have a revolver. I'll go up and get it."

"Now hold on a minute," Mrs. D said. "Everyone just calm down. This wife of his, what's she like?" she asked Hamish.

"Well, she's younger and has a rabbity face, and Deen says she whines a lot. She says she spends the day cleaning the apartment and caring for this really horrible baby she has."

"Hmm. I see. Nine times out of ten it's the woman causing the trouble. You can leave her to me. Robert, you can come along, but you'll stay in the cab and wait."

"Long as I can bring a candlestick or something," he muttered.

When, in a few moments, they were gone, the colonel said to Hamish, "Sit down, my boy, sit down. And Ettie, I insist you have a small glass of port, for your nerves. No, no, you need it. There, that's better, isn't it? Think I need a nip myself. I'm sure everything will be fine, just fine. But naturally we'll be a bit anxious while we wait for the inestimable Mrs. D to report. No one I'd trust more to get the job done. Still, our vigil may be long, and young Hamish here needs to keep his strength up. Any chance you have some roast beef sandwiches lying about, Ettie?"

* * *

Mrs. D stood at the apartment house entrance, pretending to search for her keys. The door opened and a couple came out. "Oh, thanks," she said, grabbing it. She wanted to give Kristen as little warning as possible.

For the same tactical reason, she didn't ring, but beat on their door with the flat of her hand.

It was just as she'd expected. A scared, ferrety-faced woman with lanky brown hair peered out the door.

"Mrs. Dresden?"

"Yes?"

"I'm Mrs. de Angelo. I'm here to see Deen."

"Oh, well, she's gone to bed."

"It's kind of early, isn't it?"

"She wasn't feeling well, so . . ."

"I think you'd better let me in. Now."

Mrs. D looked around her, scoping the joint in seconds. It was ghastly, to be sure, but there were no signs of criminal activity, unless you counted the baby in its crib, its stomach as large as a basketball, who was grinning at her from beneath a mop of golden ringlets.

"Where's your husband?"

"In his music room. Back there. He works on his symphony at night."

"And Deen?"

"It's not really a guest room I guess, but I made it nice for her."

"What's she sick with?"

"I think she's just coming down with a cold. I brought her some orange juice and made sure she was tucked in all right."

"Why hasn't she answered her cell phone? Why'd she miss her lesson with Robert?"

"I guess she just didn't want to. Kids are like that sometimes, you know. I can't make her turn on her cell phone, or go to lessons, 'cause I only know what lessons she tells me she has. Her mom asked me to take care of her. She was all worried 'cause she had to go off to London at the drop of a hat and there was nowhere for Deen to stay and she said to me, you're an angel to take care of Deen. It hasn't been easy, I've got the baby too, but I've tried to be like a real mom to

Deen. You have no right to barge in here and act like I'm keeping her a prisoner or something. I've spent hours with her showing her how to sew and make a cake and all kinds of nice stuff. Her mom called me an *angel* for doing it."

"I need to see Deen."

"I told you, she's sleeping."

"Past that door?"

"Yes," Kristen whispered.

Mrs. D opened it quietly then turned on a tiny flashlight she had in her bag. A few steps down the hall she saw Deen. She was asleep on her futon in that state of abandon children have, one leg and an arm outside the quilt. Her face was composed and her long, reddish hair strewn over the pillow. The bedding was of the cheapest sort, but the girl looked healthy and untroubled. Mrs. D backed silently out.

"Now listen to me carefully," she said, "you're to take very good care of that girl, do you hear? I know her mother left her with you, but I'll be keeping my eye on you."

"You'll see—Deen loves me," Kristen said. "I'm really good with kids, really nice to Deen."

"Yes, well, you just make sure you are, got that?" Mrs. D left, after fixing Kristen with a look, who affected a teary, mistreated expression that Mrs. D did not buy for an instant.

* * *

Sleeping as innocently as a lamb," Mrs. D reported to the colonel. "I couldn't very well haul her out of there, it might've frightened her and after all, Sadie did sanction the deal. But I'd be far happier if she were out of there."

"The girl could stay here, and Ettie could look after her," he said.

"Hamish, any idea when your mother will return?"

"Nope, she doesn't tell me much about Brian, but I think it's bad. I think she's going to stay for a while. Like, a few weeks more at least

I'd guess. Brian's pretty fucked up, from what I read on the Internet. I think he'll probably live but if he's paralyzed, Munster might want to hang around and wait for a chance to smother him with a pillow." He looked around at the faces of the grown-ups. "I mean, she'd have to, it'd be her mission. She wouldn't leave him there all hooked up to tubes and stuff. She could never leave him like that.

"Hey, if Deen moves in here, you think I could too? I know I said staying at the Fieldings' is all right, but I'd much rather be here. Then I'd have all of you and Deen and Ettie, and I could learn cooking again."

Later, when Robert went to find a taxi for Mrs. D, he thought, She's quite a woman. Really knows about people. And even though she pretends to be all hard-hearted and businesslike, she sure has a soft side. Why, she'd felt so bad for Ettie worrying about where the Cap'n had run off to this time she'd hired a detective agency to look for him. No doubt on the colonel's dime, but that was his business. Yes, if anyone could rustle up that old bum for Ettie, it'd sure be Mrs. D. And it seemed private detectives didn't belong to any union, so that was all right.

24

Brian was alive, though he gave no sign of being so. He lay very still on his white bed, in his beeping chamber, hooked up to all sorts of gadgets and living in a richly imagined world, dreaming round the clock on powerful narcotics. As he'd always enjoyed drugs, he was quite content, though he felt a bit as if he were tripping in some very remote place.

Sadie, on the other hand, was not content. She was bored almost beyond endurance by the business of caring for someone in a coma. She spent her nights drinking herself into a sleep in which she tossed horribly, prickled by night sweats. She hated the swanky hotel the recording company had booked her into. It wasn't anything like the London she'd known, a London of gravely paneled rooms and vintage seediness. This place was a modern high rise with exposed steel beams. Of course it was in Docklands, with a great honking lobby and views of the Thames, the rooms trying like hell to be TriBeCa lofts. A nasty steel coffee table, which she'd already tripped over twice, held a tall vase filled with what appeared to be flower stems—some indie florist's wet dream, oi, why don't we cut off the flowers, see? Just do stems, like? *I say, that's absolutely marvelous, so edgy.*

Each morning at ten thirty, rocker's time, a car hired by RRC came to take her to St. Elfreda's. She spent the mornings there with Brian, but couldn't bear to be in the hospital at lunchtime, with its groaning of food trolleys, clatter of trays, and horrid smells. So she had the driver take her back to town, where she ate lunch in a café or a sandwich joint, then did some errands or visited her old friend the bog man at the British Museum. He at least was the same, had been the same for hundreds of years, pickled by the peat he'd been buried in, the garrote still around his neck.

In the late afternoon she'd return to her faux loft and make calls home, then try to nap. In the evening, after the dinner trolleys had withdrawn, she'd call a minicab to take her back to St. Elfreda's to spend another hour or two with Brian. He wasn't allowed any other visitors, and had no living relatives, so it seemed a lonely time of day for an old rocker to lie in utter silence.

She read him bits from music magazines, talked to him, and sometimes yelled at him. At other times she flung herself on the bed next to his and let out a long sigh, thinking that comatose people are not very good company.

***

At times Dr. Mendelsen, or rather, Mr., for he was a surgeon, would breeze in, his tie tucked into the lapel of his white coat like certain cinema heroes of WWII propaganda films. He'd talk to Brian and then try to cheer Sadie up, being very British and kindly toward Yanks, especially Yank widows with lean thighs. Sadie's plan to charm the surgeon had gone rather too well, though it had achieved her desired result, in that he checked on Brian often. The downside was that he'd developed a certain heavy-handed charm toward Sadie, while giving her sidelong wolf looks.

Mendel-bendel, as Sadie had dubbed him, of course never discussed Brian's condition with her in any scientific or substantive way. She was not an initiate into the Mysteries, and so must be treated as barely able to make out "the cat sat on the mat." But through charm and an intelligent question snuck in here and there, she gradually was able to cobble together a picture of Brian's medical condition.

It seemed the injuries to his spine were of a type that might mend, or might not. That they had set the other breaks, immobilized his neck, and drugged him into a very dark, quiet place, where they could study his injuries and possibly allow them to heal on their own. As far as she could tell, there really wasn't any surgery that could be performed to aid him. That admission had been won with no little effort and cunning on her part. Mendel-bendel talked of surgery that might return the use of his upper body, but it was obvious that what he meant was that they'd do it if the larger battle was deemed already lost. As far as the skin grafts went, they'd done a rough job when he was in the operating theater and left them.

One thing bothered Sadie a great deal. This was that Mendel-bendel had spent hours observing Brian as Sadie talked to him. It was clear that he was looking for some sign of response. And there had been none. He'd been unable to disguise his puzzlement, and Sadie unable to hide her disappointment. In fact, she was getting bloody annoyed with Brian.

So there was talk of lowering Brian's intake of drugs, bringing him a bit closer to consciousness. "Oi! Who stole my stash?" Sadie imagined him shouting, in his enforced sleep, how it came out as a mumble, *oi, oo to my tash?* A frown creases his brow for a flicker, and his fingers tremble fretfully. Meanwhile, inside his head he's leaping into the air, hurling whatever object to hand at the wall and going over to repeat the question, glaring right into the asshole's eyes: "I *said,* who stole my stash?"

Ah, bitter days when the last living member of a throw-it-all-away-for-the-moment rock band is neither living nor dead. Bitter days for his will, reduced to a flicker at the far end of a dark cavern, the red and glistening corpus *Homo sapiens.* Sadie sat in her gloomy hotel chamber, her feet up, the lights out, drinking vodka and staring out at the lights reflected on the surface of the oily Thames. It occurred to her that if Brian had been in the same accident back when the band was young, well, no it was too complicated a conjecture. And she was too drunk, had passed the point of composed, linear thinking.

Instead she poured herself another drink.

25

A great cloud mass, stretching from Pennsylvania to Massachusetts, moved over the metropolitan area before sunset, bringing a sudden twilight, then darkness. As it met the warmer air from the Atlantic it stopped, piling up on itself. The weight of water inside it began to fall to earth, freezing as it did.

The first flakes of snow fell on Manhattan with a glide, then melted. As they came down faster they began to cool the tepid streets, starting to accumulate. The denizens of Gotham hurried their steps. A bitter wind came up, hurling the new snow into eddies.

By midnight the streets were white with the first snow of winter. The noises of the city were muffled by it and the streetlights shone in haloes of driven flakes. Taxis shushed by now and then, but traffic was at a minimum.

Cap'n Meat clapped his hands together to warm them and kept on walking. He'd never been sorrier to see the sun set than he had that day, the last of the daylight subsuming in indigo clouds over the tops of the buildings. He felt the wind reaching to find his flesh, and noted how it had changed and was now coming from the north. He noted also that something had broken in him. That the week in the Hollanders' house had set him irrevocably apart from the desire to wander forever. And that he had nowhere else to go but one place.

He thought he knew what that place was, but needed time to approach it. Perhaps he should go into a church to pray. No, he thought, if reason is my messenger, and self-knowledge my goal, then a will-o'-the-wisp, a phantom that some men call their father will not do. I had a father, a real man of stringy flesh and blood that had gushed from a wound. The blood had pooled on the dusty soil where I laid him down beside the harvester then tied his kerchief tight above the vein. He looked near to dying so I ran to fetch Ma. He screamed after me as I ran, *Tell her there isn't any fucking God, not when you've got to slave every live long day on acreage like this, where insects and crop diseases are more plentiful than harvests, tell her to sell up and get out.*

He'd never gone inside a church again. Ma thought it was badness coming to the surface in him, but it wasn't—he'd blasphemed the Lord, so he could no longer be a guest in His house.

Instead he read the scriptures each Sunday, alone in the parlor. Ma begged and argued with him, but he wouldn't budge, so she'd jam her hat on and leave, tugging us boys to follow her.

The city had grown so still and silent the Cap'n had an odd feeling that he was the only person left alive there. The depopulated streets were eerie, as if the worst thing man could imagine had come to pass, and he was living in a postapocalyptic world.

He'd read somewhere, long ago, of the last woolly mammoth, which was found wandering, somewhere in northern Europe, around the end of the seventeenth century. The men who'd spotted it ran back to the village to raise the alarm, then the villagers had gathered to kill it.

Extinction, by its very process, means that there is eventually one sole survivor of its species. One last of its kind to roam and search for others, crying out for them. But their calls will never be returned. No brother, no parent, no ladylove, will ever make their sound.

They forage and fend and wander, looking for another. Then walking monkeys, with their lightning sticks and yells and cutting things, beset them, and beat sounds of pleasure up into the sky to hear the last sounds of the last of one creature, as they trample its blood into the earth.

Going up Minetta Alley, the Cap'n saw a pigeon lying on the sidewalk, one wing nearly torn off. Drops of blood sat like scarlet beads on its breast. A slithering blur ran from it, a rat. The bird beat its good wing uselessly, trying to get away. The rat had bitten off its feet. It let out a cheep of fear.

The Cap'n knelt, the snow wetting his knees. He wrapped a handkerchief around the pigeon's head, then wrung its neck. It was less frightening to them if they didn't see. He buried it in a mound of snow once it had stopped twitching.

It was a night for dying, he thought, trudging up Fifth Avenue. He touched Titus's pocket to feel the cat's solid warmth. Up ahead, in front of the Forbes building, he saw a fire in a trash can, a bum's fire, and felt warmer just looking at it. Maybe there would be a few good fellows there, comparing exaggerated figures of other snowstorms.

As quickly as he'd felt hope, his hopes were taken away and replaced by fear. It was the Angry One. His voice beat out like metal fists crashing on a shield, in the abandoned city canyon. The Cap'n dodged behind a scaffolding, hiding from those demented eyes.

"I *know* you're in there, motherfucker!" The Angry One was screaming. He was looking up at the Forbes building, and gesturing. "Come on out, Stevie-boy! I got a date with your *ass*. You and me gonna fuck like queens, do *all* that shit. Shotgun joints, have us a party, a real fine time, laugh and fall in goddamn, motherfucking *love*! Yeah, you and me, Stevie-boy, I'll make you my bitch yet. You're gonna want a tattoo with my *name* on it, right on your shiny white ass, when I'm done with you, man.

"These people down here, they don't understand the capitalist *system*. Not like you and I do, hey my main man? Come on, come on down—I wanna *play*!"

No towheaded boy in spectacles came out of the towering bronze doors. The Angry One held his arms out, keening, but no playmate appeared.

"Ah, he's hidin' up there. He just does *not* know what he's missin'. Well, if that wonderbitch won't play, maybe I'll find my pleasure elsewhere. Where's that fat bum and his cat? I thought maybe I'd kill the old man first, then that goddamn cat, but I can't make up my mind, maybe it should be the other way around. Either way, when I'm done with that I don't think you'll mean so much to me anymore, Stevie-boy. Maybe I been fooling you all along, maybe I don't love you at *all*."

The Angry One's voice fell silent at last. The Cap'n was blocks away before he realized that he knew now who had been rousting and menacing him.

He wondered why. Why did this man have an ache in him to kill him? What limpet attached that man's rage to his life?

His feet were frozen. It didn't matter. Ill luck had plagued him all his days and here was just another outbreaking of the clouds that thundered down arrows at his head. The logical thing was to suppose that a life so cursed would end badly. No great surprise there. His feet bore him toward the river. The Hudson would take him, end all this claptrap.

Realizing that he was truly ready to choose death, he thought suddenly of Titus. He took off his left glove and stroked the cat's head. No, he couldn't plunge in and listen to the cat's screams, feel it fighting for life in his pocket. So he'd have to kill his friend first, then himself. But Titus had not decided to die. What should he do? There was little time left. It was far easier, he realized, to kill oneself than to leave another who needed you behind. Quick, think harder. He looked up and saw that he was on West Tenth Street, only a couple of blocks from the Hollanders. They would care for Titus.

He'd leave the cat tied to their doorstep, with a note around his neck. And Titus would yowl at being tied up, then see him leave. And he'd hear his yowls and feel his friend's eyes on his back. Why are you leaving me?

Because I must. Or, he could wrap his wool scarf around his hand, break the window into the basement kitchen of the Hollanders' house, shove Titus inside, and then seal it up somehow. Scribble a note. No, damn the soft explanations of a suicide note. All right, but he'd be obliged to say something to explain why Titus was there. . . . Look, the very thing, a square of plywood, pick it up. There, the plan was set. He wouldn't stop to say good-bye to his friend, it would be too hard.

Looking up at the brick house that had sheltered him, a house where he'd known kindness and safety, he saluted it. He knew that what he was doing was right, and that this house would care for Titus.

* * *

Is you?"

The Cap'n started. He looked over his shoulder and saw a small woman wrapped in a check coat. "Oh, meester Cap'n, it's Ettie. I been looking out for you for so long. Waking, always waking, so many nights, looking for you."

She shone the flashlight in her hand onto her own face, to show him. Feeling suddenly so very tired he could barely move, he took a few steps toward her.

"It's in here," she whispered, shining her flashlight on the garden gate. "Look, here, I open with key. It's back there. A place for you. See?"

The Cap'n followed her into the garden and over the bluestone paving. Shrubs made dark shapes around him. He was sure he was in the clutches of the river, and that contrary to common belief, a drowning man does not see the past, but this, a neatly made cottage, with a porch and lamplight soft within.

"That's your house. The colonel made it. I go now, you and your cat sleep. I lock the garden gate. Talk in the morning. Then I'll cry, so happy you came back, all right?"

He nodded and she disappeared with a shush of cloth and the snap of a lock clicking home.

The Cap'n stood, looking at the tiny cottage. He saw that lamplight fell from windows at its sides. That it had a door. A door it seemed he was invited to go in. He thought of running, there must be some way to climb over that garden gate. But a deep ache, running through the axis of his being, held him still.

Slowly he mounted the steps to the porch, then opened the door. He poked his head around it, looking in. Two lanterns burned in brackets on the wall, another on a small table. To the left a bed folded out from the wall on ropes. It was made up with white sheets, a pillow, a wool blanket, and a quilt. He really couldn't see the rest, the bed swam in his mind so large.

He stepped fully into the cabin, closing the door behind him. No alarms went off, and no one leaped out to challenge him. He didn't know how quite to describe it but the place seemed new, unoccupied. That either it was really for him, or he was sinking down inside the cold waters of the river, his hair floating and swaying, his mind at last free. Gingerly, he touched the bed.

He drew Titus from his pocket and set him on the quilt. Titus wouldn't take that, had to march around in ever decreasing circles, then sank onto the quilt, curled into a loose ball, and kneaded his claws into it. He let out a purr.

Very carefully, the Cap'n took off his coat and boots, then raised the chimneys of the lanterns and blew them out. He felt his way over to the bed and snuck between the sheets. He never remembered putting his head down on the pillow, because he was asleep as he did.

26

The storm blew out to sea before dawn, leaving the sidewalks and trees covered in a hard, white snow. As the first light showed through the windows the Cap'n opened his eyes. He was warm under the quilt, though he could see his breath in the air.

He looked around the cabin; as the light strengthened he could make out its contents. There was a pot-bellied stove at the far end, with a simple kitchen counter next to it. There was a table, two chairs, a wood bin, a small bookcase, and an upholstered armchair. Everything fit just so in its place and it was all as neat as a pin.

On the table there was a tray with two thermoses and a napkin-covered basket. Propped against one of the thermoses was an envelope.

He decided to stay in bed just a little bit longer, before reading what was in that envelope. He'd sunk as low in his mind as a man can the night before, and needed just a few more moments of quiet and comfort, then he'd get up and face what was next. It had been so kind of them to let him stay here for a night, they didn't know how kind.

Soon enough he'd be on his way, but first he needed to do a bit of thinking. He felt that having come that close to throwing himself in the river, then being saved from it by an act of kindness, that he needed to make some gesture of thanks.

It seemed that it was time to settle a few things in his life. He'd go that day to the welfare agency. He'd tell them calmly, politely of his troubles and ask for their help. He'd go to one of the public bathrooms first to clean himself up. No, first he'd go next door and ask the Hollander girl if she'd keep Titus for him, until he got settled.

He'd heard they had billets for the homeless up in Albany. He'd do whatever they said and pitch in to whatever they asked him to. Perhaps he could get a bed in a dormitory and work in the kitchen, washing pots or peeling vegetables. Maybe if he were very good and worked hard they'd help him find a little place, a room somewhere. A place he and Titus could share together. Though he knew, much as it hurt him to know it, that places like that have rules against pets.

He couldn't bear it, but it seemed he must.

There was no point in putting off reading that letter, now that he'd already faced the worst. He opened it and read it through, then took it closer to the window to read again.

"Dear Captain," he read more carefully this time. "I would be honored if you would consider this little place yours for as long as you like. Ettie will show you the arrangements for water and so forth. I look forward to meeting you, when you find it convenient." The signature was illegible but he knew it was the colonel's.

He sat down in the ladder-back chair with a thump. There must be some mistake. People didn't just go around handing out snug cabins to bums. But Deen had said the colonel was a bit batty, yes, but surely not that batty?

A Post-it stuck to the back of the envelope came to his attention. In a different hand someone had written: "The outhouse is to left, in back." A rough map made no doubt as to its placement. It was welcome news—the Cap'n had been dying to take a leak, but had been holding it in.

Coming ever so quietly back in, he thought, Well, I'll just see what's in the thermoses, and wait. Ettie will explain it all.

When she tapped on the door he'd cleaned himself with a handkerchief and some water from a bottle, made the bed to military precision, and wiped the damp handkerchief over the toes of his boots.

She led him into the garden, to a terrace behind the house. The colonel was standing at an open window, above the Cap'n's head. He smiled, saying, "Welcome. I trust you slept well?"

"Wonderfully."

"Good. Now, I thought it better we don't meet in the house," the colonel said. "Independence and all that. You have your territory, I have mine. That shed there is yours for as long as you like, keep it neat and be careful with fire, and everything will be just fine. I inquired into city aid for the homeless, but it is a most unconscionable system. Couldn't understand one word they were saying. Seemed far better to forgo all that and make a bit of a berth here for you. Now, you keep things secure there, don't impinge on my comfort, and I won't impinge on yours, agreed?"

"Yes sir, Colonel, sir," the Cap'n said, saluting.

"You are also a military man, I understand?"

"Yes sir. Corporal Meens, U.S. Army, sir."

"Not, in fact, a captain?"

"No sir. They gave me that name as a joke."

"Well, in any case, I outrank you. Serve in Vietnam, did you?"

"Yes sir, I did."

"Kill the enemy?"

"When I had to."

"Nasty business. My generation didn't do a very good job of providing you youngsters with a good, clean war. You needn't comment on that. Now, a few ground rules. I understand you don't drink. That saves a hell of a lot of trouble. First, be careful of fire in the shed. Keep the key to the garden gate on your person and spend your days as you please, but be chary of telling others where you live. It's all highly illegal in any case. You and your cat may have full use of the garden. If you get in trouble, tell Ettie. If you're sick, tell Ettie. If that cat of yours is sick, tell Ettie. I will respect your privacy but I will also wish to know that you are well, that understood?"

"One hundred percent, sir. May I say something sir?"

"Certainly, Corporal."

"I am so grateful, and so is my cat. Thank you, sir."

"That's a hell of a fine cat, soldier. I never felt such fur. Now, you settle in and get some rest." The colonel lowered the window.

"I show you things," Ettie said, touching the Cap'n's elbow. "Just simple things now, I tell you more later, okay? This is a well, but covered, so no one fall in, over here is hose tap for your water. You can throw dishwater down the grate here. This is your key, for the gate. This is a lot of stuff under this tarp for you to make your place nice, it's all for you, the colonel, he thought it better if you fix it up inside yourself. I make you food and leave it on porch. Anything you need, you tell me. The colonel, he really mean it, you tell me if you need the doctor or anything. The children next door, he listens to them, they say help our old friend. They gone now, their uncle in England is sick. I tell you everything later, yes? For now, you sleep, rest. It's okay, the old man up there, he's good man."

Cap'n Meat listened attentively, nodding to show he understood, which he did, while also feeling as though he were sleepwalking.

Ettie stood looking up at him, a kindly, concerned expression on her face. He pulled himself together and said to her, "I think I might sleep quite a bit for a day or so, I don't seem to—"

"Yes, we talk later. I understand." Her brown eyes expressed more than she could convey with words.

The Cap'n nodded his head, then went to the cabin, where he fell into the stunned sleep of a person who's been through more than they could take.

Dusk was just falling when he woke. He lit the kerosene lantern on the table, adjusting the wick and putting its glass shade back on carefully. He pulled the curtains shut over the windows and did something he hadn't done in a long while—he undressed and pulled his spare set of clothes from his knapsack and put them on. Then he knelt in front of the stove and made a fire. He fed Titus, putting a sheet of newspaper down for the saucers, and tidied the quilt on the bed. He sat down in the armchair. A long while passed. It was deeply quiet inside the little cabin. He sat there for some hours, not looking around him. Instead he felt his surroundings, the heat from the stove snaking into the air, the hiss of the burning wood, the pale light on the yellow boards. He didn't move. Titus jumped onto the bed and went to sleep. The quietness crept into the Cap'n's being.

Water streamed down his cheeks, and into his beard. He didn't blink or make a sound. He felt a great many things but they were nameless, his hurt a blank washed by a rain. He saw images flicker in his mind, then go, replaced by another, unaware that his cheeks were soaked. Eventually he felt tired, so tired. He blew out the lamp, closed the damper on the stove, and went to bed. The tears that had salted his face came back in the middle of the night. He woke, letting out a muffled howl and cried knowingly then, with the abandon of a child.

***

The Cap'n slept for most of the next two days, getting up once in a while to feed Titus. Early on he left a note for Ettie on the porch: "Just sleeping, all is right." He knew she'd worry; she had a face for worrying.

In this he was correct. Without wishing to look like she was spying on him, Ettie had nonetheless kept a worried glance aimed at his cabin. And though she would never, ever tell anyone, she'd woken that night and heard the Cap'n sobbing like a lost child. It had nearly killed her not to go down and smooth his forehead and say words a mother would to a poor, sorrowful child.

On the third morning the Cap'n woke feeling a jauntiness he hadn't felt in a long while. All the things in his mind that had been confused seemed to have left him. He had no idea if this offer of the cabin were for real, but he'd make the best of it and that was all a man could do. Titus, who'd crept under the covers to sleep next to his stomach, let out a purr. Yes, that's the way to see things, the Cap'n thought, no use guessing and fussing, just find pleasure in what you have.

He got up and made a fire. He hadn't made one since that first day, and it had gotten cold inside the tiny structure, so he made it well and tended it for a while. He thought, as he did, that he'd look for a nice tin can, one that he could bank down a pile of live coals with each night, keeping them for a good blaze each morning.

He remembered what Ettie had said, about a pile of things under that tarp. Peeking out the window by the front door, he saw that Ettie was in her kitchen and the lights were on in the colonel's back parlor. Very quietly he went out and pulled back the tarp. There were all sorts of things under it. Boxes of tools and nails and screws, sawhorses and boards, what looked like a rug rolled up in paper, and a stack of plastic cartons. He opened one: it was filled with crockery. Another contained a set of well-seasoned iron skillets and a percolator.

He put the lids back on and went inside the cabin to think. It seemed the old colonel really did want him to fit the place up to suit himself. A thought snuck into his mind, one that was as pretty as a birthday cake hidden in a pantry—that he'd do a real job of it, make the place as tidy and practical as the cabin of a boat he'd once seen.

And maybe, a thought came that was so pleasing that he smiled, maybe Miss Ettie would poke her head around the door when he was done, see how bright and snug he'd made it. Why, he'd make a real job of it and scrub everything until it shone.

Another thought came into his head, but he quashed it as being too good to hope for, so please understand that he never did think it, but he did, just for a flash, imagine that Ettie would see how nice he'd made it and then tell the colonel, and that the colonel would nod approvingly. He never really thought it though, mind you.

He worked through the day and when he was done he sat to admire his labors. There were shelves over the counter now, covered in a red paper he'd edged in points. They were stacked with dishes and pots and supplies, which he'd taken a good deal of trouble to make orderly, and the teacups hung in a row from hooks. A mirror for shaving was hung by the window, with a crate below it that held towels and soap. The buckets and cleaning supplies were below the counter, which he'd skirted with a piece of blue checked fabric, carefully tacking it up with evenly spaced thumbtacks. The rug, a handmade wool oval with a pattern of ivy, covered the center of the red linoleum floor. His clothes and his pack were stowed under the bed. Beside them were a pair of the handsomest slippers he'd ever seen, which had come from one of the cartons. The last thing he'd done was to put the set of Dickens on the little shelf, where he added the few things he carried with him—some letters in a worn cloth pouch and his own book, *The Count of Monte Cristo.* It was a book he'd always found had something that reflected a day's hardships or joys.

He sat in the armchair, stroking Titus, who'd leaped onto his lap. Titus seemed to approve mightily of the arrangement of the cabin; he worked his claws into the Cap'n's trousers, just barely digging into his skin, his thick tail switching against the Cap'n's thigh.

And maybe a [illegible] expression [illegible] so alarming that he studied [illegible] Miss Elliot would press her hand around the [illegible] was done [illegible] [illegible] anything [illegible]

Another thought came [illegible] [illegible] [illegible] [illegible] [illegible] [illegible] and [illegible] the [illegible] and that [illegible] [illegible]

[illegible] the day, and when [illegible] was done [illegible] [illegible] over the [illegible] [illegible] paper [illegible] were [illegible] with dishes and pots and supplies [illegible] [illegible] and the [illegible] [illegible] which [illegible] [illegible] [illegible] [illegible] a [illegible] the centre of the [illegible]

[illegible]

27

Deen had now been incarcerated *chez* Dresden for nearly two weeks. You might not recognize her, if you happened to see her on the street with Kristen. Her face had grown closed-in and pinched, and she moved dully. Even her caramel-colored hair was limp and lifeless.

At night, on her futon, she imagined scenarios of revenge, but lately even those had ceased to interest her much. In fact, she'd taken to going to bed as early as possible and sleeping heavily until Kristen screamed at her to get up.

Her lessons with Paul were the one element of her old life that remained as before. She'd tried talking to him about her situation, but he'd cooked up a surefire way of dealing with what he didn't want to know—he ignored it. He pretended now that she went home as normal between lessons; at all other times Deen's presence and voice went unseen and unheard by him. He'd accused her of not practicing enough, which was perfectly true—she wasn't allowed to. He'd even taken to walking right through where Deen stood in the kitchen, making her step aside.

Naturally, Deen had thought of escape many times. She kept an eye peeled for ways she might, but Kristen had the instincts of a jailor. The door of the apartment was always locked and bolted, with a chest dragged in front of it for extra security. The sole phone receiver was kept at all times in Kristen's pocket, then taken to bed with her.

When they went out, which was rarely, she'd warned Deen that if she tried to run off she'd scream that the girl was being abducted by a child molester, a call that would rouse every citizen to grab her. It was, Deen acknowledged, a highly effective approach.

The windows in the kitchen were barred, being not much above street level, and Paul locked his studio each night. Kristen had also dug out a baby monitor, which she hung by the door; the other end was next to her bed.

In any case, Deen was sensible enough to realize that while she could perhaps effect an escape by night, that wandering the city streets in the dark might not be the wisest plan.

Kristen also held another threat over Deen's head—the threat to expose Deen's secret boogie-woogie to Paul. She worked Deen over, telling her that Paul would dismiss her as a pupil at once if he found out.

It was not a very good threat, but it worked. Deen carried a certain guilt regarding that other music, not so much out of a feeling of disloyalty to Paul but as a disloyalty to classical music itself. And, more potently, it was a secret of her inner self, a half-formed philosophy she was not ready to voice.

As always, in matters of guilt and subservience, there were also practical, self-serving considerations. As you know, Deen was a hard-headed little thing, and though she looked around her and saw that Paul was as mad as a fucking March hare, and his wife and spawn the bane of her existence, she wanted to continue her lessons with him. She wished to be a great musician more than she cared about a few weeks of misery.

***

On this day though, Deen woke from fevered dreams with a sudden lucidity. She realized something that filled her with worry—that humans adapt.

Everyone has felt this fear from time to time. How a desire to fit in, to cut oneself a little slack, can involve compromising certain elements of one's will. Send even the most ruggedly individual teenager off to boarding school and they will begin to model herself after whoever is in power among her peers. It begins with little things such as hairstyles and vocabulary, and can end with the worst—being a recognizable product of a particular boarding school for the rest of their life.

Send a person to prison and the same thing applies, though with admittedly higher stakes. But as anyone who's lived in an enforced environment knows, whether summer camp or boot camp, they come out in some way molded by the system.

What Deen realized that morning was that you could be placed in the very pits of hell, with imps poking at you day and night with red-hot pitchforks, and you'll begin placating an imp or two. That if Munster didn't return soon, she might start trying to win Kristen's favor.

With a small groan, she got up. There was no lesson that day, so she'd be stuck with Kristen's scintillating company for every hour of it.

The Blob was sucking its thumb in its high chair, the remains of a banana flung about it. Paul stared through her, then tried to walk through her, as he went to the sink. Deen twisted away just in time.

Later, as Deen was mopping the floor, Kristen decided to give her a lecture regarding female comportment.

"I told you, rinse the mop in hot water after each swipe. Look at little Miss Fancy, taking such dainty dabs. Put some elbow grease in it! Anyways, I've decided to give you a few pointers about life. Deen, at least nod, show you're paying attention, I'm telling you important stuff, like, older sis to younger sis, okay? The thing is, women and men are so different. Your mom probably told you that they're equals but you know what? She was lying to you. I'm sure she's all women's lib and that stuff, wants you to grow up with every opportunity and all, but sometimes we women have to tell one another the truth. Guys don't want women who are as good as they are. Or at least ones that don't know when to be quiet about it. You ever see me talking back to Paul? And you know why he married me? Because he's a real man and wants a real woman, one who's ladylike and keeps a nice home and cares more than anything about his baby."

Deen allowed these priceless insights to fall unheard around her as she stared down at the grimy floor. Her knuckles were swollen and red from repeated contact with hot water.

"I've got to tell you, Deen, it's only because I want to be like a real older sister to you, you're going to have to stop kidding yourself that you could ever be a great musician like Paul. I'm telling you that because, honey, I really care about you."

Deen clutched the mop handle, ready to break it over her knee, then beat the woman senseless with it. Instead she took a breath and reached behind her back, lighting one of the gas burners. She moved the mop across the floor, toward where the Blob lay in a plastic cradle. Pretending to stumble, she swung the mop up, running the wet strands over the Blob's head. It let out a howl like that of a witch being burned at the stake.

As Kristen rushed to it, Deen took the *Post* off the table and tossed it onto the stove burner, where it caught fire with a *flump*. As she moved to the door she flung the trash can behind her. The smoke alarm went off in a series of ear-destroying bursts of electronic noise.

Deen was out the door and on the street before she even realized it. Above her the sounds of Kristen and the Blob and the smoke alarm fought for primacy. She sprinted away, taking the opposite direction from home. She ran until she could run no more.

Gasping, she caught her breath and walked at a normal pace. She felt exhilarated. She'd finally taken action and escaped from that cow and her crazy-ass lectures. She let out a laugh—even all that caterwauling and fire alarms hadn't gotten Paul out of his studio.

It wasn't until she was on Grand Street that she realized she'd run away in jeans and a T-shirt. That she didn't have a coat, a cell phone, or two nickels to rub together. Kristen had made sure she never had any money.

Hell, she'd manage. She walked past a firehouse where inside a fireman was washing the engine. He stopped to stare at her curiously. She smiled at him and moved away. Shit, Hames had told her that if the DHS people got their hands on her she'd be dogmeat. That they were raptors, that children with AWOL mothers and dead fathers got snapped up by them and sent into foster care.

Goddamn Munster. Uh oh, people were looking at her, wondering why she didn't have a coat. She straightened up, taking her arms away from her chest, tried to look like the kind of numb kid who's impervious to the cold.

If only she had some change to make some phone calls. She could try asking someone who looked sympathetic for some quarters, but that kind of person might easily start asking questions.

As she walked through SoHo, her hands and feet began to freeze. The sidewalks were crowded, filled with strangers who pushed past her, making her move out of the way. A worry began to grow inside her chest. There had to be some way she could find someone to help her. The city she'd thought she knew so well suddenly felt strange to her, and the people frightening.

Maybe Elizabeth, her old piano teacher, would help her. She lived only a few blocks away. Deen made her way there and rang the buzzer. No answer, not even that troll she lived with was home. But it gave her an idea, so she walked north, to the Fieldings'. No one was there either. She thought about sneaking into the lobby and waiting for them, but it was one place Kristen might think of looking for her.

There was a cop on the corner, so she veered away, toward MacDougal. If only she could call Hames. Or Liall. Liall would understand, and Brenda had a key to the house. Wait—of course the colonel would take her in, would be glad to let her stay. Turning, she walked back toward Tenth Street and safety.

Feeling warmed already by the fire in his back parlor, she set out eagerly. Ettie would make a fuss over her and cook something special for dinner—oh, it was all going to be fine. She felt as if a great burden had been lifted from her.

But as she reached her block she saw a woman with a stroller standing before their front steps. Dammit, it was Kristen, she'd know that limp down coat anywhere. Deen hid behind a lamppost, thinking. There was no way she could get to the colonel's door unseen. Shit.

Despondent, she went back toward Washington Square Park. The light was getting that lemony, thin quality; it wouldn't be long till the sun went down. Panic rose in her throat like a creature trying to crawl out of her stomach. She went over to the dog playground, lurking, watching the faces of the people watching the dogs. The dog's antics were comical, as they sniffed at one another's asses and played at aggression. The kind of person who'd stop to watch them and smile, maybe that was the sort of person who'd give her a couple of dollars without asking all sorts of questions.

She was just sidling up to a woman when someone shouted, "There she is!" Without looking around, Deen moved swiftly away.

She stepped behind a tree near the chess tables, breathing hard. She stood quite still, then looked back. Letting out a sigh, she decided that no one was following her.

"That bishop is goin' away for life!" she heard one of the chess players cry. "The jury listened, then they came back and said 'Guilty, your honor' and now that bishop's goin' away."

It was Bed-Stuy, one of the regular chess hustlers. He'd always called out hello to her when she passed, and for some reason asked her for tips on the ponies. They weren't exactly friends, but surely he'd let her have a few bucks. She went closer to his table and waited till the game ended. She hoped he'd win, but he didn't.

"Hey, kid," he said. "What's up? What's surefire for the fifth at Belmont?"

"Can I talk to you for a sec?"

"Sure, kid." He got up and led her over to the path away from the tables. "What gives?"

"Can you lend me some money? Only a few dollars? I lost my pocketbook, my cell phone, and everything. I'll pay you back."

"Okay, okay, now keep your voice down, kid. No use in everyone knowin' your troubles. Where's your mother?"

"She's away. And I don't have my keys, or anything."

"Damn. Thing is, shit, I only have a dollar. Luck wasn't with me today, you know? But here, kid, you take it. You gonna call someone to come get you?"

"Yes, I'll call my brother."

"You gonna be okay? Hey, you want my Metrocard?"

"I'll be fine." Deen pocketed the quarters and turned away, calling out, "Thanks!"

Phone booths were becoming as rare as dinosaur eggs, but Deen found one on Sixth. She dialed Hames, only to get his voice mail. Upset, she hung up without leaving a message. Feeding another quarter into the slot, she dialed the number again.

"Hames, I'm in front of Charlie Mom's, on Sixth. I don't have my cell, don't call that number. I've run away. I really need help, I don't have anywhere to go. Call Charlie Mom's and leave a message for me, or come there. I'll check in there every half hour, okay? I really need your help. Don't call the Dresdens either, or tell them anything about this. If you have to, order a big take-out dinner and I'll say I'm waiting to meet you there, okay? Put it under Hollander and I'll know."

Looking at the two quarters left in her hand, she used one to get the colonel's number, then her last to dial it.

"Meester Harrington's."

"Ettie, it's Deen. I'm in big trouble. I've run away and have no place to stay. Could you help me?"

"Hello? Hello? Is someone there?"

Deen rattled the phone and jiggled its steel cord. "Ettie, it's Deen! Can you hear me?"

"I wait, is there someone there? Hello?"

"Ettie, please."

"Sorry, I cannot hear anyone. Sorry. Call back, I wait."

Deen wanted to smash the phone into pieces and burst into tears as she heard Ettie hang up. Her last goddamn quarter was gone and who knew if Hames would ever even listen to his fucking messages.

God, home was only a few blocks away. She wandered around the neighborhood glumly, hoping that Hames would get her message. The streets were dark now, the people on them lit by streetlights and the lights from shop windows. She hoped to see a panhandler with a coffee cup for change, so she could ask them for a handout herself, but none appeared.

When a half hour had passed she went to Charlie Mom's, to ask the man at the counter if there had been a message for her. No, he told her, there had been no calls for someone named Deen. He was so pale he looked as if vampires had drunk all his blood. He never looked up at her as he went on putting packets of forks and duck sauce in paper bags.

She went back out to the street. It was six o'clock and the people getting out of work filled the pavement, buffeting her this way and that. Trying to concentrate, figure out how to get some more quarters, she saw a great lumpy figure on the other side of the avenue.

"Cap'n! Cap'n!" she cried. The figure stopped, looking around. If only the streetlight would change, and she could run across, it seemed like he'd heard her, but ages passed before she could finally dash across the wide avenue. She ran between people, toward where she'd seen him last, all the bigger, taller people blocking her view.

He was still exactly where he'd stopped, looking around him with a worried expression. "Oh, Cap'n," Deen gasped. "I'm so glad to have found you."

"My dear, what's wrong?"

"I've run away. From these horrible people who were keeping me captive. I've been on the run all day and I'm so afraid the DHS might catch me, or a cop might call them, and I don't have any money and Hamish doesn't answer his cell phone."

"Tuck your arm under mine. All is well now." He steered her off the busy avenue to the quiet of Eleventh Street.

"I have no place to go," Deen told him. "Oh, and everyone's been crazy with worry about where you've been, I'm so glad you're all right. Cap'n, do you think you could help me find someplace safe to stay tonight? And this is awful, but could you possibly give me a few dollars?"

"My dear, it'll all be fine. I'm living at the colonel's, and I'm sure we can have this all sorted out in no time. We'll go straight there." He patted her arm and Deen felt lightheaded with relief.

He felt the girl dragging on his arm, and, his street instincts kicking in, he wheeled her smartly about.

"I forgot, she's waiting for me," Deen whispered.

"Who?"

"The woman I ran away from. She's been waiting in front of our house, hiding by the steps. Munster left me with her, so she thinks she's in charge."

The Cap'n never questioned Deen's need to avoid this person. He led her away. He knew all about avoiding the law. But he hadn't noticed that Deen was not dressed for winter until an involuntary shake ran up her arm.

"My dear, you must be freezing! Here, you take this five and go into this café, order a cup of tea. No, I insist. You must get warm. Tell the waitress that your mother is coming to pick you up, play it by ear, but get her sympathy without attracting too much sympathy, you understand? I'll have a bit of a think about how to get you to the colonel's past that sentry, all right? I'll make some phone calls. Here, you pretend to be looking in this shop window, while I adjust my bootlaces. I keep some money hidden in here. Look, here's a twenty, you take it, it may take two cups of tea. Order a wedge of pie too, and make sure you eat it. You're as cold as a block of ice. Now, go on in, I won't be more than a few steps away."

The twenty the Cap'n had pressed on Deen was his only money, from a secret emergency stash he kept in his boot. But he still had a number of quarters. What he really ought to do was scare that woman patrolling the Hollander house away. But it'd be no good for Deen if he were hauled off on a charge before he could see her safely to the colonel's. Goddamn it, he thought, but he knew how fragile life was without money, and he and Deen had so little. He'd explain everything to Ettie, she'd know what to do.

Twenty minutes later, he walked by the window of the café, giving Deen a thumbs-up sign. Seeing that no one else was looking, he signaled that it would be a half-hour wait. The girl nodded. She would've made an excellent soldier.

***

Mrs. D, when reached by the colonel, twigged to the delicacy of the situation immediately. As resourceful as ever, she called in a favor to an antiques dealer and had the entire campaign mapped out in minutes. In slightly less time than the Cap'n had signaled Deen to wait, a white van with a handsome gilt logo on the side pulled up in front of the café. Mrs. D stepped out of the passenger seat, as rigidly groomed as ever. She played the part of Deen's mother beautifully, kissing her and leading her out the door. She rapped twice on the back door of the van and when it was opened, helped Deen in. She got in next, then tugged and pulled to help the Cap'n aboard.

***

Kristen stood upon the frozen deck, her duty clear and her back straight. The girl had run away on her watch, and on her watch would be caught. The cold ran up from the pavement through her feet and up her legs to the crown of her head, but she was not going to fall down on the job. Any minute now, she could feel it, the miserable brat would come slinking toward her. And she, Kristen, would be waiting. She wouldn't say a word, just march the brat home and put her to bed. There'd be time enough to deal with her punishment in the morning.

A van pulled up, double-parking in front of the house next door. She turned to stare at it. Huh, some hoity-toity antiques shop uptown. Two burly men carried a wooden packing crate from its rear, then carefully took it up the steps, where they rang the bell.

Rich people, she thought, turning back to scan the street. All these rich people like the Hollanders and this neighbor of theirs, they act like owning antique treasures is nothing. Oh look, here's my new ruby centerpiece, as if the emerald one wasn't enough. When real people did just fine with a clean table and some nice casseroles.

She didn't notice that only one of the burly deliverymen came back out. From her spiderhole in the shadows by the doorstep she waited, lonely, ever vigil. The muted sound of voices seeped out of the house behind her, then the lights were turned out in the front. Still she waited. Someday someone would thank her for being so selfless and true.

28

Munster?"

"Deen, darling! I've been worried about you, Hames kept telling me you were all right, but I was beginning to think he was lying."

"I've run away from the Dresdens."

"Have you, darling? How resourceful."

"I'm staying at the colonel's. And you mustn't tell Kristen, it's a secret."

"Really? What a good idea. I'll worry about you far less there. I did worry, you know, did realize that leaving you with Kristen was a pretty terrible idea."

"Yes, Munster. It was. How's Uncle Brian doing?"

"Well, you know, a bit off really. He doesn't seem to be making much progress. The doctor seems quite puzzled, in fact. It's as if he doesn't *want* to wake up. I'm doing what I can."

"Well, don't worry about us, we're all fine. Hamish is moving in here too, we're going to arrange things to suit ourselves from now on. I need your Amex number—I want to order a car service so we can go up and see Gretchen. And I need some money, I ran away without a dime and I don't ever want to be in that situation again."

"Of course, darling. Got a pen?"

* * *

Kristen sat holding the phone, staring at it and chewing a ragged spot on her lip. Her eyes were circled by olive stains. She'd had a terrible night, the poor girl. The police had chased her away from her vigil by the Hollanders' front steps, after which she'd lain awake all night, fretting about that rotten, ungrateful child.

She looked again at the phone, knowing she ought to report Deen missing, but unwilling to admit her own part in the matter. She'd been sitting like that for hours, only getting up once in a while to tend to Rinaldo.

Paul had not said a word about Deen's absence that morning, but now he came into the kitchen and stood, staring down at her.

"It's half past two," he said. "Where's Ondine? Why isn't she here for her lesson? What have you done with her, you evil cunt? Have you let your foul urges get the better of you, done something you shouldn't have, woman? Out with it, where is she?"

"Oh, Paul," Kristen sobbed. "I've tried calling, but no one answers the phone. I'll go, I'll walk over there myself and leave a note if no one answers the door."

Paul stared at her as she jumped up and began putting on her coat. She avoided his eyes as he continued to stare. Then he turned and went back to his studio.

The tears froze on Kristen's cheeks as she practically ran toward Tenth Street, shoving the stroller before her. Oh please, oh please, let the little wretch be hiding behind a curtain, let her be in that house, rather than murdered in some alley, oh please, oh please, she'd be in such a shitload of trouble if Deen wasn't safe.

As she neared the house she slowed down, dreading her fate. She was jibbering, saying "Help me, help me, help me" in a whisper. She stood, looking up at the blank house. It stared back down at her, uncaring.

A last instinct for self-preservation rose in Kristen's mind—she turned to throw herself into the street, fall on her face, and have a tantrum. She didn't think it all through, simply wished to end her responsibility in life, let someone else pick up the pieces. She was adjusting her mittens, for she didn't want to hurt her hands, when a sound stopped her cold. The sound of a piano being played nearby. Her eyes squeezed shut in her fit of madness, she felt for the handle of the stroller, and inched toward it. It was coming from the house next door. And it was Deen in there, she knew it, playing some ringing sounds, ringing out behind those heavy curtains she saw, as her eyes flew open in fury. Sitting there like some fairy princess in some goddamn fairy tale, eating cakes and wearing a bow in her hair, playing the piano as if nothing were wrong, the miserable, ungrateful little *brat*!

Now the consequences of what she'd nearly done came home to her, how if she'd thrown herself screaming into the street, her darling, her angel, would have been taken away from her, while she was hauled off to Bellevue. How the cops would go and knock on the door, take one look at Paul, and haul him off to Bellevue too.

She had to think hard. No, she wouldn't run up those steps and beat on that door. She wouldn't take any more chances. She'd wait for her revenge, would exact it in the fullest way, but only when it was safe. She'd get that girl and good, for nearly making her lose her precious one. It was all that miserable brat's fault.

When she got home Paul was waiting in the kitchen. It scared her—he never came in there before supper.

"She's hiding out with some rich people, in the house next door," Kristen told him as she began unwrapping Rinaldo from his winter gear. "I suppose she's decided we aren't good enough for her, don't have enough silk drapes or servants. I talked to her, she said she didn't want to come back. I told her how much we love her and care, but she was so snotty to me. After all I've done for her too. Paul? Come back, I want to *talk* to you!"

But Paul had locked himself back into his studio.

***

With an imperceptible lurch, the earth began its progress toward a new season and the sun began to wrest the frozen hues of winter from the city. The last traces of snow packed into shadowed corners began to melt, the crusts of soot on top carved away like a shell. In a garden in front of one of the old brick houses on Washington Square a flower bed showed the green spearheads of tulips poking through the soil.

Deen stood, gripping the iron palings to look at them. She felt much gladder to see them than she could explain. She decided that she'd make a trip here every day to check their progress.

She ran catty-corner across the park, skipping around oncoming pedestrians, feeling like she could leap up in the air and stay there. She was going to buy some new sheet music and was deliriously free. As she flew past a popular NYU eatery something caught her eye and she stopped, peeking inside.

A boy with long brown hair was sitting alone at a table. Deen stared at him, wishing that she knew him. He had an awfully nice face, long and rather sad with a beaky nose, not at all movie-star handsome, but she liked it very much. He looked intelligent, and as if he had sophisticated ideas about books and things. She wished she were grown up and could go in and talk to him. It was utter hell being fourteen.

She skipped off, a child again in an instant, happily thinking of digging around in racks of old scores.

Most girls Deen's age had already flirted and kissed, gotten crushes and perhaps even encountered what seemed like unbearable heartache at the time. But Deen had lived in a world of grown-ups, had no school chums or brothers of school chums, in fact, had never known a presentable man under forty. There was Liall, of course, but he was just a kid. Her only contact with a boy her own age had been the son of a friend of Sadie's from London, who had held hands with her furtively as they watched TV one night. Even she had not been able to spin a great romance out of it.

***

Gretchen got out of bed and opened the window. She looked out at the acres of lawn, scattered across which the trees were looming black shapes in the faint moonlight. The night air smelled of plants stirring. It smelled of damp and red twigs and things uncurling beneath leaves. It was not time yet, but soon. The moon rose over the woods, it was just past the new, a fine sickle. When it was full, she decided, she would go out and run beneath it. Her bare feet would bring up the scent of the greenness.

***

Deen was playing Bach's *English Suite,* one of the colonel's favorites. Normally he took a nap upstairs between lunch and tea, but nowadays he liked to sit in his parlor listening to her play. As he lay back in his armchair, he felt a contentment he had never known. He'd felt much of it lately, in his new life here in Greenwich Village, but never so keenly as when listening to the girl play.

Next she played Beethoven's *Appassionata* and a groan of love for that piece rose from his throat. There could be nothing better than this, after all those years confined to a home for the insane. To live again in a real house with all his family furnishings, listening to Beethoven played by a girl he'd grown to love, and wondering what sort of sandwiches there would be for tea.

Ettie, in her basement kitchen, knew not to run any equipment or smack the fridge door during Deen's music. The old man, he likes his music so well, she said to herself. And Deen, what a good girl. She does her lessons and is quiet, sets the table, and always offers to help with trays.

Ettie doubted though, that playing long-haired music would ever be much of a way for Deen to make a living. But she was sure in her heart, which was decorated with cupids and three layers of lace, that some tall handsome boy would one day hear her play so nice and full and kneel right down then and there to ask her to marry him. She thought about what she'd wear to the wedding. A suit, she thought; a really nice suit, maybe lilac, with some fur or metal embroidery. She could ask Mrs. D to help her find a really nice one, but no—Mrs. D would find something good for sure, but too plain, no touches or ruffles that would show how glad she was to see her little Deen marry a nice tall rich young man.

"My dear, that was just grand," the colonel said to Deen as she joined him for tea. "Can't say when I've been so happy. You know, your playing has advanced quite a lot, there is a certain *je ne sais quoi*—"

"That's the problem," Deen said.

"*Je ne sais* nothing," Robert said, coming in. "I was outside listening the whole time, still as a statue. That was the thump-thump, she's got the heartbeat in the notes now. Hey, what problem, Deen?"

"Well, because I ran away, Paul won't want to teach me anymore."

"That's a problem," Robert said, looking thoughtful. "Man, that's a big problem. I didn't think about that. There's about nobody you could get who's a finer pianist. Yes, thank you, Colonel, I think I will take a drink. I'll need one to puzzle over this here problem."

"Ah, that'll be Mrs. D," the colonel said, hearing the front door. "We'll lay the situation out to her. Fear not, she'll have an answer. A most remarkable woman."

"What've you all got your bonnets together for?" Mrs. D asked as she came in. "What're you plotting? Christ, this house is such a hotbed of activism. Hell yes, I'll have a drink. Cheers."

"We were discussing the possibility that Deen, having absented herself rather abruptly from the Dresden household, might no longer be able to continue her studies with Paul," the colonel explained.

"Oh, that!" Mrs. D said, waving her hand—*pff!*

Deen glared at her—how dare she treat her music so offhandedly?

"Don't give me that look," Mrs. D said to her. "I've taken it all in hand. I sent the great Paul a letter. I gave him all the details, including what sort of piano the colonel has. It was coded in a rather obvious way and written on faked letterhead from a music company; naturally I assumed that that creature he lives with would read it, but she's not very clever, is she? In fact, I invited him to join us here this evening."

"But he *never* goes out," Deen said.

"Yes, that is an issue, Deen," Mrs. D said. "But there are ways around it, if we have to go to another plan. I have a few thoughts."

Hamish came in. "You started drinking without me," he said.

"Have a ginger ale, my boy," the colonel told him. "Have a double. Look, Ettie made ham salad sandwiches, as well as the usuals."

"Ham salad?" he said, doubtfully.

"Indeed, my boy. Ham and tiny bits of hard-boiled eggs and paprika and celery and mayonnaise. Your innocent belief that chicken salad is the best the world has to offer is about to be exploded."

"Can we be members of the Thursday Night Imbibers' Club, now that we're living here?" he asked.

"Certainly. But remember, the real imbibing's for grown-ups only."

Ettie came in to refresh the trays just then, so she was there when the front bell rang, and so was a party to what occurred next. The members of the TNIC sat rigidly silent, listening as Ettie opened the door. They didn't dare look at one another as she showed in a small man with disheveled brown hair.

"That cunt tried to stop me from going out," he announced. "I thought about hitting her with a hammer, but find I'm over that phase of my life."

"Have a drink?" the colonel said to him.

"No, I don't drink. In fact, I'd advise you to put that bottle under lock and key."

"Are you going to come and give Deen her lessons here now?" Robert asked.

"Where's the piano?"

"In there."

Paul went to the front parlor and played a series of scales, some delicate and some so fortissimo that the lusters on the candlesticks rattled.

"Yes," he said, coming back in.

"Well, that's just splendid," the colonel said. "Just splendid. We'll make sure that everything is just as you like it—say the word and it's done."

Paul had picked up a tea sandwich, finished it, then picked up another. He took another and ate that too. He took out a handkerchief, unfolded it, and put a stack of them in it, folding it and putting it back in his pocket.

"No crowds like this, I can't stand having anyone lurking about. No telephone calls, no socializing, and no one lets that cunt I'm married to know anything about it. Also, I must never be touched, that has to be quite clear. Oh, and I think I'll need a tray of sandwiches just like these. Did you make these?" he said, turning to look at Ettie.

"Yes," she said, blushing.

A strange thing happened to Paul's face—his mouth opened and stretched at the corners, showing crooked brown teeth.

Ettie made the sign of the cross as unobtrusively as possible.

***

Hamish went down to the kitchen to help Ettie with dinner. She was just finishing a tray to take out to Cap'n Meat. "I give him sandwiches like club on Thursdays," she explained.

"Can I take it out to him, Ettie?"

"Oh yes, that's nice. Stay and talk to him, dinner just some little things you already know how to make. Here's something for that cat, and here, tulips for him, smell of spring. That's good, yes, that Deen's teacher came? Is he, you know, a motherless one? I see in him no mother."

"I'll find out for you. What did you think of his face?"

"All twisted up, like no part match another. A most sad face. I don't see the hammer there though."

"Well that's good, there are an awful lot of fragile things upstairs he could smash with one," Hamish said cheerfully. He peeked under the tea towel covering the tray. "Say, the Cap'n ought to have some of your lemon squares, don't you think? They're about the best thing I ever ate."

"Oh, I forget! So much excitement. The doctor, your mother's friend, was here today. He give the Capitain medicines and tell me, Ettie, don't give him much sweets. A real doctor, he talks to *me*, in his fine coat. He smokes so much!"

"Yeah, he's a real walking chimneystack," Hames said, picking up the tray. He disappeared before Ettie could ask him to tell him what that word meant. So she wrote it as best she could on her pad, to ask him later, carefully writing "shimneseck" in her schoolgirl's hand.

Hamish never saw the lamplight glowing from the windows of the cabin without wishing he could live in just such a place one day. He stopped for a moment to savor it, then knocked on the Cap'n's door.

"Hamish, my boy," the Cap'n said, opening it wide. "A cap to a most perfect day. Come in, come in."

Hamish put the tray on the table by the woodstove, in which a fire burned brightly, the flames leaping up to show themselves behind the grate.

"Here, my boy, sit down. You're smaller, so I'll give you the stool. I found it in a trash heap only yesterday, isn't it nice? Oh, but perhaps you have other things to do."

"Nope. I thought I might stay for a little while. Would that be all right?"

"Share dinner with me, my boy. Here, I'll give you a glass of pink lemonade. Made it myself, from pink lemons. Ah, just look at these sandwiches. And what are these?"

"Tulips. Ettie said for spring."

"Flowers. A woman's touch," the Cap'n said quietly, holding them.

"Women are weird about flowers. Munster would spend her last ten bucks on a couple of roses, I don't get it."

"Women *are* flowers, my boy, they are pretty and vivid, while we men are but shapeless lumps. I'll put these in a jar. Go ahead, dig in, have some dinner, I know you can eat for an army, it's natural in a boy your age."

"Well, I might just have a bite. . . "

After Hamish had left the Cap'n tidied everything away. He wiped each plate and glass and stacked them, to wash in the morning, with hot water he'd heat on the stove. He fussed after the crumbs on the table, picked up some bits from the floor, then tweaked the stems of the tulips so that they looked nicer. He put them a bit closer to the center of the table, where he would be able to see them better from his bed. He turned all the lamps down but one and banked the fire for the night. Seeing a smudge on the linoleum he took a cloth to it. He wouldn't like to think that if the colonel made a spot inspection of the cabin he'd ever find anything to criticize. He took off his shirt and trousers, folding them neatly and placing them in the tin trunk under the bed, then put on the wool bathrobe the doctor, Mrs. Hollander's friend, had given him. He sat at the table and read another one of the letters from his oilskin packet. It hurt less to read them now.

Titus was curled like a pill bug at the foot of the bed. Except for occasional spells on the Cap'n's lap, or a turn around the garden, he slept there, seeming to think that a bed was about the best place a cat could be. He was still afraid, the Cap'n knew, that this bed could go away, so he needed to spend as much time on it as possible.

The Cap'n closed the grate and blew the lamp out. He hung his robe on the hook by the head of the bed. He felt for Titus in the dark, running his hand over his fur. Titus let out a rumbling purr. Carefully he edged into the bed, sneaking his feet past the cat's form to make a hollow for him. In a few hours, when the cabin became chilly, the cat would wake him by tapping with a paw on the edge of the sheet. The Cap'n would roll onto his side to let the cat under the blankets, then man and cat would warm each other, sleeping well till dawn.

and no one [illegible] them [illegible] the [illegible]
[illegible] the [illegible] and [illegible]
[illegible] had [illegible] at the [illegible] and [illegible]
[illegible] to [illegible]

This was [illegible] at the foot of the bed. Except for
[illegible] in the [illegible] the garden [illegible]
[illegible] the best place [illegible]
[illegible] was [illegible] the [illegible] that [illegible]
[illegible] as possible.

The Captain [illegible] the grave [illegible] He [illegible]
[illegible] in the [illegible] the [illegible]
[illegible]
[illegible] into the [illegible]
[illegible] the [illegible]
[illegible] The
Captain would [illegible] that
[illegible]

29

"Quite honestly, I'm at a bit of a loss," Mendel-bendel was saying to Sadie. They were having a private chat in his office. "I've treated numerous such cases, am in some way an expert in these matters, and by all reasonable expectations Brian should be fully conscious by now. All indications are that the neck is healing, and all other signs, reflexes, EKGs, and so on, show normal activity. I can find no injuries or lesions to the brain that would explain this persistence of nonresponsiveness.

"May I ask you something? Not merely as a friend of Brian's, but also I hope, as a friend to me?"

Christ, the old lecher was flirting with her again. She was getting bloody tired of his little smirks and glances. She'd looked into getting Brian another surgeon but had discovered, much to her chagrin, that old Mendel-bendel was the best in the business. What the hell, play along with the old goat, after all, she'd gotten herself into this mess.

"Of course," she said. "Fire away."

"Thank you, Sadie." *The old goat liked saying her name, it gave him a tingle. And he always says it with that little smirk.* "I appreciate that. What I want to know is this—now, leaving out the natural mental ups and downs of the artistic type, tell me honestly, would you describe Brian as capable of a profound depression? I'm going to treat you as informed and sensitive enough to know what I mean. Did he have any tendency, hidden perhaps, to dark thoughts?"

The old goat had a point, Sadie had to admit, because it just wasn't like Brian to be pulling this shit. So she thought carefully, looking back, checking Brian against other templates.

"No," she said eventually. "I really can't say he does. He was getting a bit older, that can be a bit difficult, and his teeth aren't top notch, but hell, he's English. He had projects and plans and hopes and was getting laid pretty regularly by vastly younger women. He's always been a thoughtful person, but not terribly fraught—I never saw him afraid. He did do heroin back when, but actually got himself off it quite early on. He's always been very sturdy about life, took the knocks that came his way with a good deal of fortitude, and has a true enjoyment of the good bits. And by what I know about the accident it was simply that, a case of overly high spirits in one a bit too old for such tricks. But I agree—something doesn't add up. I feel it when I touch him—he's here but he's very far away."

"Well," the doctor sighed. "We'll just have to carry on. I'm sure your presence is the thing he needs most now. You are talking to him?"

"Christ, yes. I babble at him all morning and every evening. Then go back to that ghastly hotel and get royally drunk." *Oops, I shouldn't have said that, his goat eyes just registered a flicker—so, she gets drunk all alone each night? Might be interested in company? Move on to a different topic, one that says strangers need not apply.* "I've left my children alone for weeks now, and my eldest is in a psychiatric institution." *Oh, dearest Gretchen, forgive me for using you that way.*

"May I ask for what?"

"She stopped talking about a year ago. Then began cutting herself. She went too far several times, nearly died. Worse, actually, is that she simply does not seem to engage in life now in any way."

"I'm very sorry. Perhaps you should go home to see her. I assure you I'll give Brian my full attention. I've even made some inquiries into whether those vultures from the press can be removed from the front steps. It's horrible the way they circle around the dying."

There was a silence. Sadie looked at him for a long moment, her eyes very serious. She stood, leaning over the desk to really get the message across. Dropping all pretense at coyness or charm she gave him the real Sadie, in fact, gave him the Look.

"If he's dying, for no good reason whatsoever, under your care," she told him in a low voice, "if that's what you really think's happening here, you're going to do something to change that, understand? No, *everything*. This is *your* patient and *your* conscience on the line here.

"I'm going back to my hotel and think about what *I* can do for Brian. I advise you to do the same, to get out his file and think hard about some way out of the bollocks you've made of his treatment. I expect you to have some ideas in the morning, when I will want to meet with you to talk them over. Is that quite clear?"

He nodded, looking stricken as Sadie wound her shawl over her shoulders and left.

Sadie looked longingly at the vodka bottle in her faux loft, then looked resolutely away. She'd been keeping off the booze in the afternoons so she could arrive for her evening visits to Brian sober, then hitting the bottle hard when she came back.

Rain was falling on the gray waters of the Thames. She stood, looking down at it, too disturbed to do anything but stare, to hold herself fast. She *must* be able to think of some way of reaching Brian. Instead, inane thoughts crowded her mind, mixed up with Polaroid images, memories of Brian that flashed and shuffled inside her retina. Then the stricken look in the surgeon's eyes when he realized what he'd said, how she had read in them the truth, that Brian was very likely dying. Ever since reading about the Styx as a child she'd had an image of it, of a twilit, cindery shore by a wide, silent river, beneath a dome of rock. She saw Brian lying on the cinders, strapped on his back into a stretcher, waiting. All the while the vodka bottle burned its image into her back.

Throwing on a coat, a hat with a floppy brim and dark glasses, she left the room hurriedly. A cab was just dropping someone off at the entrance, she got into it and asked the driver to take her to Harrods. King Harrods', she used to call it, back when life was all a wheeze.

She had to take action. Do something to jump-start Brian's mind, and the only thing she could think of was hitting his senses. She asked the driver to pull up at a Barclays across the street. There she cashed a check from RRC for a thousand quid, asking the teller to give it to her all in new twenties. Feeling more than a little mad, she explained to the girl what she wanted them for—to strew over the bed of a dear friend who wouldn't wake up from a coma. "Because nothing smells more redolent of life than newly printed pound notes," she explained.

Dashing across the street to Harrods, she bought raspberries, a boom box, a stack of CDs, an insanely expensive silk paisley dressing gown in tanager shades from lemon to scarlet for Brian, presents for her children, a velvet scarf that was almost exactly like the one she'd worn until it fell to pieces in the sixties, and a bottle of L'Heur Bleu, the scent she'd always worn, but had forgotten to pack in the rush.

One of the liveried doormen helped her get all the bags into a taxi, tucking them around her with grave politeness.

"St Elfreda's Hospital," she told the driver. Gawd, it looked like she'd bought half the store. It was going to be hell on her bank balance. Oh, fuck it. Wait, there was something else Brian needed, what was it? Cannabis, he needed some really good sticky bud waved under his nose. If that didn't make him want to sit up and join the party again, nothing would.

"Driver, could you stop at that pub, please? I need to pick up a bottle."

"They can't sell no bottles, you got to go to an off-license."

"Yes, but you see, I'm engaged in a fight against death itself."

"Well then missus, you better find one very good weapon. Go on, I wait for you."

***

Gawd, this is such a nightmare," Sadie said to Brian. "Why don't you bloody wake up? Oh, Brian, wake up, won't you please?" She leaned over to kiss him, they'd taken that plastic thing off his neck and he was far easier to kiss now. She'd doused her own neck in about twenty quids' worth of L'Heur Bleu, so she hovered over him to give him the full benefit of it.

"This is boring the holy living shit out of me, you know that, you lying there week after week with nothing interesting to say. Do you know your piss is going out of you in a little tube? How undignified. I have no idea what they're doing with your other excretions and don't want to. No," she said, holding her hand up, "I know you'd love to tell me, but please, spare me that.

"Jesus, I'm so bored! So bored I can't even *begin* to imagine having a lively time again. It's no good your saying that I'm exaggerating, I simply won't believe you.

"In any case, I've decided I'm bloody fed up with not having a nip in the evenings, like a normal person, so I brought all the fixings."

The bartender at the pub had not just been the sort of person Sadie could talk to, he'd been the sort who liked women like Sadie. Which boomeranged right back to the sort of men she liked. It almost invariably went that way, she found. He'd provided her with a bottle of Stoli, a bag of ice, and two sliced limes, which he'd folded into a paper napkin.

She put the bag of ice in a bedpan and fixed herself a drink. "Ahh," she said, plumping up the pillows on the other bed and sitting back to take a sip. "I should've done this ages ago, Brian. What was I thinking? Here, have a whiff of what you're missing." She jumped up and waved the glass under his nose.

Sadie drank and talked to him, recalling old jokes and describing small details of her days that she found amusing. As she got drunk her chatter became more animated and she began imagining his responses, talking back to him as if it were just like one of the many evenings they'd spent together.

***

Drunks are not terribly heavy sleepers. Well, they are when they pass out, but as the booze is gradually broken down by their livers their bodies begin to clamor for correctives, for water, fruit juices, aspirin, platters of French fries, and so on, waking them in jolts.

Sadie woke in the hours before dawn. About to reach an arm out to search for water, she froze. Something was wrong. It took her a minute to figure out where the hell she was, then locate the source of her unease.

It was a whistling sound, coming from Brian's bed. Getting up, she went over to look at him. He looked even worse than usual, his face greenish and waxy, as if he were practicing for death. The whistling sound was coming from his lips. Quickly, Sadie scanned the machines he was hooked up to, but everything seemed normal. But she knew in her heart that he was near to giving up, and she could not let him.

Moving her hands to the top of his head, she willed her fingers to draw out the bad then send an entirely different juju back in. Putting all the force of her will into it, she went into a sort of trance. Later, feeling very tired, she sat by his side and spoke quietly to him.

"Brian, I couldn't bear for you to leave me. I'd be so alone. I'd have to start life all over again, and I don't know if I could. I've been turning things over in my mind, taking stock. There's something I believe you've always wanted. I hope I'm not making a complete ass of myself, but Brian, if I'm right and you do want that, we could give it a whirl. We've always been so close, much closer than to anyone else. All those years we were all together you and I trained ourselves to never even think about it, which was of course the only way to do it, but possibly I let myself become boxed in by that, stopped looking at you as a man, only saw dear old Brian. Oh, Brian, if you'll only wake up I promise to try to please you. I love you. Please don't leave me alone here."

Sadie keeled gently over and fell asleep by his side. Outside the window the dawn gradually became a gray London sky and the sparrows cheeped in the streets.

Just before breakfast the day duty nurse peeked in. She was touched at the sight of Sadie curled up by his side. She stepped in softly, trying not to wake her. She noted with approval that Sadie had not jostled her friend, but had fitted herself in like a mouse in the small bit of available mattress. It was a pretty sight, with her hand holding his. No wait—his was clasped around hers. Disbelieving, she leaned closer to make sure. And look, his color was better too, she was sure of it. That was odd—why was there a great wad of pound notes under his pillow?

Longing to fly at once to find Mr. Mendelsen, she nevertheless crept out quietly, closing the door behind her, then began to run down the corridor.

***

Later, when the surgeon had gone, looking pleased at Brian's progress, Sadie turned to Brian. "I do hope you're going to make an effort today," she said. "Begin at least by opening your eyes. Otherwise I shall be quite put out with you."

As she chattered away she prayed mightily that Brian didn't recall all the details of her semi-drunken offer. She did hope he had felt the spirit of it, the love bit, but not the other bits.

Brian was thinking hard. *Hmm, all right then, I think I've got it. I'll hint just enough that I do remember her half-drunken offer. So she'll know I'm thinking about it. It'll be a long campaign, because I can't begin the next phase until I'm really fit again, will need to wait until I'm back in fighting trim. After that I'll make her wait a goodish while, worrying, do I remember or don't I? She'll go through all the stages of embarrassment and remorse, then start to get curious as to why I'm not making eyes at her. I'll act like I'm really not all that interested, in actual fact. Then, because she's a woman and vain as hell, she'll start to get shirty, wonder why I'm not? Start to wonder if she's not attractive enough anymore. Get right ticked off about it, begin to flash a bit of boob in the morning, fall languorously asleep in front of the fire, brush up against me. Christ, I'd better swear off alcohol during that phase. Then, when she's worked herself up into a nice state of rage at my indifference, then and only then will I take her to my bed and show her finally and once and for all, what a good man's love is.*

30

A carved figure of a cow, made of stone, sat rather disconsolately on a table in the living room of the house on West Tenth Street.

It was many hundreds of years old and had been made by a man who carved temple figures for a living, a master carver who had turned the reddish, fine-grained piece of stone in his hands to study what form lay inside it. He had felt it to be a she-cow. He saw how she sat, her legs folded under her, her left hind leg tucked beneath her stomach. She had a gentle, gazing face, and around her neck she wore a garland with a bell on it.

It was lonely. Where had its latest owner and her children gone? It worried a bit, in its stone head, that they might never come home. Then it would be sent off again to another place. It was inevitable that it would go to many places in its time, this was to be accepted, for being made of stone it had, and probably would continue to outlive, its owners, who were made of flesh.

But some places were far better than others. There was that time it had lain in a heap of rubble for ever so long, for instance. And that very nasty man who'd used it for a doorstop, those had been exceptionally dull days. There was no use in complaining about it, of course, but it much preferred a bit of liveliness around it, some talk and dancing even.

It liked its present situation very much. Its latest owner had always been exceptionally kind to it, and the house was filled with music of a very superior sort. The woman even talked to it from time to time; it had been a long while since anyone had been so civil. And her children had petted it, enriching its skin with the oils from their fingers. The woman had even seemed to have a certain reverence for it, had always placed it carefully among her other things, according it a respect it most certainly had not known during that spell it spent in a dark, untidy curio shop in Hammersmith, where she'd found it.

So it worried, as a mantle of dust grew on its back. It knew from experience that as the layer of dust grew, so also did the probability of change.

It sighed. Well, there was nothing to be done about it. It would try to be good and not cry, as a hand reached out for it, to wrap it in paper, then shut it into a box.

***

Brenda unlocked the kitchen door and hung up her coat. A huff came from her lips, leaking from her soul. "Liall, you get out your schoolwork and sit quiet at the table there to do it, now," she said. "Later maybe, you can go to the park."

Muttering to herself, she got out her arsenal of cleaning supplies. Mutter, mutter. Only the mouse that lived under the dishwasher could make out her words, and even then with no very great precision. She seemed to be complaining about cleaning some big empty house that no one hardly set foot in. The mouse felt sympathetic to these thoughts—it was perfectly understandable that the vacuum-woman should feel irate. In fact, he quite agreed with her—why dust and polish this great barn of a place where no one dropped crumbs or left packets of food lying about?

When she'd gone, Liall and the mouse shared the silence that wrapped itself around them. The boy put his mind to his schoolbook, then a gust of April wind rattled the area door in its frame, causing them both to look up hopefully, then go back to what they were doing, for there was no one at the door.

The fifth time the door rattled, Liall put his hands over his ears. He'd figured out that it was the gusty wind making that sound, but each time felt disappointed that it wasn't one of the Hollanders. Each time he'd feel a heart-jump of hope, so he did the only sensible thing, he tried to blot it out. The mouse, a more instinctual creature when it came to sounds, had long since given it up as a bad job, and fallen into a disgruntled sleep.

* * *

Kristen had become fixated on finding Deen. She patrolled the area around the Hollanders' block, hoping to waylay the girl. She was determined to have a mother-daughter talk with her. You see, Kristen knew that she herself was a good and caring girl, and only wished to straighten a few things out with Deen. It was important that she do it before Sadie returned though, for the girl might tattle all sorts of nonsense about her to her mother if she didn't. Though she kept an eye out for that blond woman, Mrs. de something. She didn't want to cross her path again, risk another chewing out.

She carried her mission out on the afternoons Paul went out for his mysterious meetings, something about a recording contract was all he'd tell her, screaming at her not to ask any more questions and forbidding her to follow him with all sorts of horrible threats. He hadn't been at all nice to her lately. He'd even stopped eating the food she cooked so lovingly for him. She knew she wasn't any fancy three-star chef, but what she cooked was always wholesome. He'd thrown a perfectly good turkey sandwich at the wall the other day, saying it was an abomination against man and God.

Oh, if only she could catch that brat, where was she? If Deen tried to run from her she'd make sure she got a hold of her hair and *make* her listen. There were important things she had to tell her, about manners and being grateful to grown-ups who do things for you, and how we women need to stick together. Oh, if only the miserable brat could see how she'd really tried to be a good, caring mother to her, how she'd even *liked* having some female company around for a change. How if Deen could've just stopped being so sullen and looked around her, she would've seen that Kristen really cared for her, loved her in fact.

She was bending over, adjusting Rinaldo's snowsuit, when a voice said, "I want a word with you."

Straightening up, she was dismayed to see that sharp-eyed blonde, the one who'd come banging on the door that night.

"Let's have a little chat, shall we?" Mrs. D said, taking Kristen's arm. "No, I wouldn't pull away if I were you, I'm quite capable of making life very difficult for you. I've thought it all out, you see, and it's quite a good plan. You might not end up in jail, but you will find yourself in the clutches of the legal system. And in those cases they always send someone around to look into the welfare of any children in the household. Perhaps place them in foster care until the suitability of the parents can be determined. We'll walk this way, shall we?

"The weather is nice, isn't it? One can really feel spring coming on. Now let's make this as plain as possible. If I catch you anywhere near the Hollander house again, I'll put my plan into motion. And I promise you, I'll see it through. I'm known for my efficiency.

"It might also be helpful if you took a good long look at yourself. You see, locking up little girls and subjecting them to verbal abuse is not a nice thing to do. I might even characterize it as borderline sociopathic behavior. I've had a difficult time actually, wondering if I should call in Human Services anyway, to make sure you're not doing anything to harm your own child. But Deen's quite a brave girl, did you know that? She insisted that while you might not be the best of mothers, you'd never do any real harm to your baby.

"Psychiatric help would be in order. Though of course you'll lie till you're blue in the face to the counselor. Still, I think it would be best. Here's my card, have your counselor call me within a week to confirm that you are having regular sessions. I'll follow up to see that you do continue, be very sure of that. I think a year would be the least one could hope to see some improvement, all right?

"This is your door, I believe. Good-bye."

* * *

A figure slunk by the town houses on West Tenth Street, making notes in his crazed mind. His rage-filled eyes were hidden by his hood. He looked up at the lighted windows, knowing that there was warmth and comfort behind them. He whispered his curse upon them. Them that let old bums camp in their gardens. For hadn't he finally tracked down that fat old bum, followed him, seen with his own eyes, that damn bum letting himself in that garden gate, with his own key?

Later, in a foul pocket of the undercarriage of the city he screamed up at the sky; "Motherfuckin' idol worshippers! Greenback fuckers, livin' in houses the size of a fuckin' king's! Roll on piles of money till it brings up *blisters*. So fine and rich that if they take a shine to some old fat bum that they feed him off plates of *gold*! Cook up twenty chickens to feed him with, fillin' the air with chicken juices. All for one solitary, goddamn bum."

The Angry One let out a bloodcurdling scream, raising his arms to the sky. "All that food? That they fed him off of plates of gold? I'll cut it out of his belly! Watch it *spill* to the ground!"

***

Gretchen had been watching changes in herself. She saw first that she loved books again, then nature, looking for hours out the windows at the trees and plants, noticing their leaves growing.

Also, the place inside her where she stored her hatred of the wicked nurse was nearly complete. She could almost describe its shape. It felt good to hate someone. Lately she'd been very canny, had eluded the wicked nurse's pinchings. And she'd drawn a picture of her, one that looked just like her, but subtly showed all the ugliness and evil in her, and left it lying in the cafeteria. The staff had passed it around, snickering. And no one tried to pin it on her, everyone knew she just drew that dog, which had to be drawn quite badly.

She'd also decided to cut down on the pills. Keeping them under her tongue until they could safely be disposed of, she pretended to still be pliably medicated. In a week or so she'd be off them completely. It wouldn't do to stop taking them in one go, she knew, having a certain knowledge of drug lore through her upbringing.

That morning someone had opened a door in the back, bringing in a smell, a smell of damp leaves and another, one that tugged at her mind. Jonquils. She said the word aloud in her head, testing it.

The moon had risen over the treetops beyond the great lawn. It shone in the window, bright enough to see by. Lifting the top of her pajamas she looked at her scars. They were almost healed. A sensation buzzed through her. When she recognized it as pleasure at seeing her skin nearly whole again, she knew that soon she'd be ready.

Touching the copy of *Jane Eyre* under her pillow first, a ritual she did not dare to ignore, she got quietly out of bed to look up at the moon from her window.

It looked down at her and spoke. "Wait for me, I will guide you," it said. It had a lovely voice, sort of shivery and smooth at the same time.

"I'm most awfully grateful," Gretchen replied. "But I'm sure I could manage on my own."

"But my dear, it would give me such pleasure. This is a particularly dull part of Connecticut. Hardly anyone walks about at night here. They drive their cars right to the door, and scurry in as though night were not the most beautiful part of the day. Amorous teenagers and a few inept thieves—why can't thieves learn to consult an almanac?—are my only entertainment. I must be off, till next week then?"

"Yes, good-bye," Gretchen said, holding up her hand.

31

Colonel Harrington sat in his armchair by the fire, in a sleepy post-tea bliss. Deen was playing a Debussy etude, while Hamish and his young Scottish friend had gone next door to play their guitars.

He lay back, a dreamy look on his old, whiskered face. He delighted in picturing what the Cap'n had done to fit out the inside of his tiny cabin. Fortunately Ettie and the children brought him news of the Cap'n often, describing the shelves he'd put up and lined with red paper. He reveled in the fact that the Cap'n had cut the edges of the paper in zigzags, something he thought was straight from the pages of a Victorian lady's magazine. Ettie had told him that the Cap'n had made several pictures to put on the walls. Beautiful ones, she said, all over with flowers and birds and animals. Apparently he'd painted them himself, had quite a dab hand with a brush. Was there perhaps a budding Douanier Rousseau in his garden shed? What a lot of clever and artistic people he'd fallen in with.

Except for Deen's music, the house was quiet now, but often it hummed with the sounds of tea trolleys, bottles being opened, and chatter. Such delightful sounds. The house had become precisely what the colonel had always dreamed of—a comfortable home filled with his family's furniture and the sounds of children. The girl and her brother had decided to take the top-floor bedrooms next to Ettie's, and at night he could hear their scrapings and small feet, well, that might be a bit rosy, for the boy did clump quite a bit. Still, it cheered him even in his bed to know that the house was being used as it should, as a place of shelter for a small tribal group.

The Cap'n, he noticed, was very, very careful to be quiet in the garden; clearly the good man was concerned that he not disturb him. But the screen door to the cabin had a squeak, as all good screen doors should, and sometimes his cat let out a questioning meow. What a very fine cat that seemed. He knew from petting it that its tail was as thick and soft as a cloud, and also what Ettie had told him—that it was striped orange and white. Striped like an animal that sat in a tree and had very wise eyes, she said, like one she'd seen on a nature program. He supposed she meant a lemur.

His hands folded over his stomach, he slept, his feet stretched out toward the fire. He dreamed of pleasant things, especially so because he no longer dreamed of more troubling parts of his past.

* * *

The Harrington family had lived in an old and rather fine brick house that had been built by his great-grandfather. When the colonel, as he was now known, was born, it had already accumulated all it could hold in the way of furnishings, and his mother, whose family home it was, left untouched what she had grown up with. She was a Harrington twice over, having married a distant relation.

The colonel was an only child and not a happy one. He might have liked to have been happy, but happiness was not something his parents encouraged. His mother, born at the end of the nineteenth century, had been raised in an essentially Victorian consciousness, one that led her to regard the birth of her child as a highly disgusting episode.

The bloody primality of it, in fact, had convinced her that what she'd gone through was not what God intended, that her own body was aberrant. Being of a very private nature, she asked no questions of the doctor, but became convinced that her insides had putrefied.

The colonel's father did not find it inconvenient to no longer pretend to woo his bride. He cared only for the properties she had brought him. Sitting at his desk each day, he tallied them endlessly. It was his great scheme to add to them, to budget down to the decimal point their incomes and expenditures, greedily assessing when he might buy another with the profits.

The colonel had gained his sobriquet in the Institution. His parents had placed him there after his eyesight had gone, in 1952. He'd graduated from university three years earlier, at which time he'd done as his father requested, returning home to learn the ropes of the family holdings. He lived at home and spent a good deal of his time touring the state, making reports on building conditions and tenants for his father.

The truth was, his father was a slumlord. He'd held on to all the office buildings, farms, and industrial properties that had come with his marriage, then used the profits from them to buy housing in rundown neighborhoods. The worst of it was, the rents paid weekly for these atrocious hovels were higher than the going rate. His father explained it to him as if displaying a wonderful piece of business acumen: *You see, they have to pay it. And if they don't they can be turned out at once, and there is always someone even more desperate than they to take their place.*

The colonel often wondered, those first few years at the Institution, if his blindness had not been brought on by his fervent desire not to see the misery of his father's tenants. He hadn't argued at all when Dr. Matheson told him they'd decided it was best that he be cared for at an institution. He didn't realize until he got there, that it was one for the insane. But by then he had no wish to be anywhere in particular. And he supposed he had been acting a bit odd lately.

At the Institution he had a private room and was allowed a few comforts, such as an armchair and a gramophone. And there, because he treated everyone, the cleaning staff, orderlies, doctors, and fellow inmates, with great courtesy, he was treated with courtesy also.

As the years passed and his hair grew gray, he became a sort of statesman there. The staff and patients turned to him for advice or to settle their disputes. His room had become a cross between a study and a drawing room, as various bits of furniture were offered to him. It had a carpet, a chesterfield, two more armchairs for visitors, some small tables, a sideboard, a desk, a radio, which he prized, and a hot plate on which he could make tea.

It is surprising that as the decades passed no one inquired as to why someone so clearly sane was still there, but it was a rather parochial place, as institutions go, and they'd gotten to think of him as a fixture. He certainly never complained, and as keen younger doctors with more modern ideas tried to shake the place up, somehow he remained inviolate, in his cozy chamber in the old wing, a structure dating back to the prewar era, which in the South, meant the Civil War.

His father died in 1967. His mother, on the other hand, saw out her hundredth year. She never had visited him once, in the forty-four years he was there.

With her death came documents and a very large estate. She hadn't wanted to leave him a cent, but he was the only true Harrington left, and the devil if she'd leave it to some half-breed Harrington. She did, though, have the satisfaction of leaving a large sum to her doctor, on the condition that as executor, he see that the boy never be freed from the confines of the Institution.

The doctor promptly put the idea of a large sum of cash out of his mind, and, rejoicing that the old bag of bones was truly dead, studied up on the medical and legal procedures for springing someone from the loony bin. He'd secretly made a number of visits to the colonel and had no doubt whatsoever about his sanity.

The judge surreptitiously wiped her eyes and even the lawyers looked less blandly indifferent when the colonel rose at the hearing. "Ma'am, ladies and gentlemen," he said. "I should like to live life in a real house for the years left to me. I would also, should you grant me the ability to do so, establish a trust for the amelioration of the tenants that have passed into my keeping, to offer certain properties to them for below market rate, build a system by which each of them may be able to rent to purchase, or, in the very least, live in far better conditions.

"As to my own plans, I would be lying if I said I would like to learn Braille, or improve myself very much. I fear I'm too old for that. I would, though, like to live quietly in a real home, where perhaps I could make the acquaintance of some friends, hear the sound of talk around me, and share a drink with them."

* * *

The colonel woke with a snort. Ah, that was the sound of the dumbwaiter that Mrs. D had had installed; that woman thought of everything. Ettie would be wheeling in his supper any minute. The children had theirs in the kitchen with Ettie. They hadn't discussed it, but he thought it a highly civilized arrangement. It wasn't that he didn't wish their company, but being blind, he found it difficult to concentrate on maneuvering a fork and to make conversation at the same time. Though Ettie was awfully good about preparing foods that he could manage and keeping a strict order to their arrangement on the tray.

Mrs. D had interviewed all the applicants and hired Ettie, of course. But what luck to have found Mrs. D. It had been the real estate lady who'd mentioned her name, another rather terrifyingly efficient woman.

What a trouper Mrs. D had turned out to be, with a heart like a lion when it came to defending her own. And she'd understood at once his wish to appear sighted, had colluded with him to effect it in the most diabolical ways, making him maps with raised lines showing the exact layout of the rooms in the house, then helping him learn the numbers of steps. What a remarkable woman. Why, she'd even done a recce of the Hollanders' main floor for him, rehearsing him until he felt confident to try it, and painting a most vivid picture of the style of the room and its mistress.

* * *

Robert had spent the afternoon redoing the gas line to Ettie's stove, having declared the original workmanship a criminal act, one no doubt perpetrated by some union dude. Having saved the household from being blown to kingdom come, he was naturally invited to stay for supper. Ettie and Hamish had made crab cakes with lemon aioli, asparagus, and pommes Anna. Hamish did not display the same fascination for baking as he did for what he called "real cooking," so Ettie made the dessert, a flourless chocolate and walnut torte. Though he ate three slices of it, his snobbery being solely one in which he deemed that men don't make cakes.

"No, you kids go on upstairs, I'll help Ettie with the washing up," Robert said, waving them off. "I know for sure it's good for you to wash dishes and all, but you two seem to have character to spare, so go on, watch TV or something."

"Look what the Capitain make for me," Ettie said, when the children had gone. "So nice, is it not? I show him the pictures you give me, of the children and I tell him, Oh, I cried when you did that. How you are such a nice man to say, Ettie, she needs pictures of her young ones. So he say, Ettie, may I make you a frame for them? Look, he painted it all over with flowers."

"Hunh. Yes, it's nice, anyone can see that, but kinda sloppy, don't you think? What's this supposed to be, a tulip or some chicken's foot? You think you ought to be letting that old guy give you presents?"

"Yes. I do think this. I think it's good that he is nice and has many things to paint. And that he lives so neat in that little house and washes everything and shines his boots and is quiet like a mouse. Never one thing out of place there. You don't say that! All the sadness in his eyes? You give him something he paint for you—his eyes not so sad when he paint, and he like to do anything for you."

Robert looked at her, what a little spitfire she was, with her fists on her hips and her cheeks blazing. What a woman. "Now, here's our coffee, calm down, guess I owe you an apology. Guess I just got a teensy bit jealous and all. Now sit down and talk to me, I want to ask you something.

"Ettie, you think that old man upstairs might like a part-time handyman? A place like this sure needs someone after it all the time. I mean to say, if someone were here and did, say, two days a week work on the place keeping it up, maybe just for room and board? The other days I could carry on with my regular jobs, keep earning some money. I don't make a whole pile of it, that's for sure, but enough to keep off the streets and I give a little help to my daughter, she's got her firstborn now and while her husband's a steady enough fellow, there's never enough to go around, is there, with a new baby in the house."

"Tyrell, the best, best baby," Ettie breathed. "See, I put his picture with the children's, in the frame."

"Now that I look at this frame again, it strikes me as a real thing of beauty. You understand what I'm asking?"

"Maybe. First I ask Colonel, then we talk more, yes?"

"That old man, he's too proud to tell anyone he's blind, isn't he? Goes around acting like he can see as good as you or me. Has all sorts of dodges."

"You can't know this, I never tell anyone!"

"But it's true, ain't it?"

"Yes. Meez D know and I know, now you know. Don't ever tell him, please. If you do, it will hurt him so much. Maybe later, if, well, if you are here more, maybe he tell you himself."

Maybe he should've had a ring or something, he thought as he walked to the subway station. Maybe he'd blown it bad. Maybe he'd thrown away his chance for that woman's love. But no, it would've been crowding her—first he had to find out if she wanted to change things, might consider the idea. She was the kind of person that once she gave her loyalty, would never look away, so he'd have to slip into her world. Not that he had anything at all to give up if he did—two lonely rooms in a building in Brooklyn, with a sofa, a TV, and a bed. His daughter was all grown up and living in Philly, she loved him all right, but didn't need much of him.

The one thing that worried him was that if he became one of the colonel's employees, he might lose his right to sit and drink sippin' whiskey with him on Thursdays. Might have to toughen up his insides and pretend not to mind about it. It could be done though, and he might find that after a few months he didn't even mind. After all, there wasn't a thing he wouldn't do if he could take Ettie's hand and call her his own. Imagine her, keeping so mum about the old man's blindness. Never peeped a word, always acted like he was just fine.

It must take a mountain of courage to bang around, acting like you can see. That's why Ettie did what she did, she admired him. Sure she did, anyone with a bit of gumption would. Everyone on the planet was screaming about their little teensy problems, crying out that it was somebody else's fault they couldn't make do, while a few other ones sat still and took it, made the best of it. You just didn't hear about them or read about them in the papers, because they kept their own counsel.

The train car rattled and shook as it dove beneath the harbor. The power supplying the lights inside failed, then flickered back. With a screech and a hiss, the train pulled into city hall. The occupants of the car waited, then the train pulled away, swaying around a curve as the driver built up speed.

32

The moon rose over a great clean sky, a sky punctuated by a few clouds as lovely and palely white as fruit trees in full bloom, which sailed across it on a soundless wind.

Gretchen bound her slippers onto her feet with some strips of cloth she'd hidden, tied her bathrobe tight, then put her shawl around her. She picked up the framed photo (no glass) her mother had given her of the family, and peeled the paper backing away. Under it she found the credit card Sadie had whispered that she'd put there, *just in case, darling*. She put it carefully in her pocket.

Rollingbrook prided itself on having no obvious signs of wishing to keep the "guests" in—the windows were neither barred nor locked, but they were covered with heavy screens that were removable only from the outside. Gretchen cut the screen deftly with a scalpel she'd stolen from the emergency station. She cut enough to be able to push it out, then stepped over the sill and into the night.

There was no time to linger to enjoy the beauty of the spring night, her bathrobe and pajama legs were much too visible, but she put her face up to feel the moonlight for a moment, then moved swiftly toward the woods beyond the mowed lawn.

Once within the safety of the trees, she let out her breath. Stock still, she listened, but there were no shouts or sounds of pursuit. She looked around her, determining what direction to take. The one that said to her to follow its path led straight into the densest part of the woods. It was very dark that way, there where the trees ruled the land. But her father had given her a second name, had called her Mab. Mab, he'd said, was queen of all the woodlands, a girl who could turn herself into a sapling and whose long hair was combed each morning by the wind. She put her hands out before her and walked into the shadowy world.

As she entered its penumbra the pupils of her eyes expanded; now she could see how the moonlight fell down between the branches, etching everything in a pale aura. It was like a song, a tune coaxed from a pipe, it was everywhere, every twig, every leaf, was given shape by it. Stepping lightly, she trod with sure feet through the forest, winding between the tree trunks and over rises and dips, making her way around outcroppings of rock. She traced her fingers over the fronds of last year's ferns, leathery and dry to her touch. She came to a small stream and crossed it, the mud on its bank soaking her rag-wrapped slippers. Skunk cabbages poked up from the black earth, letting out their pungent smell. Kneeling on a stone she scooped some water from the stream to her mouth. She sat, looking around her. Above, a pair of screech owls called to each other, their sounds as infinite a part of the forest as all the other parts of it, the silver of the moonlight reflected on the ribbon of water, the scent of bark, the glimmer of a spider's path drifting on an eddy of air, everything woven together in a world far from that which man strove to alter.

She wished she could stay there, never leave this night-lit world of the forest, become part of it. But she knew that when the sun came up, as it must, she'd then be subject to its rule, and far from her purpose. So she stood and went on.

Some time later she came to a place where the trees thinned. Beyond them was a pinkish, unnatural light, with the sound of traffic tearing the air apart. She changed course to the right, away from it. The moon had set and it was quite dark, but she knew she was near. Following a small ridge she came to the edge of the forest and peeked out. She saw a house below, its walls taking shape in the gray, predawn light. Stepping out a little farther she looked at it carefully. It wasn't the right house, though why she couldn't quite say.

Following the ridge, keeping within its shadow, she made her way along its flank. The nearing sunrise was just beginning to tinge the sky with seams of pink when she stopped to venture out again, looking below her at another house. It was a huge, elaborate thing, far larger than a house needed to be. Content with her travels she lay down by an outcropping of rock where a pile of chestnut leaves had drifted. Burrowing and wiggling, she tucked herself into them, leaving only her eyes and nose exposed. She breathed in their dry, brownish scent. A slow-moving insect crawled over her hand and she sighed—it was good to have company. She made sure not to move, so that she wouldn't crush some tiny part of it.

The sun was well up when she woke. She stretched, brushing the leaves from her shawl. Moving cautiously she left the woods to get a better look at her house. It had a garage built to look like a stable block, with a cobbled forecourt and a green mansard roof. It simply stank of money. And though she couldn't say how she knew, she was sure there was no one at home. There was another house across the street, but it could only be guessed at through the trees.

Gretchen picked her way down the hillside, unafraid of being seen—the house had no eyes. It simply waited for her. She walked along the back, looking at the doors, waiting to find one that would tell her it was unlocked. There it was.

She went inside, stooping to take off her muddy slippers first. Wrapping them into a bundle, she deposited them behind a sofa.

Going through the rooms she glanced at them, starting once when she saw a thin beggar-girl staring at her, but it was only herself, reflected in a large gilt looking-glass.

When she at last found the staircase she ran up it, opening the first door she came to. She closed it; she was looking for milady's room, and that clearly was not it. The next one was.

A large room, longer than it was wide, it had French doors onto a balcony at the far end. It was a room that could only belong to a woman, with its Chinese wallpaper painted with peonies and birds, and its apricot velvet chairs. Or perhaps even a countess, judging by the bed, with its cascade of figured silk descending from a gilt coronet above it.

Gretchen was the only child of Ree Hollander's who had known him. She knew his burnished, floating hair, how he strode about in frogged coats with wide cuffs, his jeweled peacock presence. She remembered her father as she floated barefoot through the mirror-paneled door, into the Connecticut contessa's bathroom. She heard his voice rising above the guitars, and smelled the dust burning on the spotlights, saw him raise his arm in a gesture of magisterial grace.

The bathroom was done entirely in dusty pink marble, with a sunken bath. A gilt dolphin spat water into it when she turned the taps. Adjusting the temperature she left them on, then took a tour of the dressing table, where she found a bottle of Diorissimo. She poured a dollop of it into the bath, stripped off her clothes, and got in, letting it fill around her.

She sniffed an armpit, enjoying the earthy scent, then soaped herself thoroughly. When she'd done she lay back in the water, floating. Time passed, in which she thought of nothing, her mind as suspended as her body. Much refreshed, she washed her hair with some very superior shampoo she found, then rinsed it with a jet from the hand-sprayer. Ahh.

Sometimes, when things seem to be going too well, one gets a feeling of insidious worry that comes creeping along behind, a shadow that must follow even the best-loved thing. But sometimes, contrary to what might seem tainted by too much luck, things actually do go well. So Gretchen rose from her stolen bath surefooted and clean, scented with soap and Diorissimo. No ogre came stamping in, no door banged below. Lazy and warm, she walked into the bedroom and opened the other mirrored door.

Recessed halogen lights inside came on at the summons of the door. Gretchen looked into a gallery, a temple, as it were, of women's clothing. Being Gretchen, she naturally did not gasp, but her face was expression enough. Running like a nymph to the first dress that caught her eye, she took it up on its hanger and laid it along her body. It fit. She, milady, was her size.

In fact, the Connecticut contessa was a wonderfully slim woman in her forties and very proud of keeping her figure, but more than that, was a woman who cared deeply and truly about clothes. Who had never thrown anything out that she'd looked good in, which meant very little had ever been tossed aside. She put tissue paper over her padded hangers and had been something of a fashion star in her day, when she'd looked so utterly fetching in a wide-brimmed, candy-spun hat and a strappy dress.

Her shoes were arranged on white shelves and her hats on Styrofoam mannequin heads. Rows of drawers were filled with belts and shawls and boas, every conceivable sort of handbag, hair ornaments and scarves smelling of faded Diorissimo.

Gretchen did not speak, it's true, but you mustn't think that her head wasn't stuffed to the brim with words. The words to "Ziggy Stardust" cued in her mind as she tried on a madder of rose silk shirt. *Woke up as a rock 'n roll staaar,* she sang as she found a white camisole to wear beneath it. A pair of white leather jeans went on next, then a pair of high-heeled suede boots. She studied herself in a mirror. It needed a belt. One made of silvery mesh with squares of turquoise took her fancy, yes, that was it. Perhaps she'd nick the necklace with the jade ankh as well, it was awfully nice. And that narrow eau-de-nil scarf to wind around her neck, the way her father used to wear them.

Now she needed a coat, what about this ankle-length suede one in the same light brown as the boots? And sunglasses—the Jackie O's, she decided. The pocketbooks were arranged by color. She chose a knapsack style in black leather, carefully zipping the Visa card in its pocket.

Finally, she looked at hats. A wide gray one with a floppy brim looked just the ticket, but you never knew with hats till you tried them on. She did, looking critically at the effect, but it was just right. She was a rock star incognito.

Rolling up her old clothes, she found a suitcase to hide them in. She was sorry to leave the shawl, it was quite a nice shawl, so first she touched her lips to it, then said good-bye to it politely.

Downstairs she found a book-lined room with a desk that held a copy of the Yellow Pages. Looking through a stack of bills she made a note of the address. The next part would take some effort, so she massaged her jaw with her fingers, practicing opening and closing her mouth. Marshalling her nerve, she dialed a number.

"Yes, this is Sadie Hollander," she said. "Could you send a car at once, to take me to Manhattan? Tenth Street. Yes, that's fine. Can I pay for it now with my card? And could you add twenty percent for the driver, please?"

When she had hung up, she went to the bookshelves, to calm herself with the feel of their spines. Oh, look, a copy of *Jane Eyre,* and in ever such a nice blue morocco binding. She slipped it into her pocketbook.

When the limo pulled up in front of the house, Gretchen got in, giving the driver the address.

As the several tons of Cadillac rolled onto the highway, the driver offered a pleasant observation on the weather, but Gretchen did not respond. Every barrel has its bottom and Gretchen had hit hers, had used up all the speech she could muster for the time being. She felt sad, knowing that he thought her terribly rude: he'd probably go home later and complain to his wife what a stuck-up girl he'd had to drive today. She might have nodded to him, but it didn't occur to her.

She thought about how she still had one more thing she must say. When she arrived and the family all came running, she had to say to Sadie: "I'm better now, Mother."

Sadie would probably not cry, she hardly ever did, instead she'd kiss her and promise never to send her back to that place. Then Gretchen would point first at her mouth, then at her heart, to show that she had a promise too, to never let the screams inside her get so strong again. Later she'd make some new drawings, to show her that she didn't have to do that dog drawing anymore.

The caddie came to a stop in front of the house on West Tenth Street. The driver, correct in every gesture but truly hurt by Gretchen's refusal to respond to his few, cheerful words, opened the door for her and then drove away.

Sadie had not thought of also taping a key to the house in the back of the picture frame. She should have, it's true, but life is made up of such small oversights. So when Gretchen rang the bell, then began to kick the door and beat on it, a small oversight became, as they frequently do, a large problem. Gretchen sank down on the top step, put her head in her hands, and sobbed, pitifully but soundlessly.

A boy came walking down the street, his gait a skipping, awkward one. He stopped when he came abreast of the steps and stared at her.

Gretchen raised her head. He was looking at her with frank curiosity. She thought he looked about her brother's age and had the nicest face, square and dark, with the most wonderful eyes and long lashes.

Liall, for it was Liall, had never seen such a beautiful girl. He'd stared so many times at her photographs in the house, but even those hadn't done her justice. She'd been crying but her face wasn't all blotched and puckered, it was more like her eyes just swam in spring-water. Her clothes and her hair were all sort of flung out around her, like a doll that had been dropped on the floor.

"You're Gretchen, aren't you?" he said. "Did you run away too? Don't cry, please, I mean, go ahead if you want to, but I'll help you."

Gretchen gazed at him, her eyes still awash.

"You locked out? It's okay, your brother and sister are staying right next door. I'll show you."

Gretchen nodded, then pointed at her mouth, looking questioningly at him.

"Oh yeah, they said you didn't like to talk. I'm Liall, Hamish's friend."

Gretchen fought a battle inside herself at that moment, wanting very much to win it. She did. "Are you the boy with one white leg?" she asked him.

Liall smiled and pulled up one pant leg, revealing part of a beige plastic limb above his sock. "Come on, I'll see you safe to the colonel's. That's where your brother and sister are for a spell. Your mamma's in London just now, but you'll like the colonel. He kind of acts like everything's just wonderful, so you get to thinking like that too around him. You can take my hand if you're scared."

Gretchen stood and went down the steps. She looked at her young protector with a smile and put her hand in his.

* * *

Ettie knew pretty much everything there was to know about the Hollanders. She knew these things not because she was a busybody, far from it, but because she loved them. Their aches and bruises were her aches and bruises, their good things and presents tied with bows were hers too. So when she opened the door and saw Liall holding the hand of a girl like one of the daughters of the secret places in the mountains, but who she instantly knew to be Gretchen, she let out a cry of welcome and held out her arms.

33

Mrs. D made her report to the Thursday Night Imbibers the next evening.

"First, and most important," she began, "I've talked with the girl. She was quite clear and said simply two things—that she never wants to go back to that place she was in, and that she would like to become normal again. No thank you, Colonel, I'll wait to have a drink until I've given my full report. Oh Goddamn it, all right, just a snort.

"I explained to her that naturally she'll stay here until her mother returns, and that she wasn't to go out unless one of us adults is with her, that I had to take that precaution if we are to keep her safe in her mother's absence. She agreed, was very sensible about it.

"Now, I did some research on the subject and it appears that not only do we have no right whatsoever to keep her here, we are, in fact, acting firmly on the wrong side of the law."

"Hear, hear," the colonel said, pouring himself some more whiskey.

"I've told the children never to answer the phone next door unless they're quite sure who's calling. There have been a number of messages left on the machine there from that place. They sound slightly panicked, though I'm sure they're more worried about any possible accountability for their neglect, than concern for Gretchen. Legally, it's quite clear that we should let them know that Gretchen's safe, but I say to hell with them. I say we protect the girl and hide her from those jackals until her mother gets back and can sort it all out.

"As to Sadie, I spoke to her this afternoon. She was a bit, shall we say, euphoric, but I think she understood most of what I told her. I'll call her again tomorrow, earlier in the day, to make sure she's clear about what we're proposing. But she seemed perfectly happy for us to keep Gretchen here, and was overjoyed that the girl seems so much better. By the way, she said that Brian's making excellent progress and is sitting up and doing some exercises.

"As to the matter of the girl's state of mind, I've spent a good many years dealing with all sorts, and in my view, that girl's sane. I understand from Hamish, whose frankness can be a real help in putting things together, that she was in a very bad way when she was put into that place. I'd say she's pulled herself up by her bootstraps and made a recovery. She's making a real effort to talk again and is doing everything to behave like a good girl. Hamish also tells me she's making the kind of beautiful, detailed drawings she used to before she cracked up. I gather while she was ill she'd only do one drawing over and over, of a dog. These things and the fact that somehow, God knows how, she managed to get out of that place dressed only in pajamas and a robe, then make her way to Manhattan, shows remarkable cunning. In fact, it seems she arrived in a limo. And dressed in those wonderful clothes! She won't talk about it but clearly she must've lied, stolen, and cheated to manage all that, which I think proves her mind's working perfectly well."

Mrs. D poured herself a well-deserved drink.

"A most excellent report," the colonel said. "As usual, a remarkably thorough piece of work. But tell me, is she as beautiful as our young Scottish friend says she is?"

"Colonel, I'm an Irish girl by birth, and that girl's not just beautiful, she's like something my granddad was always yammering on about—he used to cry over the old country, the way the sun shone over the hills covered in spring grass and how it smelled. I used to think it was all just hogwash but now that I've seen that girl, I'm not so sure. She has something of the old country and the smell of new grass to her."

"My, my," the colonel said, sighing. "I must say, I do hope she'll come and see me. You did tell her that she's most welcome to join me whenever she likes?"

"Yes, I made that perfectly clear. I gave her a full description of the entire household, including the fact that there is a bum living in the garden."

"Excellent, excellent." The colonel reached for a sandwich, then remembered that Ettie hadn't brought in the trolley yet. Odd, he thought, it wasn't at all like Ettie to be late. Well, she was probably doing something for Gretchen, she'd taken a rare, almost worshipful fancy to the girl.

Robert had been as quiet as a judge, or at least as quiet as a proper judge should be, listening and considering the matter carefully. He'd been aware that there was another Hollander child, but mostly from Ettie, who'd described her as some kind of mythic apparition, which wasn't much of a help at getting at the truth. Now he felt he was on firmer ground, and could offer an opinion.

"Here's what I think," he said. "I think we need a plan to protect this here girl, keep her from those grasping fingers of the people at the funny farm. I mean, it's all very well us agreeing that we'll keep her safe, but how're we going to do it? I think we need a real plan, to set up a system of communications and patrols and rehearse what we'd do if the law shows up. For sure get a hidden video camera on the front steps for starters. I can install it, that's a piece of cake. But we also got to train those kids in emergency maneuvers, what to do if those people from the funny farm come a knocking, or send the police."

"Yes, excellent thinking," the colonel said. "Perhaps we should have steel barricades installed inside all the doors, and possibly rig up a way to repel invaders. The children could be trained to deploy it on anyone who tries to force their way in."

"Now look, let's not go off on a boiling oil tangent," Mrs. D said. "Let's stick to protecting the girl, while keeping ourselves out of the hoosegow, all right?"

"I guess we got a bit carried away," Robert said sheepishly. "Guess I just felt so strongly that that girl's had a rough time of it that I got plumb mad. But here's something else I was thinking—Deen told me that the girl's taken a real shine to Liall, and I think we ought to ask Liall to come whenever he can, to spend time with her. It seems like she talks to Liall more than anybody, feels easy with him. Now Liall's quiet like, but has a way of asking direct questions about things he doesn't understand. Says things some other people might be afraid to say, if you get what I mean. Ettie's a fine, fine woman and will mother that girl and rock her to sleep every night if she wants, but it might be good for her to have someone else around who doesn't just smooth the problems away, if you get what I'm saying."

At that moment Ettie came in with the trolley. She gave Robert a hard look.

"Oh, Ettie," Mrs. D said. "Look, all my favorites. Cress sandwiches, smoked salmon and cream cheese, chicken salad, and homemade potato chips! Is that caviar?"

"Yes, beluga. On endive leaf. The colonel, he say Ettie, spend money, so I spend money. I say you three sit up here, deciding everything, and me I sit in the kitchen, crying and praying for that girl. I never saw such a good girl. I tell you, Colonel, I leave right now if you don't take care of that girl. Find someone else to make you roast beef sandwiches."

"My dear," the colonel said, looking very contrite, "You don't possibly think we might send her back to that institution? I assure you, all we were discussing was how best to care for her. And I solemnly deputize you to be her mother in absentia, so you cannot leave. I'm awfully sorry, I should have included you in the conversation, have blundered in not asking you especially to join in making plans for her. Will you forgive me?"

"Oh, everything's all right?" Ettie said.

"Yes, quite all right. We've agreed to keep mum about the girl being here, so you mustn't answer either the door or the phone if you think it might be anyone coming to look for her, do you understand?"

"Oh yes, if anyone ask, I know nothing of such a girl. And I make sure the Capitain he know nothing too."

"What if you made her some of your famous duck broth?" the colonel suggested. "There's nothing like your duck broth to fix someone up."

"She a vegetarian."

"Oh dear," the colonel said.

"She can hear the animals scream. I make her vegetable broth, with mushrooms. Even better than duck."

Ettie went down to her kitchen, happily thinking of a bouquet garni, new onions, celery, carrots, leeks, and oyster mushrooms. With some juniper berries, she decided, and a turnip. It would be the best broth ever made, clear and rich.

She stayed up late to reduce it in a heavy copper pot. The vent over her eight-burner stove fed out a pipe to a small fan above a window in the area, and people passing sniffed the air, wishing the smell were coming out of their own kitchen. One of them, a distraught, drunken bum, sank down on his knees and moaned, clutching the iron bars of the area railing as he stared at the woman in the kitchen below. Fortunately Ettie did not see him, for she would surely have taken pity on him and offered him a mug of broth, and just as surely he would've been back every night after that, yowling outside the door like a stray cat. A nightstick pressed into his side by a cop eventually moved him along.

***

The next morning, as Ettie was preparing breakfast, Gretchen came quietly down.

"I'll make the toast," she said.

"No, no, you sit," Ettie said.

Gretchen stayed where she was, looking at Ettie.

"Okay, yes, you make toast," Ettie finally said.

When the colonel's trolley was ready Gretchen reached for the handle, asking Ettie with her eyes, could she take it up, please?

Ettie argued back with her own eyes, but Gretchen's will was stronger.

***

Ah, breakfast," the colonel said, turning down the music. "What wonderful things have you made this morning, Ettie?" The colonel broke off, realizing that it had not been Ettie's tread. Nor Deen's. "Why, it's Gretchen. My dear, I'm so charmed to see you, what a pleasure. Won't you join me?"

Gretchen looked at him; he was exactly like Hamish had described him, basking in his chair like an old seal, his fat belly covered by a tweed waistcoat. There was something though, that he hadn't told her.

"You're blind," she said.

"Yes, my dear."

"Hamish . . ."

"Never said? No, I don't suppose he would have. Afraid I'm a terrible old fraud, pretend to be able to see. Think I've fooled the boy, and your sister. Most everyone, for that matter. Ettie and Mrs. D know, they are my eyes."

"How long?"

"Since I lost my sight? Let's see now, a very long time, almost half a century it must be now."

Gretchen sat and tentatively put her hand on his.

"I'm so awfully glad you're here," he said. "May I touch your hand? My, what a delicate hand it is. You know, as a southerner I never feel quite right when a house isn't filled with visitors. In the South, you know, once a visiting relative or friend comes through the front door they may stay until doomsday, and we cry terrible tears if they have to leave before that. Let's have some breakfast, shall we? Since you've found out my secret you won't be shocked to see me spill a good many crumbs. Have you made the acquaintance of the Cap'n and his cat, who live in the garden? A quite remarkable cat, with fur as rich as an empress's sables. The Cap'n lives in a little cabin, which I am told he keeps as neat as a pin. He rescued your sister, you know, when she ran away from that poor madwoman. I find your presence immensely soothing. I do hope you will come and sit by me whenever you like."

34

The colonel stood at the open window of the parlor, his face held up to feel the spring sun.

"Morning, sir!" the Cap'n said below him in the garden.

"Morning, Corporal," the colonel returned, saluting. "Fine day. Billet all right, is it?"

"Yes sir. Very much all right, sir."

"Fine, fine. Carry on the good work."

***

The Cap'n sat on his pocket-size porch, the door to the cabin open behind him to dry the floor, which he'd just washed. He'd taken his boots off and cleaned their soles with his knife, now he was polishing them with a rag and a bit of Crisco. There was nothing like Crisco for keeping boots in good order. Titus was also attending to his person, he was giving himself a thorough washing from the tufts of his ears to the end of his tail, which he'd caught between his paws.

Hamish came out the kitchen door, having finished off a stack of pancakes, three poached eggs, two English muffins with jam, and a half pound of bacon. He was less weedy these days, the Cap'n noted, but still thin—all that food Ettie shoveled into him was just being burned up as his bones grew.

"Come join us, my boy," the Cap'n said. "We are grooming. Look at that cat, at the contortions he does to get every speck off his coat. He always does his whiskers last. That cat has been a shining example to me. I was down and out and quite frankly smelled, when that cat showed me better ways."

"Deen says my hair looks like something that's washed up on the beach after a storm," he said, sitting next to the Cap'n.

"Well, you might consider running a comb through it now and again. I recall when I first saw young men with hair as long as yours. I confess, I was a bit shocked. Now look at me, with hair down my back and a beard as long as Methuselah's. Hair, my boy, is an essential part of self. It grows out of our heads after all."

"I guess so. It's funny stuff when you think about it. Kind of like an alien life form."

"That's it, my boy, in a nutshell. I was wondering, do you think you and your sisters might like to come to the cabin this afternoon, for some lemonade? And a cake?"

"Sure. I mean, Deen and I can come for sure, but Gretchen, she's a bit hard to predict. But I bet she'll come. Anyway, I'll ask her."

* * *

The Cap'n roamed the Village, panhandling. He needed some money to buy a nice cake for the children, something special. He hoped desperately that Gretchen would come, each small way she rejoined the world was so important.

He'd never been much good at begging though; it was an art he'd never quite mastered. The only reason he'd survived at all was that once in a while, against all odds, someone would give him a much larger sum than normal. Usually someone who'd stopped and actually talked to him.

After three hours he'd garnered only a couple of bucks and was feeling dejected. Then a man gave him a dollar—maybe things were looking up. He spotted a woman who looked likely, not too old—old ladies were almost always hopeless, and not too young, young ladies were far less hopeless but more easily frightened. This woman was well dressed and didn't have one of those hard, city faces.

"Ma'am, some money to buy food?" he said.

She looked the other way, as disdainfully as she could while still seeming not to notice his existence.

"I only asked because I wanted to give some children who've been nice to me a little cake," he said sadly, after she'd passed.

"Really?" a young man with spiky lemon hair said. "That's so cute. How much do you need?"

"I'm not really sure. I've never bought a pretty cake."

"Oh my dear, one *lives* to buy pretty cakes. I always say, the prettier the cake, the prettier life is. Do you know *where* to buy a pretty cake? No? Well I do. Come on."

Taking the Cap'n's arm, he turned him uptown. "There's the most marvelous pastry shop, just a couple of blocks from here. I'll show you. Are they really nice children or just a set of your own phantods? No, don't answer that, I might be disappointed. You really smell quite nice for a bum, you know. I'm sure they are the most delightful children. Do they have names?"

"Oh yes. Gretchen, Hamish, and Deen."

"Names that simply could not be made up on the spot, names that have the jangle of reality to them. Look, behold yonder window! Oh my *God*, just look at those darling pink cupcakes! Forget the cake, honey, you've *got* to have those divine little cupcakes. One for you, three for me, yummie yum yum. Let's see, three children and you, three apiece and two extra to fight over, that makes fourteen. Don't be silly, I shall certainly buy them for you. Really, I work for what they call a 'major' magazine, and a few cupcakes will hardly break me. Wait here and I'll just nip in and get them, all right?"

The Cap'n waited outside, hoping he didn't look too conspicuous, but not wanting to move out of sight of the shop window, in case his benefactor might think he wasn't on the up and up about wanting a cake.

"What a dragon!" the yellow-haired man said, coming out with a large striped box. "First, I thought she'd roast me with her hatred, then gouge my eyes out. I'd thought that breed had died out. At least here, in the birthplace of *la vie Bohème*. Ah well, clichés are so eternal. Here, not like that, silly—put your thumb out, there, that's how you hold a cake box.

"And if anyone asks, especially any man under the age of fifty, do be an angel and tell them that I'm slipping this twenty into your pocket because I'm the most charming and kind-hearted girl on this planet. I always feel one should *act* beautifully, because there are so many beautiful people around one. You know, your teddy bear's tea gives me the most *wicked* idea for a photo shoot. Like that terribly sick book about a doll that I stole from my sister as a child. It made me weep absolute rivers of tears. Must dash, love you."

With that, he disappeared into the whirl of bodies on the avenue. The Cap'n stood still, looking for him, catching a glimpse of crocus yellow hair in the throng heading uptown. He reached into his pocket, and sure enough, there was a bill there. Pulling it out he saw that it was a twenty. Gretchen must surely come now, he thought.

When he returned to the cabin, telling Titus the news, he fussed about, getting everything ready. He lit the fire, set out lemonade and glasses, then arranged the cupcakes on a platter. I'm afraid he was a bit clumsy and got a fingerprint on the shell-pink icing of one, a rather grimy fingerprint, for he'd added some more newspaper to the fire. He didn't see it though, as he stood admiring them on the willowware plate.

Gretchen reached for that particular cupcake and ate the bit with the fingerprint before anyone could notice it. Then she smiled up at the Cap'n, who was handing round glasses of lemonade and beaming. She was entranced by the cabin, how everything in it was so tidy and fitted into corners and under windows. The Cap'n had lit the lamps against the growing twilight and she admired their haloes of golden light. She picked up another cupcake and nibbled off a layer of icing, then took a bite of cake, enjoying how the drier, floury bits jumbled with the melting sweetness of the icing in her mouth.

Smoke drifted from the stovepipe on the roof, carried slowly away to the west by the wind. The Cap'n had brought out a picture he was working on, with a file of cut-out paper animals, birds, and flowers he'd painted. Three young heads and one old one bent over the table, studying ways to arrange the creatures and plants, as Hamish carefully ate the last cupcake in tiny bites, so that it would last as long as possible.

* * *

When the Hollander children had gone the Cap'n tidied up, wanting to have everything shipshape before Ettie knocked with his supper. She always left it on the table outside the door and let him do the rest, serving it from the sealed containers to his dishes, or rather, the dishes in the cabin. It was in no way his cabin, or they his dishes, he knew. The Cap'n felt that Ettie's system had a delicate balance, that she gave him food but otherwise expected him to be independent. It was one of the thousand or so things that he admired about her.

After supper he sat reading in the armchair, feeding the wood stove from time to time and as often as not staring at the flickering flames beyond its grate rather than reading. His mind kept wandering back to the children's visit and the young man who'd been so interested in getting a special cake. It was the first time he'd asked any visitors to the cabin specially, and he felt it had been a great success. Gretchen had even spoken a few words, and had seemed to enjoy those silly cut-out tigers he'd made, the ones that looked just like Titus, and the owls he'd done, in checked waistcoats, with faces just like the colonel's.

Finally, he put the book down; it was no use. He couldn't recall a thing about Little Dorrit, except that she'd been a very serious child. He thought, Why not celebrate this most wonderful day by taking a late stroll around the neighborhood? A fellow he knew, a bum called Frankie, who had a specialty act in doing an exact imitation of Al Pacino, and who the Cap'n was friendly with, could often be found on MacDougal in the late hours. He'd like to meet with him again, tell him that he was doing well and inquire after Frankie's health. He could even give him some money, by gum.

He banked the fire down, blew out the lamps, and lit the battery-powered night-light. That was for Titus, who didn't like being left alone in the dark. He patted the cat's head after he put on his coat, telling him he'd be an hour or two at most.

* * *

Not long after the Cap'n had let himself out the garden door, a figure slipped down the quiet street, then slid into a shadow across from the colonel's house. Watching from under his hood, the Angry One observed the lights going out in the house, from the downstairs rooms to the bedrooms upstairs. He also observed that all the lights were out in the house next door, as he waited patiently for that one last light on the top floor to go out. Finally, it did. Moving silently across the street the Angry One swarmed up and over the wooden gate to the Hollanders' garden. He slithered across it, around the mulberry tree, then slithered up and over the fence to the garden next door. Crouching behind some shrubs he stared with rage and disbelief at the miniature house, a perfect tiny house with perfect pretty porch, and wood smoke coming from its chimney. Here at last was the lair of that fat bum someone seemed to love so much. The place where he would die. Where he'd stick a knife into his belly and watch all that food they fed him on golden plates come sliding out, along the tip of his blade.

Knock, knock, he breathed, holding his carve-up knife as he stood before the door. Then he took a deep breath and blew the door down.

The bum was not at home. Not at home. He knew it at once. He closed the door behind him, edging in, the knife ready in his hand. *Why* was that fat bum not home? *Why* was he not where he'd watched him be every night for the last six nights? Why was he not in his little-bitty kingdom?

Look at that bed, will you just *look* at that? All cozy and covered with a quilt, a clean, Mamma kind of quilt. He took his knife to the bed, stabbing it and stabbing it, ripping it apart with the point of his knife.

He saw a movement, an orange tail beneath the table. He grabbed at it and clutched it, heard a squawk and pulled the cat up. He fought off its claws, taking it by the scruff of its neck, holding it out and shaking it. He ran out to the garden and spotted something exactly to his purpose, an old stone well. As Titus fought to get free he pulled off the wooden cover and flung the cat down the well. There was a splash, then the Angry One put back the cover and fled.

Titus tried to climb the stone walls, tried and tried. Cried out, Help me. Scrabbled again and again to find a purchase, but always slipped back down to the cold water. It was pitch black inside the well as he struggled to get out. He tried with all his strength, but with each try grew weaker.

Eventually he hung there in the water and felt it fill him. His paws churned the water a last time and then his lungs filled and he died.

***

The Cap'n walked happily home, cheered by having seen his pal. He was very careful to make no noise as he opened the gate and went into the cabin. He sat in the armchair sighing, reaching to take his boots off. But something was terribly wrong. With a heart frozen by fear he saw the bed and knew its murderous intent. He looked around, but the one who had done it was clearly gone. Inside his icy reason he feared one thing over all others.

"Titus," he called softly, going down on his hands and knees. "Titus?" Very carefully he explored every spot the cat might hide in. There were not many. Oh Titus, where are you?

Wait, there's a chance he escaped to the garden and is hiding there. Taking off his bulky coat and picking up a flashlight, the Cap'n went out and began quartering the garden in a crouch, whispering: "Titus, Titus."

The hope that had filled him when he began searching the garden leached from his mind as he came to the back fence. Sitting very still he listened for an answering meow. He sometimes thought he did hear one, at times was almost sure of it, yet he knew that almost sure is a long way from reality.

Aiming his flashlight over the stone terrace he saw something in its beam. A tuft of silky hair, which the breeze had already begun to scatter. He picked it up and touched it, a hair floated up and clung to his nose. Unheeding, he let out a cry, an uncomprehending note of despair.

Deen woke with a start. She looked over at Gretchen in the other bed but she was sleeping soundly. The sound, whatever it had been, caught on the hem of sleep, had not come from her. Concentrating on what the sound had been like, she thought it had come from below, in the garden. Putting on her bathrobe and slippers she went downstairs, taking a flashlight from where it was kept by the back door.

Cap'n Meat was standing on the terrace, looking down at something in his hand. Deen touched his arm and saw that it was a tuft of orange and white fur. She shook him, mutely asking him to tell her what had happened?

"I went out. Someone very bad came while I was gone. Titus is missing."

"Have you looked for him everywhere?"

"Yes, everywhere."

Deen looked around the garden. "Titus, here kitty," she called out softly, moving to look under some bushes. A queer feeling came over her, as if she could feel Titus's presence, feel some trace of pain or fear in the air, no, she could smell it. Walking across the terrace, her eyes half shut, she traced it, traced the tingle of molecules through the air. "Over here," she said. She was standing next to the old well.

The Cap'n went to it and pushed the heavy oak cover aside. Deen pointed her flashlight down. Titus floated below them, his tiger-striped fur caressed by the vagaries of the water, flowing out then flowing closer to his body, silently and slowly in the black water.

Cap'n Meat fetched a plank and placed it over the well, then crawled onto it to reach down and pull up the body of his cat. He saw that his paws were bloodied by the attempt to climb out, so he hid them from Deen.

"I know!" she cried. "How he tried and tried to climb out. How all alone he was and how he tried time after time to get out. I wish I'd never known him, wish I'd never loved him or knew anything about him. I wish I couldn't see how much he suffered."

Crying as if she would never be free of her grief, Deen turned and ran back into the house.

The Cap'n's eyes followed her sadly. The poor girl, if only she could have been spared seeing that. Taking the lifeless body of his cat in his arms, he carried him into the cabin. He carefully dried Titus's fur with a towel, then sat in the armchair with him on his lap, stroking him. I'm sorry, he said, so sorry. Oh, my dear friend, if only I'd been here to protect you. I am so sorry. Oh, please don't leave me, I'll be so all alone. I loved you so much. You were the best and noblest companion a man has ever had. You were my friend.

He sat for a long time, with the body of his cat on his lap, absently stroking it. Eventually he got up and wrapped it in a towel, because it seemed that as a once-living thing traveled closer to its own cellular destruction it needed the dignity of a shroud. But he couldn't lay it down all alone, so he held it on his lap for the rest of the night.

35

Gretchen went down to the kitchen the next morning to find Ettie hunched over the table, weeping. When she heard Gretchen's step and looked up, Gretchen asked with her eyes, *What's wrong?*

"Oh, missy, something terrible. The cat of the Capitain's who is so nice? A devil, an evil one, came into his cabin last night, when the Capitain he is gone, and threw the cat down the well. Yes, he drown. The bad one, he cut up the Capitain's bed too, into many, many pieces, like he want to kill him. Mother of God this a bad world sometime. And what will the poor Capitain do without this friend of his? We know to love him, when we see how he love his cat. Such a good cat, always so clean." Ettie put her hands over her face, her shoulders shaking.

Gretchen put her arms around Ettie. When her shaking had quieted, she went to make her a cup of strong coffee, putting plenty of sugar and heated milk into it. She set it firmly in front of Ettie.

Ettie, being a good girl, wiped her eyes and drank. And when Gretchen pushed some buttered toast before her, she ate.

Feeling she could safely leave Ettie now, Gretchen patted her hand and went off in search of Deen.

***

Next door, Brenda wielded the vacuum with more than her customary ferocity, aiming it over the rug as she narrowly missed furniture legs with it, all the while muttering to herself. Switching it off, she took an oiled dust cloth from her pocket and began attacking the surfaces.

What am I thinking, she muttered, not doing the dusting first, then the vacuuming? Everything's at sixes and sevens lately, and that's the truth. Liall had told her that some crazy man had thrown that old bum's cat down the well. Lord, and why would a person want to go and kill a cat? Sure enough, aren't pets the most trusting of Your innocent creatures? But that old bum's just another forlorn human, can't even keep his own cat safe, probably went out and got himself all liquored up. Boozing and paying no mind to his own kind, just like all men.

Her dusting brought her to the piano, which she swatted and rubbed at. Glancing out the French doors, she saw Liall, Hamish, and the Cap'n digging a hole in the next garden. Oh Lord, just look at that old bum, every line of him one of misery. Fooled everyone into being nice to him just because of that cat of his, when he's just some worthless layabout, who ought to be doing a job of work like the rest of us. Only it doesn't seem right, him losing his pet that way, not right at all. I guess maybe I just might go and pay my respects, that sure was a nice-looking cat. Throwing some poor cat down a well, that's the Devil's work.

Gretchen could not find Deen because she was tucked behind the boiler in the cubicle next to Ettie's kitchen, her head on her knees, feeling and puzzling her way through a miasma of such abject misery that she felt herself unfit for human society.

***

The colonel walked heavily up to his bedroom to put on a more somber suit. He chose the dark gray, rather than the black, which he decided would be too gloomily Victorian. He exchanged his brogues for a pair of black shoes, lacing them carefully and tying the bows. Picking up his watch and chain from the leather box on the dresser, he fed the chain through his vest and tucked the watch into its pocket. He hadn't been able to read time from it for nearly fifty years, but it was a repeater and chimed the hour when he opened it. It had been his grandfather's watch, and with it he'd not only been able to keep a sense of respectability, he'd also been able to maintain the fiction of his sight, looking down at it to say, "My word, nearly half past six."

He went slowly downstairs, counting the steps, until he reached the kitchen. Turning his head from side to side, as if inspecting his domain, he said, "Hello?"

"Oh, Colonel," Ettie's voice answered. "It's all ready. You go out first, I walk behind you. If you give me your arm, like you're being nice, I'll show you where to walk."

"Right we are," the colonel said. He was carrying his family prayer book, in which had been inscribed the names of his ancestors, all the way back to the first Harringtons in the New World, who'd arrived in the Virginia Colony in the 1620s. Their descendant, Blaylock Harrington, had fought with his four grown sons in the revolution, going to war with the rifles they hunted for food with.

It was a beautiful spring day, nearly as fair and warm as early summer. The leaves budding out were fresh and palely green. The quince was in bloom and the wisteria beginning to show trails of lavender. It was a day so lovely it mocked sorrow.

Brenda looked very churchy, in her navy blue coat and hat. Ettie whispered to the colonel: "Liall's mother." The colonel turned in what he hoped was the right direction and bowed to her.

Hamish, Liall, Deen, and Gretchen stood to one side. Deen clutched a bunch of daffodils, which she'd mangled rather badly in her grief. She was blubbing quietly yet unceasingly. Hamish had tried to get her to shut up, but decided that it was hopeless, as she'd only blubbed louder.

The Cap'n was very much touched by everyone coming, even Liall's mother, who he knew did not approve of him. He patted Titus's form and whispered to him that he was being sent off in state. He'd sewn the cat's body into a canvas sack at daybreak, placing a bit of plank under him first. He'd had an idea that if Deen saw the cat's limp form, she'd take it even worse. In this he was quite correct, and saved Deen from howls of pity, as he carefully placed the stiff bundle into the ground.

"Ahem," the colonel said. "Perhaps a few words to see this very fine creature off to the next world. I thought I might read the burial service. It was written, of course, for man, but in this case I think is more than appropriate for the friend who we mourn today."

Opening his prayer book to a random page, he recited the service. When he'd done, there was a silence, then Brenda said "Amen!" The Cap'n, helped by the two boys, filled in the grave.

As people went quietly away, Brenda shook the Cap'n's hand, saying she was sorry for his loss. Hamish and Liall went off to throw a basketball around, both of them feeling the need to hit something quite hard. Later they discussed some elaborate plans for catching the person who'd killed Titus, and killing him in turn. They weren't terribly practical plans, but not lacking in gumption, and the grit to carry them out.

The colonel went back to his parlor to consult with Mrs. D by phone. There was no question in his mind that that woman would not only make sure that fellow never got in again to harm them, but would personally see to it that he was put in custody. He didn't like the idea of causing another human any harm, but in this case, shooting was too good for the fellow.

Only Gretchen, Deen, and the Cap'n remained in the garden. Gretchen knelt over Titus's grave, smoothing it and tucking bits of sod into place. It was a fine grave, well mounded up, and wouldn't sink into a pitiful hollow after a few months.

Deen sat hunched on the step to the terrace, crying in ragged gasps, while the Cap'n patted her hand, looking wretched. Suddenly she let out a howl of pain. "I can't stop thinking of him in that well, trying and trying to get out, all alone!" she wailed.

Gretchen got up and went over to stand in front of her sister. Taking her by the shoulders, she shook her, forcing her to look at her.

The old bum and the young girl looked up at Gretchen, startled. It was clear she had something to say. They waited.

"The world has sadness in it," Gretchen began at last. "Suffering is always with us, and inside of us, and around us. Once, I felt it too strongly, heard too many cries of pain, too many whimperings of the cast-off and broken. Until it drove me mad. Worse, I forgot the other voices, the ones that must exist too if sorrow does, the sounds of joy.

"Yes, your friend struggled alone in his last few moments to live. And he did not live. We are all animals, awaiting our death. But think if we only had that, birth and survival and then death, never knowing friendship or love? You rescued that cat as a kitten, Cap'n, were his friend and protector. He spent nearly all his life with you, loving you and knowing that your voice and touch could be trusted until the end.

"What you cry for, Deen, is his trust. Your tears honor him, but they also find too much meaning in the random cruelty of the world. His death was not just the result of man's cruelty, but also the cruelty of existence, the unknowing, spinning world that we live on that brings to a place, an hour, a creature's fate.

"The two of you are children. Good, kind-hearted children who put yourselves in his place and cry with pity, imagining him calling out and lonely as he died. It's you who are calling out and lonely now, tormenting yourselves in your own well of suffering, while around you everywhere are others who've never known what that cat knew of love."

Deen blew her nose into a sodden Kleenex, which promptly fell into pieces. The Cap'n offered her his bandana. "Did you feel like you'd been thrown down a dark place, when you were taken to Rollingbrook?" she asked Gretchen.

"No, Deen. I was lost inside my own wandering then and didn't know what I was, or how I felt. Later, I did feel abandoned, but as my reason came back I realized that I'd been smashing up everything around me. Even then I couldn't stop wanting to undo things, make a mess.

"I had to think very hard. You see, I didn't want to lose that part of myself, the negative. As objects are defined by shade, so is the psyche. But when it grows destructive, blots everything else out, well, they cut that part out of a person with drugs, they have to. I had to find a way to keep it inside me, but not let it tell me what to do. Maybe I had to take that part out and touch it all over, in order to keep it where it belongs."

"Do you think you might actually have been beset by demons?" Deen asked, quite interested by the idea.

"Oh, I don't think there's any doubt about that."

"Are you going to be normal now?"

"No, Deen. I hope I shall never be normal. Now you mustn't talk to me for several days, I've used up a year's worth of words."

* * *

Oh look!" Sadie said, "it's the dear old Brooklyn Bridge." She was burbling, addressing herself first to the driver of the ambulance, then to Brian, in back. "Gawd, it's been *two months*. Since I abandoned my children for this git here, the one strapped in the back," she explained to the driver.

"Do you think my children will recognize me?"

"I'm sure something about your face will ring a bell," Brian said. "Stir up all sorts of bad memories."

"Darling, I never should've let you have that coffee. The doctor warned me you'll need to be reintroduced to stimulants very, very slowly."

"Oh, get stuffed."

"You hear how he talks to me?" Sadie asked the driver. "What's your name?"

"Dennis."

"I should change that, if I were you."

"What's the matter with Dennis?" he said.

"She's a right snob, our Saids is," Brian shouted from the back. "But she's onto something; Dennis is never going to get you anywhere."

"We can't help teasing you just a tiny bit," Sadie explained to Dennis. "After all those grisly weeks in the company of the most direly serious people. Doctors are so humorless these days, don't you find? They seem to think anyone with a few kinks in them is headed straight for hell. While Brian lay there pretending to be dead for weeks and weeks, and I had to stay in the most wretched hotel, the most ghastly place you can imagine. And I had to abandon my children for all that time, and they've all run away from where I left them, taking the law into their own tiny hands—oh look! It's our block! Do honk the horn, dear Dennis, please. Oh for Christ's sake, don't be such a lump, honk the horn. Live a little, signal to all that I'm home, with Lazarus back there, in tow. I don't know, how about two bits and a shave? Whatever grabs you."

***

Walk back now, away from the house with the blue door and the tarnished brass knocker in the shape of a dolphin. Stop for a moment to let the ambulance driver get that man in the wheelchair out, stand considerately out of his way. And wonder a bit about who they are, the runnelly faced man and the woman with the untidy hair helping to tug him up the front steps, then dumping her pocketbook upside down to find her keys. There's a story there, it's clear, but this is New York, where people don't stare, so walk on, past the basement Suds Café with its Formica tables strewn with yesterday's papers. Past that restaurant that always looks so chic, its window seats piled with jade green silk pillows. Back toward Seventh Avenue, below the tiny office built into a turret that juts over the street from the white brick parking garage, the one that looks so neat, with its vintage metal desk and red swivel chair. Back to the noise and traffic on Seventh that thunders and roars like a great river, past sushi joints and newsstands, head shops, book shops, and solid brownstones, their shutters prudently closed against the curious gaze of those passing by.

About the author

About the book

Read on

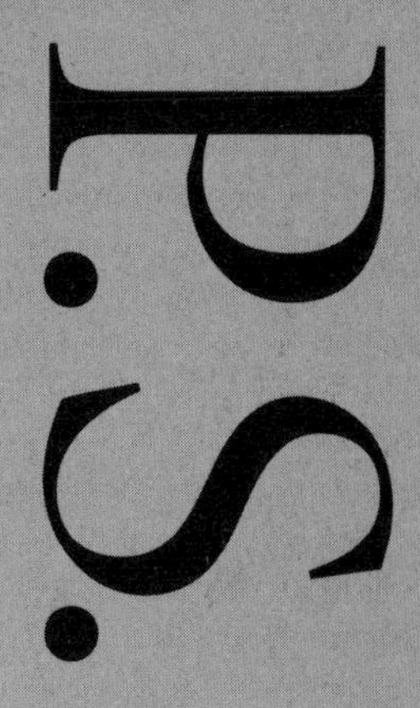

Insights,
Interviews
& More . . .

About the author

Meet Marjorie Kernan

© Laura Brunelliere

MARJORIE KERNAN was born in New Haven, Connecticut. As a child she was determined to become an artist. Later, she dropped out of high school to take studio art and art history classes at Princeton University, having talked her way into auditing classes there. She studied at Princeton for three years, with Jeremy Gilbert-Rolfe, Tony Smith, Richard Serra, and Lynda Benglis, among others.

Later, she studied at Carnegie Mellon University and the School of Visual Arts, in New York City. She worked for a florist in New York in her early twenties, then moved to Maine, where she took a gallery job for room and board. She has been a house painter, crewed on a wooden boat, been a freelance designer of lighting and textiles, and, for the past fifteen years, has run an antiques shop, where she and her husband sell the antiques they buy in France.

Several years ago, while sitting in a truck cab in France, bored out of her mind, she began to think of writing a novel. When she returned home she wrapped her brushes in linen, cleared out her small studio, and turned it into a writing room. She has never looked back. The daughter of Alvin B. Kernan, the writer, critic, and professor, she'd been brought up to think, and breathe, literature.

She and her husband of twenty-one years, a photographer, live in a house that began as a one-room shack, which they've added to over the years. The studio she writes in sits on four stones pulled from the meadow, which she looks out across as she writes at her desk.

She is currently working on a second novel.

"Several years ago, while sitting in a truck cab in France, bored out of her mind, she began to think of writing a novel."

On Reading

A LONG TIME AGO, in a farmhouse in Connecticut, I stared in amazement at a piece of paper on which I'd just formed my first word. The crudely made letters were some sort of juju. Drawing pictures of dogs and cats and the sun radiating lines was one thing—this was a new, hard-core concept, shapes that made the sounds that made the names of things.

Later, when I could read simple books, a whole world opened to me. I didn't even have to make the sounds with my lips anymore, could absorb the doings of Flopsy and Mopsy unhesitatingly. There was a young maple tree in the garden that with some effort I could climb, up to a limb where I would lean against its trunk and read, hidden within its broad green leaves. I read and read on my secret perch there, of witches and little English girls who were very, very poor, and boys who discovered buried chests of gold.

“There was a young maple tree in the garden that with some effort I could climb, up to a limb where I would lean against its trunk and read . . .”

Books were treasured objects. Birthdays and Christmas would bring new ones, each to be gazed at for a long while, its cover illustration traced with a finger. Then, when sufficient pleasure had been derived from simply looking at it, the great moment would arrive, the reading of the first sentence. Each part of the process was to be hoarded for as long as possible.

I named my dolls after characters in favorite books, and believed that when I went to sleep the diminutive figures in my dollhouse could finally stir to life, go about their business. My world was informed not simply by reality, but by the fantastical things I read in books, and believed wholeheartedly. One memorable birthday I received a wooden doll exactly like Mehitabel, known as Hitty, the doll heroine of a book by that name. My mother even made her a dress just like one described in the tale, of calico, with a drawstring purse to match.

In the playroom there were shelves with books for young people, oddities of books that spanned the Edwardian era to the 1920s. They were long on extremely well-behaved children in clean pinafores, boys with ringlets, and horrid children who died in vats of boiling oil. None lacked a hard-hitting moral conclusion. I read my way through them—they were books after all—but stumbled over the longer words, yearning for the day I could understand grown-up books properly.

I can still feel that visceral sense of not knowing enough, and trying to get there, building vocabulary and ▸

“In the playroom there were shelves with books for young people, oddities of books that spanned the Edwardian era to the 1920s.”

comprehension, that slow, impatiently hoped-for accrual. I proceeded from babyish books to books about children my own age, and continued to eye books beyond my grasp, occasionally foraying into a few pages of them, then retreating in defeat. One word stands out in my memory from one of those forays—"melancholy." I stared at it for a long while, then gave up, knew I'd been hurled back down the rock-strewn hillside. The other bugbear was an old copy of *Gulliver's Travels* that looked liked a children's book, and actually had illustrations, but was too awful to even peek at again. I tried not to think of it, but it sent shivers of worry through me.

Then it seemed to happen in a moment: suddenly I could read real books. I think it was *Jane Eyre* that was the password, a book I loved so well that I strained to follow every word properly. It gave me a glimmering of something the grown-ups called "literature."

Dickens was next. My father had a complete set, with reproductions of the original illustrations by "Phiz." I began with *David Copperfield*. There was a wide bay window in the house with long curtains that could be pulled across its front, providing a hidden place to lie on my stomach on the window seat, absorbing the world Dickens had invented. That furious Mrs. Jellyby and her causes for the poor in faraway places, while her own family suffered neglect. And Mr. Gradgrind, an industrialist from the north, who boasted of his rough, pragmatic origins. There were people like that now, I realized; in fact, the woman at the Whole Earth Center was exactly like Mrs. Jellyby. Reading all of Dickens gave me an enormous quantity of new words, and a more sophisticated perception of narrative.

"Reading all of Dickens gave me an enormous quantity of new words, and a more sophisticated perception of narrative."

With Dickens under my belt I discovered that at last I was able to read anything. My father's library was the first point of attack. For a long while it had stood as a kind of faraway castle on a distant hilltop, serene and unassailable, filled with books with somber cloth bindings.

To begin with, I read anything that might be salacious. *Lady Chatterley's Lover*, Henry Miller's series of "Tropics," and Alain Robbe-Grillet, whose books I chose simply because of their covers. I didn't really understand *Lady Chatterley's Lover*, and, as for Henry Miller, couldn't imagine why people said his books were smutty, but I found Robbe-Grillet strangely interesting. Here ▸

was fiction of a kind I'd never imagined before, weird and incomprehensible as all get-out, but somehow able to raise a signal of born-bad rock 'n' roll, which was also beginning to interest me at the time. So I read the books quite carefully, getting a jolt of meaning here and there, without understanding in the least bit why.

From that first realization that I could at last read anything in print I threw myself into the process. Having no particularly developed sensibility or taste, there was almost nothing that didn't interest me. There were degrees of pleasure certainly—comic books and Thackeray's *Vanity Fair* were saved to be read with lunch, but all the others were almost as big a kick. A pile of ancient *Saturday Evening Posts*, paperback thrillers with their covers torn off, the works of Henry Fielding, Maupassant, and Hawthorne, Dashiell Hammett, Japanese poetry of the Edo period, *People* magazine without fail (only a buttered roll for lunch those days), books on film, *Artforum* (dictionary to hand), *The Autobiography of Benvenuto Cellini*, *Dune*, Greek drama, Victorian smut, "true love" comics, which were especially treasured because they were so cheap they reprinted stories from the '50s and '60s. To this day I can recite the woes of the nice girl in the pillbox hat, who is sadly deceived in her love for a poetry-spouting beatnik.

I had access to the university library, and would play a game there that involved choosing an elevator button at random, then a shelf on the gloomy, subterranean floor, then a volume, one hand over my eyes. Then I'd read it, even if it were a book about Paracelsus. There was always something quite fascinating to be learned, ideas to be traced from its thesis, in the same way that truths can be discovered in the *I Ching* by those who are willing to delve into their inner thoughts.

Now when I hold a new book in my hand I still study it and linger over it as an object, before reading that first line. Feel that same promised thrill of some new voice or insight. Though I have to admit, I am far less easy to please. But I can still feel the cool green shade of those maple leaves, and the smoothness of the limb I perched on, where I read so many hours as a child, in that filtered world of greenery. And still feel that slight tinge of guilt ticking in my mind—how much longer can I hide here reading, before being called in to set the table?

“I had access to the university library, and would play a game there that involved choosing an elevator button at random, then a shelf on the gloomy, subterranean floor, then a volume, one hand over my eyes.”

Author's Picks
Ten Books

Here are ten books I'd suggest to a friend who's a big reader, but who might not have come across them.

THE BLITHEDALE ROMANCE, Nathaniel Hawthorne, 1852

One of the best novels of New England, based on the Brook Farm experiment, an early attempt to create an idyllic community in which to foster the arts and live off the land. Zenobia, one of Hawthorne's most vividly rendered characters, is a temptress who becomes the unraveling point for the community.

FLICKER, Theodore Roszak, 1991

By the author of *The Making of a Counterculture*, this novel follows the life of a young film buff through his education by a dauntingly intelligent mentor to his eventual rediscovery of an obscure German Expressionist filmmaker turned Hollywood schlockmeister, and his bizarre techniques.

THE BALKAN TRILOGY, Olivia Manning, 1960–65

The three novels issued as her first trilogy (followed by *The Levant Trilogy*) describe the author's own experiences in Budapest, and then Athens, during the Second World War. Manning's characters are detailed and complex, and hers is one of the greatest descriptions of the displacement of people and the disintegration of states as the Axis powers pushed to capture all of Europe.

SHACKLETON'S BOAT JOURNEY, F. A. Worsley, 1933

Frank Worsley, the captain of the *Endurance* on Shackleton's ill-fated attempt to reach the South Pole, tells the story of the *Endurance* simply and in classically restrained prose. The *Endurance* is beset by ice in the Weddell Sea, and the men survive an incredible crossing to Elephant Island in three open boats after the *Endurance* sinks.

HEED THE THUNDER, Jim Thompson, 1946

Thompson's writing is gradually finding legitimacy, long after his death. Born in Anadarko, Oklahoma, Thompson wrote like Dostoevsky on poppers. *Heed the Thunder* is his most traditionally limned book, and is a view of the American West that ought to have set the literary world ablaze, but was ignored, pushing the author further into the world of dime-store pulp. I often imagine some sailor home on leave picking ▸

up one of Thompson's books to read on the Greyhound bus, and wondering, *What in the hell kinda weird shit is this?*

MRS. SATAN, Johanna Johnston, 1967

Did you know that a woman ran for president in 1872? Her name was Victoria Woodhull, and she ran on the Free Love platform, with Frederick Douglass as her running mate. Women were not allowed to vote at the time, so Woodhull, a fiery suffragette and orator, sailed into politics, filling the hall at Cooper Union for her speeches. She was a stockbroker, a denouncer of hypocritical preachers, and was jailed in the Jefferson Market women's prison, just around the corner from Sadie's house.

ZULEIKA DOBSON, Max Beerbohm, 1911

Considered a classic, this novel seems to have fallen out of favor. Probably the most perfect example of the fantastical presented as probable, and written with the most feathery touch, it is a book I go back to year after year. If any book could be described as a particular influence on the fable-like quality of my book, this would be it.

“If any book could be described as a particular influence on the fable-like quality of my book, *Zuleika Dobson* would be it.”

LOST ILLUSIONS, Honoré de Balzac, 1837–43

Many of us were set *Père Goriot* in school, and probably loved it or hated it. What seems to be left out of discussions of Balzac's *La Comédie humaine* is his one vast, great novel, *Lost Illusions*. Two men, bound by family and friendship, seek their fortunes. One toils honestly in the provinces, in an attempt to invent a paper made from cheap natural materials, and the other goes to Paris to conquer society and seek his fortune as a writer. This is Lucien de Rubempré, whose evolution in waistcoats, boots, and breeches, and gall at the slights he first meets with in the capital, are as sharp today as they were then.

SEVENTEEN, Booth Tarkington, 1916

No one reads Tarkington any more. Hardly any of his books are in print. But *Seventeen* is one of the funniest novels I've ever read. All the petty miseries of adolescence are boiled up in it then reduced to a light broth. The next time you wonder why you're reading some book about a mass murderer who turns his victims into hat stands, throw it away and raid your grandparents' shelves for a copy of *Seventeen*.

“No one reads Tarkington any more. Hardly any of his books are in print. But *Seventeen* is one of the funniest novels I've ever read.”

LOVE AND WAR IN THE APENNINES,
Eric Newby, 1971

Newby's account of being sent on a mad WWII mission from a naval sub to a beach in Italy, where he is captured, eventually escapes, and treks across the mountains aided by the Italians, is a book I'm always giving away, in a fit of generosity. I should keep a copy in a locked vault.